The Following Years

For Ethel Graydon

A special thanks to
Hazel Romano
for her excellent proof-reading.

First Published in the UK
First Edition
© Molly Cutpurse 2010
ISBN 978-1-4457-0849-2

Timeline

Edith Jessie Graydon born	Christmas Day 1893
Avis Ethel Graydon born	24 September 1895
Edith Married Percy	16 January 1916
Freddy Bywaters murders Percy	3 October 1922
Edith leaves 41 Kensington Gardens	4 October 1922
Charged with murder	5 October 1922
Stratford Police Court and Remanded to Holloway	6 October 1922
Trail begins at the Old Bailey	6 December 1922
Sentenced to death	11 December 1922
Reprieve failed	5 January 1923
Edith and Freddy executed	9 January 1923
Edith's body moved to Brookwood	31 March 1971
Avis Graydon died	6 August 1977

One

9 January 1923.

9.00am.

London

For the Graydons, a normal family of six in all respects, 9.00am was a moment each of them would remember as being extraordinarily painful. An important moment in which each one of the horrid events over the previous three months coalesced into one singular dimension of searing emotional pain. Here was a splinter of time that would not be forgotten by those participating in it.

Here was a fracturing moment, a pivotal moment. A moment few humans would understand, or ever have to endure. Time is seldom regular in human perception. Yet occasionally an event occurs in which Hell manifests itself.

The recipients of this event, the family, six lonely human beings and one friend, were not aware of the gravity of the moment — beside the immediate crushing effect it was having. A seven-day repeating clock, whose time was known to be accurate, regulated the gathering. Its three small brass bells eventually announced the top of the hour with terrible regularity, and as it chimed, the tiny front room of 231 Shakespeare Crescent, Manor Park not only became a singular moment in space, but eventually part of England's shame.

The adult children each sat a short and respectful distance from each other on the edge of their individual wooden chairs while the parents sat on the only sofa. Their daughter, the parent's last one, clung onto her eldest brother's arm with a singular fierceness than cannot be imagined, her knuckles white with strain, her nails chewing his shirt. Both the parent's expressions, as were their four children, were hardly connected to family life. All were blasted and gripped by an unseen terror, and they remained as statues, all eyes cast down.

Only the youngest boy, Harold, smoked furiously, his long ash occasionally tumbling onto the dull red, and slightly worn circular carpet which was spread over the cheap brown and cream linoleum. Miss Ethel Vernon, the only person not related to the family, was mostly a friend of the daughter although she had been staying at the house. Yet she was tearful too. She was there to support Edith's mother, and she held Joey the family black cat closely on her lap, stroking him furiously and unendingly.

Everyone had been awake all night, unable to sleep despite medication offered to them by Doctor Wallis, their new family doctor. They were still wearing the clothes they wore when they last visited Holloway prison the previous day.

Mrs Ethel Graydon, the fifty-one year old mother, grey-haired, and as white as the sheets she boiled every Monday, in one fist she clutched her daughter's photograph, and in her other, the left side of her temple for she suffered prostrating migraines. Enough to allow her indispositions to occasionally dominate family life, and often made her uncertain in social circumstances.

To the Northeast, some ten miles distant, connected events were ongoing which dictated their misery. For there, in a wooden two-storey structure, attached to the end of B Wing in Holloway's woman's gaol, enveloped by light rain and a hastily erected makeshift screen, it designed to prevent owners of the neighbouring houses watching, twelve men and one woman observed a terrified, yet mostly unconscious and drugged young woman, no longer pretty, whose crime was no more than to be guilty of foolishness and naivety, disappear from sight as she plummeted through a trapdoor, her thin neck snapped instantly by a stout leather noose. A few seconds after nine o'clock, Edith Jessie Thompson was dead and mythology born. Because by statutory law her body had to hang for one hour, official recognition of her death could not take place. However, the doctor descended into the dark pit and listened for her heartbeat. He did not hear one. It was usual for hearts to beat for as long as half an hour after the event, hence the hour required by law.

However, what Doctor Morton, governor of Holloway Prison discovered as he approached the swaying body, was a monstrosity which would remain and haunt him for the next twelve years until his own death in June 1935. In those initial few seconds, red became the only colour he saw. Dark red drenching the dress. Dark red messing the floor. Dark red dripping. And a strong smell of iron, urine and faeces. Thereafter, the good doctor would forever dedicate his life to the campaign of abolishing hanging. As he checked for signs of continuance, it was difficult for him to believe that the lifeless body which hung before him, was the intelligent and occasionally lively woman with whom he had become acquainted over the last few months.

Many people believe it to be an act of tenderness and compassion that the condemned is allowed to wear his or her own clothing when they die, but it is not. Those with knowledge understand that the body has its own way of re-acting to the violence done to it. And that is not a clean way as Doctor Morton had discovered. Prison authorities know this, and have no wish to waste a uniform on such a person. Everything possible is reused.

To professional executioners, Ellis and his assistant Young, distress to the body was expected, although even they, after that awful wait, were shocked and unprepared for the sight which eventually awaited them. Swiftly they unhooked the body from the dreadful apparatus and laid her out. Whereupon she was stripped and washed, and her soiled and bloodied clothes burnt in the nearest furnace. They worked quickly in preparation for the required autopsy. A great deal of time was spent cleaning the pit with water and bleach, a task that particularly irked Ellis as he was not the most patient of men.

*

A short walk away, at precisely the same time, the same punishing event was taking place in Pentonville Prison as Fredrick Edward Francis Bywaters, Edith's paramour, suffered the same fate. In identical circumstances, his family too, living at 11 Westow Street, Upper Norwood held a similar vigil, praying and already grieving for the loss of a son and brother.

Back at 231, the little brass bells of the clock ceased to announce the awful time, and as an unearthly silence replaced the vulgar noise, Edith's family and their friend became dimly aware that their loving daughter and effervescent sister was no longer alive. No longer part of the world. No longer one of the living. As one person, the empty silence now allowing it, their previously suppressed agony, suspended by quite unimaginable disbelief, spluttered outward and, Ethel was the first to collapse, as if a great legal dagger had been drawn across her heart.

By the time her husband, William and Miss Vernon had caught and laid her gently back onto the sofa, her eyes had rolled up into her head and she was mercifully if briefly unconscious. Peering around helplessly at Avis, his eldest, and now only daughter, William asked her to fetch the half bottle of whisky that their next door neighbour, Mr Bristow at 229 had gifted to them during the night. As she left, William silently and with dignity, took the chintz cloth from the table and gave it to one of his sons indicating that he was to cover the room's only mirror. The oval one above the mantelpiece with the glass-cut tree on one side with which Edith used to adjust her hair whenever she left 231.

Silently, Avis wiped her watery blue eyes, and stumbled out of the room into their equally tiny kitchen just as, unaccountably, Joey the cat gave a mangled unearthly screech and shot out of the room into the hall. Its seemingly unwarranted noise froze everyone, and it was not seen again for eight days having fled into the garden. A mystery that was never solved, but one which no one forgot as it became entwined into a private family legend. For although Edith could not keep a cat at her own home due to the duties of her and her husband's working life, it was well known that she had loved Joey, and had since he had been a kitten.

Whenever she had visited, he had always headed straight for her warm lap where she would stroke him, and scratch his jet black ears continuously. The clock, as momentarily registered by one of William's sons, read one minute past nine.

The Graydons had taken up residence at 231 in 1898 and William, generally an immaculately dressed man who always used a large spotted handkerchief and a gold-plated watch, assisted by his much younger brother, who was later killed at Flanders, had immediately set about decorating and repairing his new home. Financial considerations unfortunately caused the work to be extended by some years. Up to when the last of his children arrived in 1902 in fact. Therefore, by Christmas Day of that year, Edith's tenth birthday, a sparkling kitchen with a new Ascot water heater became part of the fixtures and fittings that appeared throughout the house. Banisters and dangerous stairs had been replaced. Its roof had been replaced. Decorations and a thorough painting had brightened their home, and a new outside privy had been installed. The six occupants, especially the children, were an extremely and rumbustious happy family.

Eventually, the almost absurdly long rear, and equally absurdly tiny front gardens had been tackled. At the back, a lawn and hardy perennials had been planted while at the extreme end, a vegetable patch had already yielded and helped supplement the family's income.

However, that was almost twenty years ago, and two decades of cooking, cigarette and chimney smoke, not to mention the soot from the nineteenth century Tottenham & Forest Gate Railway line which passed only a stone's throw from the bottom of their garden, had removed the gleam off every trace of the entire house. Especially the kitchen as it was the room most used.

Avis momentarily stood next to the dresser where the bottle had been placed, for a passing express train, its loud wailing whistle, brought back a stream of memories of happier times with her sister. She remembered how they used to sit on the steep slope just on the very edge of their garden and wave to the trains as they steamed by. And all the names they had given to the trains... So many happy innocent hours they had spent.

When they had shared the same bedroom, she remembered how they would count together the coaches as they were hauled past their house, the lines causing them to clickety-click. In the distance, the hooting and engine-type noises would continue until they fell asleep, the noisy and dirty trains being very much a large part of their childhood. Once, they had an occasion to travel on that very line, and it was with much excitement that they managed to recognise their own house. And their father who was digging the vegetable patch at the time. Spotting them, he had waved back.

Avis listened to the receding train, and felt her eyes smart again as her mouth tightened. Absent-mindlessly, she drew a forefinger across the top of the family's cutlery dresser, and stared hard at the accumulated dust. An illustration of how the family had abandoned their housekeeping duties since 3 October 1922. Something that was alien to the mother of the household.

Retrieving the bottle and a glass, she furthermore, and almost as if she were seeing it all for the first time, glanced around the tired old kitchen noticing immediately the happy photograph of her entire family in a polished wooden frame on the high dark brown mantelpiece, the once new gas cooker, the dark brown and heavily stained earthenware sink with the single tap, and the wire-mesh fronted pantry on which were laid, marble shelves to keep their food cool.

The toned-down brown and white wallpaper was now detaching itself in little strips, mostly near the low ceiling. The black and cream linoleum looked tired, exposed and worn. Especially near the cooker and sink. There were two doors, the dirtiest one furthest from her leading towards the long and at the moment, hardly visible garden. There was talk of having electricity installed, but for the time being, Avis had to make do with oil lamps and gas. She had been very excited about father allowing electricity into the house but now, at least over the last four months, the subject had, quite properly, been dropped.

Avis was used to the pleasures of the electric light because Edith, in her Ilford home had had it installed some years before. Although she loved living at 231, like any young person, she felt her parents were so Victorian. Next door's cat, twice impregnated by Joey, sitting on the dividing brick wall, meowed outside before hissing at some unknown threat, unnoticeable by Avis. However, this she ignored after a brief glimpse, and poured her mother a single measure.

Who was coming around as Avis reentered the front room. Two of her brothers were now doing their best not to cry, and had turned away to the grey outside. The other, the youngest, Harold, had already fled upstairs. Miss Vernon was cradling her dead friend's mother tightly and William was composing himself, standing against the mirror as if it were still capable of reflecting. His face was stone, his eyebrows terribly straight. The fire warmed his knees through his baggy trousers.

Ethel murmured a little as Avis held the back of her mother's head, and a little of the burning yellow liquid was dribbled over her wide thin lips. Soon, she opened them, and allowed her daughter to pour a reasonable amount under her tongue. Quickly, her colour returned, and she opened her eyes, but began crying almost immediately again.

Which prompted William to spin on his heels, and ordered Avis to return to the kitchen, and bring the packet of small blue pills their doctor had suggested she take in preparation for the event that she was now undergoing, and for which she had refused. However, William was adamant, and Avis soon returned with a small cardboard tube from which she extracted a large ball of cotton wool, scooped out a pill and dropped it into her mother's mouth.

This done, William ordered Miss Vernon to take her upstairs, and put her to bed and, without kissing his wife or showing her any kindness or courtesy whatsoever, the two of them shuffled out. Soon he heard them on the thinly carpeted stairs as she battled to get the weeping woman to her bedroom at the front of the building.

Avis could not help notice how quickly the intensity of the little front room had shifted from a cliff of dark black grief to anger, and she, with inspiration, offered a glass of the whisky to her father who took it without thanks and downed it in one go. Most unlikely for him she thought. But given the circumstances...

They stood in silence, and apart for perhaps half a minute, her father turned slightly away from her, towards the mirror again. So she gently took his large and bony hand in hers, and lifted it up to her cheek. Perhaps it was the warmth of her face, or perhaps that someone touched him in his awful time of aloneness, but with immense gratitude, he turned quickly and pulled her towards him. When she was close enough, she pushed her face deeply into his chest. A signal for the remaining two sons to leave before they embarrassed themselves.

Although she could not see him crying, and for that she was thankful, she knew that she must not look up. So there she stayed, his arms tightly curled around her back, fists clenched against her spine. How long they remained like that she could not tell, but the release made her sleepy and eventually, her knees gave way. Sensing this, William let her go and told her to get some sleep. The road is quiet he said. The delivery boys have been told to respect this morning. After she had kissed him on his cheek, she left and, fully clothed, was asleep within moments of laying her head on her pillow. William sat back heavily on the sofa, brought a hand to his face and covered his eyes, whereupon he cried again for his lost and executed child. Quite silently.

Two

The household remained silent for the next two hours after Newenham, William and Harold, the three boys, as already arranged, left to stay with relatives for the rest of the week. Their sudden heavy male absence, normally one of cluttering and shouting, just after each of them had visited their mother, who was sitting up in bed at midday, drinking tea supplied by Miss Vernon, set everyone off again. But eventually, the boys left leaving their mother staring helplessly onto the rain pattering against her small bedroom window. She sat, a picture of misery, her knees drawn up, and the eiderdown wrapped around her as some protection against the cold. Rarely did they light a fire in the bedroom. Only normally if someone was ill, and was expected to remain so for a few days. Miss Vernon attempted to warm Ethel's hands by covering them with hers.

After Miss Vernon and she had drunk their tea, and the elder of the two had refused all attempts to persuade her to eat a little, Miss Vernon helped her to wash and dress. She did not have much in the way of black in her wardrobe, but they did their best.

William, after shaking the boy's hands goodbye, settled into a routine, with which he was somewhat familiar; preparing the house for mourning. In his childhood, in the 1860s, death had been a universal and constant visitor. One might even say, a companion. By the time he had reached the age of fifteen, six of his siblings had been taken across the great divide as his father used to euphemistically call death.

As this unhappy social event occurred to each of his neighbours as well, it could truly be said that death became a familiar sight on the closely knit, working-class streets of his youth. Perhaps not a month would pass by without a fully draped, polished black cortège proceeded by a tall, hard-faced, slow-walking, immaculately dressed funeral director, accompanied by his many pall bearers silently drifting its way through the narrow East-End streets on its way to a graveyard, so many of the occupants of the dark coffins, young victims of smallpox, cholera, measles and other sweeping occasional epidemics such as influenza.

The etiquette in those days meant that all men would lift their hats, offering the gift of compassion, the older ones might even bow slightly to show respect, and the experience dulled everyone's senses. All would stop walking or talking as the cortège passed. Often, as death was important to the Victorians, for even the poor, the hearse would be black, probably with glass sides, and have a great deal of silver and gold decoration. Perhaps a huge canopy of black ostrich feathers might cover it. Only the very poor could not afford these trappings.

Inside lay the coffin. It would always be polished, and often had mouldings, expensive metal handles and inscribed plates. Sometimes the coffin was covered with black, purple or dark green cloth that was attached to it with brass, silver or gilt-headed nails. The hearse would probably be overflowing with flowers and wreaths. Normally, at least four, and six if the family could afford it, black horses pulled the ensemble, and each horse would have a black ostrich feather plume mounted on their heads.

The rest of the coaches would clatter after in a somber and dispiriting fashion. Each would contain a family of mourners, and usually the blinds would be drawn. Despite their position in society, the men would wear dark suits with crape bands around their top hats if they could afford it. The women wore black gowns made of crape, with black veils and black gloves. They would hold black-edged handkerchiefs to their eyes. Jewellery made of jet was worn if it could be afforded. These processions made its way at walking pace from the house of the deceased, along main roads leading out of town to the cemetery.

Therefore, as William remembered the kind of almost monthly event from fifty years ago, he shuddered with the thought of what was going to happen later on that day. As if losing his daughter through an unnecessary death wasn't bad enough. For his daughter, there would be no cortège, flowers, respect or compassion. No final words, no headstone and no graveside against which he or his wife and children might grieve. His beautiful child would be treated with utter disrespect, like Monday morning's rubbish.

The last funeral he had attended had been his mothers, and being her eldest child, he had made sure that there had been a trace of the respect for her as he had remembered from his early days. She had been drawn along by six black horses, and was so universally liked that the entire street had come out to offer their respects. It was that almost overwhelming body of love from all he knew that enabled him to cope with his loss. Their presence somehow made the occasion natural, as if her death was something not to be opposed.

From some dim memory, combined with the final words of the judge who had presided over the murder case, William knew that the body of his daughter would lay in unconsecrated ground forever with only a mark in some governor's private notebook, and a page in some secret file at the Home Office to remind future law enforcers where she lay. And moreover, it would be in a place where he would never be allowed to visit. Already, just thinking about it, he was beginning to feel the first stirrings of indignation, for he felt whatever sin his daughter had committed, and whatever punishment she had received, was being forced upon her innocent family as well. Therefore a sense of universal and righteous injustice filled his heart that morning.

Upstairs, after he had washed, and then dressed in his darkest suit and tie, William took out seven black armbands that he had recently and secretly brought in morbid anticipation, and gave one each to his wife, Avis and Miss Vernon as they entered their time of mourning. The other three, he would give to his boys later when they joined them at Holloway. Ethel did not have a black dress, but Miss Vernon found her a skirt and coat that would be appropriate. Avis borrowed another of her mother's coats, and after she was satisfied with her appearance, her dark brown hair pressed tightly to her small head, she poured four glasses of whisky, and they sat silently in the kitchen for a short while until it was time to leave. The day was certainly going to test their fortitude.

While he was waiting for his wife to complete her dressing, William had covered the other four mirrors they owned, and closed all the curtains in the house just as he had been taught to do when his brothers and sisters had died. The street outside seemed unearthly quiet for midday, and it would not resound to the energy of children or shop-keepers completing their rounds until after they had left early in the afternoon. When they did, curtains twitched, and the tree-lined curving road was impossibly empty and quiet. Just the opposite of what William would have wanted had they really been attending a funeral, his many neighbours showing their respect by their absence.

They caught the twelve-forty from Woodgrange Park Station, which deposited them at Upper Holloway at half past one. Although the journey time was short, and the train was not too crowded, for the four of them, it was the most agonising journey they ever took. Each were silent throughout with not a word said. William was convinced that everyone in the carriages, and on both stations, knew who they were, especially at Upper Holloway.

His paranoia was not entirely unfounded, as pictures of every member of his family entering and leaving the Old Bailey had occupied the front page of every newspaper in the land. Especially since Edith and Freddy's trial began. Naturally enough, when the death sentence was issued, the reporters shamelessly fought over themselves to get the best picture and story, and each journey both there and back to Holloway Prison became nothing less than a torture and a social embarrassment. Seeing how excited they became, and how they jostled for a good place to take a photograph brought home to William just how socially important and immense his daughter's case had become.

On the train, a thrown away early edition of The Mirror caught William's eye, and the muscles of his eyes stung as he read its headline, which reported only of the morning's executions. There was a photograph of a mass of people apparently demonstrating outside the entrances of both Holloway and Pentonville Prisons, and a minor headline read No hope for the condemned. William therefore fixed his eyes on the mass of factories and seemingly endless rows of terrace homes as he tried to imagine how things had got this far.

He knew he was not an important man, not a sensational man in the sense that he had knowledge or power. Therefore he was confused why those reporters had elevated him and his wife to be more important than they were. He was head of a small unimportant family. A little previously happy family, which meshed quite comfortably with larger circumstances. He did not know what had happened to him. The circumstances surrounding the imprisonment and now, execution of his eldest daughter had left him stunned, helpless and impotent.

As a man, and as a father, he had raised his first-born female child in the best possible way. Nevertheless, given the extraordinary coverage in the national newspapers, and the gravity of the legal weight against his daughter, he had proved himself to be inadequate. It was not something against which an ordinary man could defend himself. Therefore, as he sat next to Ethel, her right arm pressed against him, his chief emotion was one of shame. He had brought Edith into the world and failed her. And now he was to see her body for the last time.

*

The afternoon before had been an artificial experience, and one he would not have wished on his worse enemy, even if he had one. For that was the last time he saw his daughter alive. After three months incarceration, that was the finale visit, and already he had told his boys that they were not allowed to be there on her last but one day for fear of unsetting her even more than he knew she would be. Everyone knew it would be bad enough with just her mother and father and younger sister.

The three boys, having visited her two days before that, dared not argue with their father, and each of them would take the visual picture of their poor drugged older sister, surrounded by guards, to their graves. Each could not imagine what it would be like on the very last day but one. It would be many years before they would talk about it to their parents.

As if to compound his nerves, a reporter had taken a photograph of them when they arrived at the ticket office at Upper Holloway Station, but William had held his temper, and did nothing, remaining silent as he, in turn, ignored him. Avis though had thrown him a look of disgust as though she had just sucked in an insect. Ethel had walked resolutely forward and was relived when they reached the business of the street outside. Miss Vernon meanwhile had busied herself getting a cab.

They had arrived from Upper Holloway in the afternoon with plenty of time to spare, but were still kept waiting for a discourteous period in one of the upper offices without offer of any refreshment. Greeting them at the main gate was Lily, one of Edith's aunts who had pleaded to accompany them. This request was granted as she was on the official visiting list.

Eventually, some thirty minutes over their appointment time, they were escorted by Doctor Morton, the governor through a virtually silent hospital wing to B Wing where Edith was being kept in the, so-called, 'death cell'. So silent was it that they were sure every single prisoner was aware of their presence, and had decided to honour them in their own fashion. Certainly, on the occasions of their other visits, the place had never been that ghostly quiet. The female guards were more respectful too.

Edith was not, this time, at the table where she usually met them, but could be seen laboriously pulling on a dressing gown wearing a discouraging and painful expression. She moved slow, obviously drugged, and dragged her heels as she eventually met them. Doctor Morton immediately lied about her state of mind, offering the phrase that Edith has been quite cheerful of late.

The woman, it was clear, was devastated. She was a human wreck, and offered little in the way of conversation, replying to all questions with a lacklustre affirmative or denial. She asked no questions, and the family became increasingly uncomfortable in the presence of the female guards. The visitors could not understand intellectually how the building could transform a happy, articulate, intelligent and worthy member of society into this ruinous and helpless woman. Although emotionally however, each knew it was the thought of death, and the extinguishing of the self that would cause her to change into the stagnant woman who appeared before them.

Ethel found herself overcome with pity rather than grief, and that helped to keep her emotionally balanced. The very last thing she wanted to do was to break down on this final visit. Their stay was longer this time, although how long, no one had any idea for it was dusk when they left the oppressive set of buildings, and walked out into the fresher air of Parkhurst Road.

Finally, as Morton motioned that time was up, they were allowed to embrace her. And all did with positive assurances that by tomorrow she would be a free woman for there were so many people working on her behalf. Avis, after she had hugged her cold sister, and smoothed her right hand repeatedly over her dry hair, an action that she would remember for the rest of her life, noticed the lips of one of the woman guards quivering rapidly, her eyes arrowed fiercely at the floor.

Then it was her mother and father's turn, and they looked into her watering eyes as if she were a rare and precious object. Never had they seen their daughter looking so miserable. So unhappy, no words could communicate. The feeling of utter helplessness and impotence was complete. The shattering atmosphere as they moved out of the cell leaving Edith behind knowing what they were going to do to the poor thing at nine o'clock the very next morning was unimaginably distressing. It was made far worse by Edith's ingénue eyes, and her murmuring and motioning. Her arms softly flailing. Her voice slurred.

'Take me home dad. Take me home.'

She was gently struggling against the stronger arms of the two wardress', and the scene burnt into the family's eyes. They were no longer surrounded by compassion, but by the unjust rule of law. No clemency. Just mercilessness, indifference and blind obedience. The last resort, and the only force left. A frail and delicate woman set against centuries of decisions. That then was the last time they saw her alive, and as they backed away, suddenly she was gone for ever.

*

After meeting the boys, walking back into the prison mortuary was as chilly as they assumed it would be, and the four of them entered its cold domain in a fearful state, not knowing quite what to expect. However, the only object in the pitifully plain marble-covered room was a single wooden coffin. They noticed immediately that its lid was to one side, and the coroner, Doctor F.J.Waldo, to whom William was briefly introduced, begin to complete the necessary formalities which included taking statements from Edith's parents. William could barely mask his grief, and Avis held on to his arm tightly as it was the most unnatural and surreal experience she had ever encountered. She could not understand where her sister had gone. Why she would not wake up. Why she was in that coffin. So young and not ill at all. William was first asked to confirm that the pale-faced body laying there so unnaturally still was actually his daughter.

Most surprising was Ethel who showed little emotion as she gazed upon the face of Edith, now composed and laid out holding a shower of white lilies, a white cloth around her broken neck to hide the extensive bruising and damage. It seemed impossible to believe that just one day before, she had been a healthy woman. The mechanics of what and why those people who stood around her did this to her daughter was beyond her consciousness and her intelligence. That is why she remained so unemotional. Because she could not understand.

They were allowed to kiss her, but even then they had to ask permission. Their daughter and sister was no longer theirs. It was their final and strongest humiliation. Doctor Morton therefore nodded his assent, and each duly paid their last respects to their daughter, sister and friend. William's grief, as the last to approach the coffin, broke though then, and he collapsed over his child as he said goodbye, and had to be helped away by Ethel. With this, almost as a signal, or permission, Avis too wept silently in a corner while the unemotional Ethel, supporting her husband along with Ethel Vernon, glared at the downcast and highly embarrassed officials who dared put her daughter to death. The boys looked mummified. They looked like ghosts.

William recovered himself in a cold and empty side lavatory, and being allowed to take Edith's last few possessions; her wedding ring being the most emotionally precious, and her fur coat, after half an hour, the little party left Holloway prison for the last time leaving the body of their beloved Edith behind its thick and dark walls. Each felt a powerful sense of madness running through them. An insanity for what had been done.

An hour after they had left, under cover of darkness, the body was roughly covered with lime, and the coffin was unceremoniously sealed. It was then uncaringly lowered to a depth of eight feet in an unmarked patch of hard winter ground next to the workshops and the transformer house. Having observed the coffin being lowered into the ground, the governor returned to the warmth of his office to write up reports leaving two workmen to backfill the hole under deepening clouds heavy with rain. No position identified it. And there it would remain for the next forty-eight years.

Three

Having certain knowledge of his child's death, and not being able to undergo any form of ceremony or funeral rite for the body, had an unusual and unaccountable effect on Edith's parents, and to a lesser extent, Avis. The boys, even the eldest, did not possess the capacity to fully emotionally understand what had happened to their sister. In their intellectual minds, she was dead and that was that. Immensely sad, but that was that. In time they would comprehend, but by the time they developed the emotional maturity, the bulk of their emotions would be spent.

Miss Vernon, being merely a friend of the family, although she was extremely upset herself, was placed in the delicate position of marshalling Ethel, William and Avis home. Being younger, and of a shy nature, she therefore had limited experience in directing and controlling the adults.

With Avis, of whom she was very fond, it was simply a case of guiding her by the simple procedure of touching her elbow. However, she did not feel comfortable doing that with the senior Mr Graydon and his wife. Nevertheless, she took charge in flagging down another taxi and, when they were back at Upper Holloway, brought tickets and managed to manoeuvre them down onto the platform with little fuss despite more photographs being taken surreptitiously from one of the station's walkways. But not covertly enough to escape Miss Vernon's eye. And the middle-aged man in the trench coat did not escape the look she gave him either.

This caring attitude continued upon their arrival home as she discovered there was very little food in the house. Ethel and William had simply found their chairs in the kitchen by their fire and sat, still wearing their coats. However, Avis, upon arriving in familiar circumstances, boiled water and made a pot of tea. Miss Vernon, not wishing to leave them for one moment more than necessary, knocked next door and asked their boy if he wouldn't mind running to the corner shop to buy a loaf. Tinned tomato soup she found.

Ethel, quite understandably, broke down several times during the evening, and was the subject of much attention by Miss Vernon. Avis continued her knitting, and William tried to read a book on gardening, but it was clear that his wife's hysterics were irritating him, and eventually, he disappeared into the little outhouse next to the kitchen. This was where the family took baths and was cold, it being January. It was clear to Miss Vernon, that there was the best place for him that first evening. Conversation being impossible between husband and wife.

The blue pills were eventually brought out again, and Ethel, by ten in the evening, was mercifully fast asleep. William joined her soon after, which left Miss Vernon and Avis alone. About the same age, although Miss Vernon was younger, now the adults had retired, they both relaxed to an extent, and found themselves sharing the best of their memories of Edith, which in Miss Vernon's case was not many, but she enjoyed the chat. Oddly, this did not depress or upset them. In fact the opposite happened, as if they were keeping her alive, and they were able to break the suffocating depression that had been flooding them. They agreed it was good that it was over. They agreed that they could now put it all behind them. They agreed that they could now get on with their lives. They agreed that what had happened, had happened for a reason, and could not be changed. They agreed that time heals all wounds.

On what they could not agree, for it was not discussed, for it was too painful, was how much Edith was loved, and how fundamentally awful it was that she would no longer be there to cajole them with her jokes and flattery. That they would never again hear her high peels of laughter, or her sudden dramatic entrances. Never again to be embraced by her long and rather thin arms. No more to be entertained by her sometimes widely inappropriate sense of humour. Or passionate stanzas of poetry. Or the beautiful clothes she brought back from her shopping trips. Or the light gay manner she had with strangers, and the way she was easily able to put them at ease.

Both women knew precisely what they were missing, and it only took them to catch each other's eye just the once to silence them during their necessary period of denial. While they were foundering for a way to expunge the images that they had had to undergo over the last two days, they sat slightly apart, convention not allowing anything more.

After more tea and another hour, the formality of saying goodnight allowed them to award each other with a kiss on each other's cheek, and an embrace of genuine friendship, although the hug lasted perhaps slightly longer that it would have done under normal circumstances. This was understandable.

Four

Wednesday morning came dull and wet again, those clouds over London having shed more tears overnight, and it was evident that Ethel had come down with something for she was coughing badly, and had a mild fever at six in the morning. Avis volunteered to fetch their new doctor while Miss Vernon made up a fire in the bedroom, tended to the kitchen one, which warmed the house, and waited for Avis to return with groceries after she had visited the surgery.

It was what they expected from delayed shock, and the fever rose during the day. The doctor explained it was as a direct consequence of the emotional strain of the last few days, and ordered total bed rest. William was examined also, and was told not to return to work for at least a week on account of a racing heart, a pronouncement against which he strongly protested.

Nevertheless, Doctor Wallis, a tall and wiry Scotsmen, although not used to dealing with such unusual and tragic family circumstances, remained firm. William was to do what he was told. Out of earshot from the rest of the family, Doctor Wallis offered his most sincere commiserations upon the most tragic circumstances ever to be wrought on a family, and told him that he would keep a special eye out for them all. William, although on the point of his eyes smarting again, for such kindness from a stranger did not occur often, nevertheless raised his chin, directed his gaze and thanked him with an enthusiasm which surprised himself.

Doctor Wallis was certainly not like their former doctor. Who had been an irascible Surrey-born man possessing a short temper, and an even briefer ability to emphasise. A short man of pompous self importance, the Graydon family, like many others over whom he presided, were glad, and not just a little relieved when he had moved on after being their doctor for five years.

Although he may have softened a little given their almost unique circumstances, each of the Graydon members were convinced that the hard unemotional line he often took, which was one of, forget and walk on, would not have been appropriate in their circumstances. One of their neighbour's children, affectionately known as Little Billy, had been hit by a trolleybus in the summer of 1922 close by East Ham railway station, and the ten-year-old child had lost his right arm, which had been literally torn from its socket. After an initial week of uncertainly as to his survival, and then after some months of recovery, his mother had made a complaint to the local authorities about the way her child had been treated once he had been allowed home. Apparently, according to gossip, the doctor had been dismissive of the boy's injuries, and had ridiculed him when he had cried.

This was one of many instances of idle talk of which the Graydons became aware. In the quieter moments during their trouble, William had occasionally reminded Ethel how thankful they were to have a more professional and understanding man. He himself had once taken a tram to The London Hospital over an accident he had had rather than be seen by their infamous doctor occasionally described by William as a man no better than a veterinarian.

Little Billy, who lived four doors away with his five siblings at number 239, since his terrible accident, had become a favourite with Edith who, on her weekly Friday visits to her parent's house, had on each occasion, called in and spoken some encouraging words to the boy, and often gave him a paper bag of illicit sweets, although it didn't take very long for his mother to figure out who the culprit was who was lovingly spoiling her son.

When Edith's prison confinement began in October, Little Billy missed her visits immensely, but was naturally not told the truth about her absence. At first it was illness they told him, then another job, which meant she could not come so often and then, after her execution, he was told she had moved to another part of the country. His mother's lies were exposed though a few months later when he overheard one of his teachers talking. When he arrived home that afternoon, he had asked his mother about what he had heard but, with some shock, she had dismissed it as idle chatter, and accused him of eavesdropping. It wasn't until he had turned thirteen that he rediscovered the truth about the lovely lady who was once so kind to him. He became another victim who would remember her kindness for the rest of his life, and in the twilight of his own years, in the nineteen nineties, would recount to his great grandchildren the story of the tragic woman who had cared for him so much.

Breakfast was an affair to be forgotten. Although Miss Vernon had cooked bacon and eggs, only she ate. Ethel had no appetite, not even for the toast placed before her in bed, whereas Avis and William merely picked. Miss Vernon bravely attempted to encourage them to eat something, but knew in her heart that only time would resolve the current sadness and all the accompanying problems that prevailed.

Excusing himself, taking a second cup of tea, William retired to the only place he knew where he could be himself. His cherished garden shed. A place of unusual chemical smells, stacks of wood ready to be chopped up for the fires, heaps of rusty tools and unfinished projects of furniture.

Locking the door, not to keep anyone out, but to keep it closed as it had a habit of wandering open due to being improperly adjusted, he sat in his favourite old deckchair, a throw out from a few years ago, and packed his pipe. The rain pattered continuously, and after he had lit his small paraffin heater, he sat back, and drew out a head and shoulder picture of Edith from his back pocket.

Some masculine side of him told him not to indulge in such over sentimentalisation. Nevertheless, as he looked deeply at his daughter's loving smile and youthful, almost innocent eyes, a photograph taken on holiday, another macabre part suddenly superimposed itself on it, his last perception of her lying so still in her coffin in that awful cold mortuary. With acute distress mounting, he realise again how unnecessary her death had been, and by how much the world had been needlessly robbed. With no abashment whatsoever, he brought his large veined hand up to his eyes, gripped his forehead tightly and silently sobbed as deeply as he was ever allowed. Then he was glad he had locked the door.

Five

Ethel recovered, at least physically, after a few days, and by the end of the week, it was universally decided that Miss Vernon ought to get back to some semblance of normal life. After all, she had been a close companion to Ethel for almost three months since she had arrived from St Ives in Cornwall to work for Edith, and her place of work, where she was an under manager in a shoe shop in Penzance, desired her return. It was only because her uncle owned the shop that she had been allowed so much time off. But as, since she had been a child, she had been able to twist him around her little finger. So he did not take much persuading to let her explore a new life in the capital.

Therefore it was on the Saturday, with Edith four days in the ground, Miss Vernon packed her carryall and waved goodbye to Ethel, William and Avis. Embraces of affection and kisses were offered and accepted, and Avis promised to visit her in Cornwall when the summer arrived. A promise which was to be broken for two years. As she had to be taken to Paddington, a taxi was summoned, and the long-legged twenty-five year old climbed into it with mixed emotions.

Because the last three months, despite being a trial of the first order, had meant a great deal to her. She and Edith had hit it off immediately once they had met at the house of a mutual friend, and to assist her family in the way she had, had meant growing up a great deal faster than she had anticipated. Although half way towards thirty, she was still an innocent country girl, not used to the modern attitudes of Londoners at all, many of which she found shocking.

Right up to the day before her employer was executed, she had been utterly convinced that Edith would walk away from Holloway prison. She freely acknowledged, at least to herself, that if she had had advanced knowledge that she would have had to witness those last extremely harrowing moments with Edith's family in the death cell, and to see her poor friend's body laid out in that hideously dark coffin, then she probably would not have volunteered to help out as much as she did.

But she had done, and as she was driven away to catch her train, she was glad that she had. Miss Vernon was a sensible woman, unusually, a single child, but that was as a result of her mother undergoing an emergency hysterectomy just seven hours after she had been born back in 1898. Her first and only child. And therefore infinitely precious.

With no sibling rivalry, adored by her parents, and given the glorious countryside in which she spent her childhood,

Miss Vernon grew into a happy adult with only the slightest hint of naivety for that time and place. Her father was a fisherman, an earthy type of man who practically doted on his daughter who was very fair and gay. So with an abundance of good upbringing behind her, perhaps it is not surprising that she volunteered so readily to help out her new friend's family in the time of their greatest need.

Nevertheless, despite all these positivism's, Miss Vernon wept when at last she found herself in an empty carriage. Faced with a twelve-hour journey, and with a limited amount of reading material, and no one with whom to speak, she finally allowed herself to cry once the train reached the countryside. As the first stop was Salisbury, over an hour away, she felt safe from ridicule and interruption, as it was a non-corridor carriage.

Her parents, who knew of course where she had been, and what she had been doing, and for what family, although shocked that their child had become involved with such notorious people, nevertheless accepted that what she had been doing was from the kindness of her heart.

Upon a good night's sleep after her long journey, they questioned her thoroughly about the perplexing and the complexities of the famous case which, of course, they had been following in the newspapers. It was not without a sense of pride nevertheless, despite his personal feelings about the infamous Edith Thompson, that he mentioned to his drinking pals just to whom his daughter had been close.

On the Monday following Miss Vernon's departure, and just six days after losing Edith, The Graydon family prepared to face normality. This was by William and Avis returning to work, and by Ethel feeling well enough to entertain for a very short while, the closest members of her family. Which were her two sisters, Edith Liles-Walkinshaw, after whom Edith had been named, and Lily Liles-Laxton who had accompanied them on that last but one visit.

They arrived together a few hours after Avis and William had left, and had traveled together from north London where they had met up previously for a coffee to prepare themselves for the visit. Each wanted to assure the other that they were not going to mention anything that might have the slightest possibility of upsetting their sister.

However, although pale and thinner than they thought she ought to be, Ethel welcomed them in with a smile that seemed genuine. The sisters knew Ethel was recovering when they were told that she had baked a fruitcake the day before, although during the time they chatted, she did not eat any of it.

They had though, considerably underestimated how little it would take for the sharp memories of the recent past to surface. Just an initial query from Edith was all it took for tears to appear. Clearly their older sister was still in an extremely raw and, concerning those who had executed her daughter, unforgiving state.

However, just as quickly, as the three settled unpretentiously around Ethel's small wooden kitchen table, she recovered, and continued in this manner for the whole of the sister's visit, dipping in and out of intense grief, and combining short periods of lucidity with unwholesome anger.

Ethel informed them that she was, when a little clearer in her mind, going to embark on a series of letter-writing to those in authority. As she affirmed her conviction, her small fists opened and closed, while her eyes flitted from one sister to the other, looking for confirmation.

William, she said, was also going to join her on this campaign to put right the wrong that had been done to her beloved daughter. It was when Lily's eyes refused to maintain contact with her sister, and momentarily dropped to the thick green tablecloth, that Ethel imagined she was being judged. With this recognition, she stiffened, and asked her sister for her opinion. To confirm that she thought she was right in her actions.

To understand Lily's thoughts, it must be understood that some form of contentment played a large part in her life. She could not be classified as a working class woman anymore, having married above herself, and therefore had no need to work. She was quite content to be a stay-at-home mother of her two children in her large north London house while her hardworking husband did what a husband was supposed to do.

Lily could quite easily be described as a sensitive woman, and one prone to biliousness and various other disorders of her digestive and mental systems. Like her older sister, she was well known for her migraines, and her constant visits to the doctor. His bill alone in 1922 would have paid for an entirely new wardrobe for Ethel Graydon.

Lily, despite perhaps possessing a genuine fault in her body of some unknown description, suffered from hypochondrias. Therefore as her doctor had advised rest as a main answer to her problems, that state of mind had become essential to her. Midway through her life, she considered quietness and contentment indispensable to her lifestyle, even taking an interest in the distinctly unconventional side of life, which involved strange and otherworldly investigations into unknown phenomena such as hypnosis and spiritualism.

Naturally she had been completely horrified when she last saw her niece. The visible condition of Edith had shocked her immeasurably. Insofar as, at the moment of Edith's execution the next day, Lily was in bed suffering with one of her heads.

It can be understood then that from Lily's point of view, extending any form of suffering was a worthless gesture. At the time when she was sat around that kitchen table, already slightly miffed at having to selfishly put off a perfectly good hairdressing appointment because her older sister wanted support, she could not have conceived of how she herself would have coped had the tragic events been caused by her own daughter.

For this magnanimous thought, she can be congratulated, but she still felt that what was done, was done, and as there was no going back, no return to normality, and nothing could be done to return Edith to the living…then what was the point in continuing the anger, the rage, the letter-writing?

Lily had long ago recognised the value of calmness, and she knew it was necessary for her. She could not see what possible good any continuation of such sour emotions could accomplish. We can see then how her thoughts became so misinterpreted, and how much real empathy she had for any situation that did not encompass her own realm.

Edith slyly glanced at her well-to-do sister, and brought a tea cup to her mouth to disguise her feelings. Both Edith and Ethel knew how their sister's mind operated, but now was not the time for her half-backed, laid-back theories. What Ethel was looking for was practical support.

Nevertheless, Lily, as part of her awareness, knew that to refuse to assist her sister on such an important issue would cause more family trouble than it was worth. And that would directly impinge on her health. So, with the immediacy that comes from practice, Lily fixed her eyes on her poor sister's lined and tragic face, reached out for her soft and well-washed hand, and promised to commit to her cause, adding the word important and confirming that anything she could do, she would.

Now confirmed as a renegade letter-writer, at least in spirit only, as she continued to listen to Ethel's literary plans, her mind selfishly wandered, and hoped that her name would not be associated in the press with her sister. But then her stomach did a little churn as she remembered how well known the Graydon family was, which meant of course, any letter written to a newspaper condemning the establishment in all its forms was sure to be published.

Which would mean that her well-to-do friends, those with whom she played bridge, and those with whom she assisted at charity auctions and functions, and met in those fine Regency West-End tea rooms they frequented, would read of her intimate and private family secret. The one that she had not released or discussed with a soul. That she was the aunt of a convicted and executed murderess.

Her stomach bumped a second time when Ethel continued to relate the extent of her plans. Which included partitioning the Prime Minister and even the King. Staring into her sister's tired eyes, she just could not imagine the laughing stock she would become, concomitant almost certainly with a bout of poor health. It might even mean a change of address.

More tea was poured, and the cake was divided into bite-size triangular portions. It was soft and delicious, proving that Ethel had not lost her touch despite avoiding her cooker for months on end. Edith quickly helped herself to another piece as Ethel continued to relate what she intended to do.

Edith's opinion could not be more in opposition to Lily's. She was already a veracious letter writer being a fervent opponent of vivisection. Although she worked as a secretary for a chiropractor, the almost new system of complementary medicine, she spent the rest of her free time campaigning for a change in the laws which govern how livestock was treated. She could truly be said to be one of the pioneers of demonstrating how poorly western society treated animals.

She had a small library about the subject, but secretly, her enthusiasm and knowledge about the injustices perpetuated upon animals were so broad that she was even writing a book herself, albeit secretly from her husband who, although not understanding her passion at all, nevertheless encouraged her literary career.

Her two children, both boys, took no interest at all in their mother's, as they saw it, eccentric interest, and fled the nest as soon as it was practicable for them, leaving her with a great deal of free time, and only one husband and his occasional few business friends to feed.

Therefore she relished the thought of sharpening her pen, convinced that with her superior use of the written word, she would succeed in bringing attention to the dreadful fate her niece had suffered. Although her sister Lily was known as the sensitive one, her awareness extended inwards whereas Edith's traveled in the opposite direction. However, as much as she loved her namesake, she felt she would not be able to properly control herself during those last prison visits. Which is why she said her goodbyes, at least in her mind, a week earlier, which was on the occasion of her last physical visit.

Leaving her niece behind knowing what they were probably going to do to her had been one of the hardest occasions, and she was emphatically ordered not even to hold her hand. Edith had sat across to her over an old and much damaged and marked wooden table while three female guards had stood over them. They had talked about the way Edith's mother had brought her up, about her dad, whom she missed so terribly, and about her own family. Just sharing common news.

Edith Thompson, at the time, was justifiably miserable, but her visitor could see that she was making an effort to appear bright. This was of course some time before the Home Secretary decided that her life was worth nothing, and that she could be disposed of as so much rubbish.

Edith, the aunt, sitting across from Edith, the soon-to-be-executed, held terrible feelings about the affair, which is why she made that day her last visit. Although she had not known for certain, in that she would not have staked her own life on it, her intuition and knowledge of the powerful men behind the scene, due to her own interests made her niece's death a virtual certainly.

Repeatedly in her mind, she cursed the dates. If only all this nonsense had taken place before 23 October 1922, then she was absolutely convinced that her niece would have been saved. Edward Shortt had been the Home secretary at the time, a noted liberal. He was not a particularly success-ful barrister, but was popular and a clear thinker. He did a great deal to prevent rising crime levels, and helping unemployed soldiers after the Great War. Although not well respected in Parliament, he was admired in certain quarters for his liberal thinking. Edith Liles-Walkinshaw had no doubt whatsoever that had her niece's representations come under his judgment, she would have lived.

It was well known that Shortt was capable of a great deal of compassion. A case from 1919 illustrates this:

A young man called Adams was seventeen years old in 1919, and had befriended a sixty-year-old man George Jones whom he stabbed with a shoemaker's awl, three times in the chest and three times in the throat. Adams was subsequently charged with murder. His trial took place at Guildford Assizes in July 1919. The jury found him guilty, and he was sentenced to death. Which was later commuted by the Home Secretary, Edward Shortt, to life imprisonment.

He also repealed, in September 1922, a death sentence on Mrs Elsie Yeldham, a woman condemned to death for murder by the same judge as would be judging Edith Thompson's case the following month. However, Edith Liles-Walkinshaw knew of the Home secretary Bridgeman, and of his Eaton educated ways, a staunch conservative who took over office from Shortt on 25 October 1922, just twenty-two days after the murder of Percy Thompson. Under the new Conservative government, he developed a reputation for harshness and resolve, actively disliking strikes, socialism, and trade unionists. This was not a man to have on one's side if one needed compassion.

It was therefore Edith Liles-Walkinshaw's superior knowledge of the guardians of England, none of which, naturally, she imparted to the family, that virtually promised that her niece would probably not get the reprieve for which everyone was praying. Even when the editor of the Daily Express, Beverly Baxter himself chartered an aeroplane to visit Bridgman at his country estate at Minsterley the night before to plead with him one last time. Even with over a million signatures signed, Bridgman remained true to his convictions. Whatever they were. If ever there were two unfeeling monsters in this story, the Home Secretary was one of them. The other being Montague Shearman, the trial judge, a noted misogynist.

Cautiously Edith asked Ethel if she had a list of those against whom she intended to petition, and upon being asked this important question, Ethel crossed to the mantelpiece, and drew a slip of paper out from under a small and cheap carriage clock. Silently she passed it across where Edith unfolded it, and after a second or two, gave a very low whistle as her eyes darted across the list of names.

She nodded impersonally, and indicated her approval with a smile, at the same time passing the paper to Lily who took it as if it were contaminated with some form of deadly disease, but nevertheless, voiced her enthusiasm too, if not with a little less emphasis.

An arrangement was fixed so that Ethel would write an original letter, in the flavour of how she wished to express her disapproval, and what her aims were, and then her sisters would append their names to it. At the moment, there were sixteen names on the list. Including King George V. In Lily's mind, the situation as it developed, was extremely unsatisfactory, but she believed she covered her feelings well enough. She immediately decided to talk the matter over with her husband at the first possible opportunity, and could only pray to God that he be as equally distressed by the idea thus, hopefully, allowing her to gracefully sever her connection from the socially ruinous idea. Edith told Ethel that she would in addition, be writing her own letters.

Once the table had agreed on their strategy, Ethel poured more tea, cut more cake, and the conversation turned to other things, although no subject ventured far from close family matters. After an hour, Edith imagined she noticed Ethel becoming rather tired, and suggested they leave.

Ethel, not surprisingly, agreed, and finishing her tea, stood and thanked them again for their support. Then after one more little speech, the two sisters found themselves in Shakespeare Crescent, and walking north towards Woodgrange Station. The three sisters had always been tall and willowy, and the two of them cut quite a dash as their well-cut clothes differed against the relative poverty of East-Ham. Something of which the two sisters were all too aware.

Hidden within their most inner thoughts, and never vocalised, both of them believed that perhaps if Ethel had married into a better class of person, that is to say, not the family of William Graydon, then perhaps the family dishonour may have been avoided. Clearly, to them, it was the loose upbringing influence by the Graydon side that had turned their young niece's mind, and filled her brain with all those silly romantic notions, which was to eventually become her downfall.

Stately, they reached Woodgrange station, and brought tickets, deciding not to visit the refreshment-room as it was teeming with schoolchildren, no doubt on some trip. Instead they boarded the first available carriage. Luckily, the train was steaming as they walked down the stairs to the platform. Once they were settled, they talked about the afternoon of course...and the letter writing specifically.

Edith could very well read the hesitation in her younger sister's eyes, face and general non-enthusiasm. It was no secret that Lily had been the more fortunate of the three sisters on the issue of marrying the most connected and wealthiest man. Almost a doctor. However, Edith had not done so badly for herself. And they both lived in fairly palatial houses with sound address', and her husband had a well-laid out career in front of him.

Certainly, as they had reflected occasionally, they had done better for themselves in the marriage stakes than poor Ethel, who believed at the time of her marriage, that moving to East Ham from Dalston was going up in the world. In much the same manner as Ethel's eldest tragic daughter in her mid twenties, believed Ilford was better than East Ham. Had Edith Thompson borne a child, it could be believed that he or she might have themselves ventured further into the Essex countryside.

Ethel was tired, and she took the opportunity of a quiet house to take a nap, which she did by the fireplace in the kitchen. Covering her thin shoulders with what used to be her mother's dark red shawl, only the two puppies next door at 229 disturbed her a little as they yelped occasionally, waiting for their mistress to return. Sitting in William's deep easy chair, for his was more comfortable than her rocking one, she stretched out her legs, slipped off her slip-pers so her toes were warmed by the gently roaring fire which she had stoked, and covered herself with a light green woollen blanket. After running a few sentences of what she hoped would be useful lines in her letters, she fell into a light sleep as the afternoon came to a chilly close.

Whereupon she dreamed of her daughter, and her husband and of a life which was no longer bearable, or even tolerable. Except she did not know, or could not understand about whose life the dream was supposed to be. She dreamt of a cave by the sea in which her daughter was trapped by a rising brackish tide, and of her efforts to reach her before she drowned. Which she did not, and therefore awoke gently perspiring over an hour later, the fire now throwing long flickering shadows around the worn furniture. After looking at the time, Ethel stretched and rose to her feet, a little cold and frightened. Their little mantlepiece clock told her it was time to cook supper. William and Avis would be home soon. But a voice inside her head, spoke to her.

Immediately the contents of the dream came into her memory, and then by swift imagination, she was in that death cell again speaking her last words to her daughter. It was momentary, but tears fell immediately. She was given no choice.

Six

William, one of three chief clerks with a tobacco company, had been well established at his firm when he and Ethel had married in 1892. The tall and well-built man had started his working life on the shop floor, and had worked himself up diligently to his semi-managerial position by no more than the appliance of hard work. Being a genuinely convivial fair-minded fellow, he was well liked, and respected by his fellow workers, both on his level and under. Athough he could become a little taciturn occasionally, that was only because he believed in getting things right, and he enjoyed the concentration.

Therefore, his work being first rate, and his sickness record amounting to just one week in over twenty-five years, when he had badly twisted his ankle falling off a tram a few years ago, the director had no difficulties in allowing him the required time off to prepare and then attend to his daughter's court case. Like all the victims in this profoundly and quite unimaginably sad saga, William was thoroughly upset when his family name caught the public imagination, and his daughter's infamous actions made the headlines on every British newspaper.

Needless to report, he did not relish the thought of his quiet and unassuming life being turned upside down and inside out, with reporters hounding him from doorstep to doorstep, and unknown people taking photographs of him and his family whilst out performing the most normal of activities, such as walking or shopping.

Within a very short space of time, as the furore grew, and Edith's case was transferred to the Old Bailey, the social pressure became intolerable. When other members of staff began to complain that the press had begun to harass them as well as they entered and left the building, all hoping for the smallest scrape of gossip, the decision was made to call William into the director's office where he was sympathetically told to take off the required time at half pay against next year's holiday until the matter was settled. It was only because Edith had been charged with a capital crime that he had been dealt with so understandingly.

William had done nothing, but profusely apologise for the trouble he was causing, and at the time, his heels burning on the director's thick carpet, his cheeks became a shade of cerise at his embarrassment and humiliation. When he had left work that last day, he was extremely angry with his daughter for causing so much trouble for the family. Eventually, with the case taking five days to resolve itself, and then taking three weeks more until her death, and one week after, he had taken six weeks off. An amount he was never to recover.

His three closest pals, the ones with whom he drank at his local, were at the factory gate upon his return to consolidate their friendship, and he shook hands with them, mutely at first, but then with a mixture of relief and awkwardness. They in turn spoke only in the broadest of terms, bringing him up to date with the latest internal news. The rest of the employees, hundreds of them, streamed through the double high iron gates, and William felt like a black marble amongst a myriad of white ones.

Yet his natural paranoia had a basis in truth, for everyone who could read, and even those few who could not, had become aware of the employee whose daughter had been put to death, and there was no avoiding the enquiring eyes. Those who took a glance, did so as if they were attempting to see a monster's monster. The last woman to be hung in the British Isles had been fifteen years previously, so naturally, to those with not even the usual slightest morbid interest, William quickly became an object of unkind curiosity.

An early meeting with the management was on an altogether different level than his last one in that poorly heated, wooden-panelled office, and Mr Jenkins, now quite the congenial boss, bad him to sit while his secretary fussed around, and poured William a cup of tea, and offered him a plain biscuit. The director made it clear that he was profusely sorry to hear of his tragic news, and that he could be put on 'easy duties and hours' for a period if he so wished.

To which William sensibly replied that he believed it would be in his very best interests if he continued to work as hard as he had before, believing that only time would heal, and the best way to act was to keep his mind busy. This was the correct answer as far as Mr Jenkins was concerned, and told William that if there were any more complications, of any sort, then he must not hesitate to speak to his secretary. At this, William had nodded with enthusiasm even though his heart was broken.

When he left the director's book-lined study he felt significantly calmer. However, when he descended from the first floor into the factory, and came under the inspection of a few hundred pairs of eyes, his blood pressure rose again, and shuffling quickly, found his own small wooden office where he quickly hung up his coat and hat.

His young apprentice, a quick-minded lad called David fetched him a batch of papers to be signed, and looking at the lad's slightly embarrassed pimply face, decided to take pity on his youthfulness, and mentioned simply that it was all right, and gave him a friendly shake of the shoulder.

David brightened up considerable after this exchange, and began to chat away in the manner William remembered.

Lunch was a quick half a pint and a cheese roll near Silvertown with his three friends in a run-down public house called the Three Tuns. Apart from a few old regulars, all of them past retirement, the filthy and nearly condemned eighteenth century building was empty. It would soon be demolished to make way for a council house complex. William found the beer rather sour, the conversation trite, and the memories overwhelming. He was therefore glad to get back to the security of his office after the token half an hour.

Apart from one uncomfortable occasion in the afternoon when, while inspecting a stock of raw material just unloaded from one of the many wagons, two women decided that they needed to add to the volume of sympathy he had already received, the rest of the day passed off without incident.

The problem with those women though was that, apart from one of them being about an inch shorter, she looked so very much like his dead daughter that it was all he could do to stop himself from rudely staring, something she noticed and thought queer.

She was also about the same age as his Edith, and wore her hair in the same fashion which was not an uncommon style for a young women in that time and place. However, her similar appearance went further than that. It was the roundness of her face, and her eyes in particular. The width of her small mouth was the same, and she had the same delicate ears.

In that last afternoon in the death cell, he had particularly burnt her alive features into his memory, despite the devastating human wreak she had become. As much as he hoped and prayed that those who had the power over her life, in his dark heart, would forgive her, he had to admit that he felt as if they, as a family, hadn't a chance. He remembered looking at her, in their closing moments, and not understanding at all the difference between his precious daughter's life, and the massive objection the government had against her living. Of course she was going to die.

The young woman, who was a new employee, felt his uncommon gaze, and mistaking it entirely, swiftly looked down and away while her friend carried on verbalising her compassion. It was all he could do to directly, make his apologies and hurry away.

The end of that first working day came at last, and the journey home was as uneventful as his going there. He wore his old dark trench coat, and that, plus his fedora, fairly well obscured his face. Walking with his head down, in the rain that had begun again, he became as anonymous as any other Londoner.

Seven

Avis did not have the four-mile journey on public transport that her father had had to endure twice a day, six days a week, as the telephone exchange where she was an operator was simply ten minutes walk towards East Ham railway station. It had been her usual practice to wait for her friend Mary Page who lived at number 95 on the corner of Byron Avenue and Browning Road, but since the disruption of her routine, they had not been in communication with each other for over two weeks.

Her story is, concerning her place of work, essentially the same as her fathers. In that she had applied for some time off (because she was a witness not because the defendant was her sister) and although initially her request was frowned on by her manager, the staid spinster Miss Brown, after the why and how was established, her opinion about the matter had softened considerably, and even more so when the death sentence was announced, and eventually carried out.

This was because, when she herself was a young child, an orphan who lived in an institution until she was adopted, she had a favourite friend who lived in the next street,

May, a girl of similar age in whom she found a fast friend. Unfortunately, May's parents, when she was thirteen, decided a new life in South Africa was what the family needed, and the young Miss Brown lost her best friend although they wrote to each other continuously.

Nevertheless, May's new life did not turn out as expected, as five years later, having fallen for the misguided charms of a wicked and evil young man, she was induced into a life of petty crime. The horrifying conclusion of which, after the murder of an old shopkeeper, led May, along with her boyfriend, to the gallows in Johannesburg. At the age of eighteen, Miss Brown lost the one person who understood her more than anyone else.

That was twenty-two years ago, and allowing no one else into her life, at the age of forty, she was a confirmed and strict maiden. She lived quietly in the house of her dead stepparents with several cats, and her only known pursuit was her love of gardening. Specifically roses.

When Avis returned to work on that Monday morning, Miss Brown's heart, remembered how she had once felt all those years ago, and invited the twenty-eight year old into her office for a cup of tea before her shift began. Avis was momentarily nonplussed at this act of kindness, and not a little suspicious, but she drank the tea nevertheless as Miss

Brown espoused her personal sorrow over her bereavement.

Avis could see that Miss Brown's affliction was quite genuine, but she had no idea why the previously unyielding and rigid disciplinarian was being so kind. Therefore she remained on the edge of her seat during the interview, and came away much confused. Even as she stood to leave, Miss Brown, having finished her speech, touched her gently on the shoulder before offering it a slight squeeze. She looked kindly at her over her black pince-nez's, and fixed her firmly, saying that if there was anything she could do to ease her pain, then she was not to hesitate to knock at her door.

Therefore, bewildered may be the best explanation of her state of mind on that first morning back as she left her coat in the ladies changing room, before she joined the other hundred or so *hello girls* in the main switch-room. The place was the usual cacophony of raised voices which never dropped in volume at all as she entered, although she gained plenty of attention. A new, finely dressed girl with a blond Eton crop had taken seat number twenty-three, her usual place, but a wave caught her attention, and with a genuine smile, sat next to Mary who, in-between calls, welcomed her back with a great deal of smiling and gesturing.

Having being employed by the General Post Office since she left school, and had long become acclimatised to the business of the work, it took but a second to attach the headphones provided, pull out a pen, arrange a sheet of paper before her, and connect to the first caller.

In between calls therefore, but falling naturally silent when Miss Brown or her deputy, Miss Howe, was on the floor, she and Mary spent the next three hours catching up. Avis was glad to return to work, even though she found the monotony a little tiresome, and some of the customers more than a little sharp and rude.

Just one or two of those that became angry, she desperately wanted to tell them that losing a connection, or not having enough pennies for a call was not the end of the world. Losing one's sister to a noose was, and they ought to put things into perspective. Needless to say, she had the perspicacity to keep her temper under control, but once or twice it was desperately hard.

Dealing with a disembodied customer reminded her of how awkward it was dealing with the faceless bureaucrats of the Home Office. Those unidentifiable men who worked behind the scenes, who made the laws, and ordered those of a lesser capacity to carry them through. There was no face-to-face honest communication, and because of that, the caller often felt they could be as rude as they liked.

It was though, perhaps an hour into her morning shift, that Avis noticed this. Or rather noticed a change in her manner towards those rude enough to raise their voices. It was as if she herself had become greater than those tormenting customers. As if she realised that there was absolutely no point in entering into an angry dialogue. And doing so would no more help the situation, or change the situation than if she had implored Doctor Morton, the governor of Holloway prison just to do the right thing and let her sister go.

Almost certainly, she *knew,* if those anonymous Home Office stooges had been required to put the rope around her sister's neck, pull the lever and then deal with the consequences afterwards, it was very unlikely they would enforce the law as it stood. In a moment of pure clarity, in which a caller was left on the line, Avis saw the pyramid of justice for what it was; an abomination of transferring responsibility or blame onto a person of lesser social value. It struck her as a thunderclap.

Before that clarifying moment, she had imagined the entire process of her sister's imprisonment and death to have something to do with the disembodied notion of justice. Now she was stunned that her sister had died not because of a murder, but because of something entirely man-made.

If Avis had been feeling generally helpless before she stepped into work, by the time her afternoon shift had finished, and she was stepping out with Mary into the cold and wet winter air, she was not anymore. The clarity of her earlier moment of recognition had changed her viewpoint more than any other thought she had had previously. Mary became aware of this softening of character, but did not mention it. She imagined that her close friend, whom she had known since primary school, was still simply dealing with her many emotions. Nevertheless, she linked arms, and dragged her back home to her mother's house.

Mary's mother, Caddie was quite unlike Ethel Graydon. In that she was loud, and prone to fits of chuckling, which did not stop just because a neighbour with a troubled family history was visiting. It had been a long time since Avis had even seen her own mother smile, and she was somewhat taken aback by the presence of so much good cheer. She accepted a cup of tea but refused supper, as she knew her mother would be cooking. After her and her father's first day back at work, she knew that it was important for the family to sit down together, and so that became her excuse to take her leave.

Much of the reason for Mary's widowed mother to be on such good terms with the world was the almost daily presence of Mr Esequiel Banks, an exceptional and light-footed dancer from the hall where she practiced her ballroom dancing twice a week. Over some months, and given a reasonable period of time for the, still young, Caddie to cease her mourning, she had allowed the kind and entertaining Mr Banks to court her.

Hence the reason the woman was in such high spirits. Mary did not entirely agree with the direction in which her mother was heading, but found solace in the fact that her two sisters, both younger, felt the same. Their father, who left the earth eighteen months previously, could never be replaced. Kind and as entertaining as Mr Banks was. However, none of them felt they had the right to mention their feelings to their mother. They had witnessed first hand how utterly devastated she had become when their father had died. Even at that moment, Mary had had no idea why he died except it was something to do with a lump, which had developed on his leg. It was just not the sort of thing that was mentioned.

Avis for a long time, used to go around there after work and, being very fond of Mr Page, she took a great deal of pleasure in reading to him passages from his Bible. When he finally died, Avis was nearly as bereft as his own daughters had been. Mary though had never forgotten her friend's kindness, and their relationship had deepened significantly.

It was Avis's father, William and Mr Page who became better friends first through their work. Drinking pals only to begin with, but which quickly turned into a first class friendship through their shared twin interests of gardening and dancing, which became compounded when Ethel was introduced to Caddie. Therefore the four of them would take trips out to places of horticultural interest like Kew Gardens or the Chelsea Physic Garden. When the children grew, it was only natural that they too would befriend each other. Especially as they went to the same schools.

When Edith had been taken into custody, and the story broke, first in the local paper and then nationally, the support the Graydon's received from the Pages was unlimited. However, it was not the Pages, which withdrew their friendship as the case deepened, but the Graydons. It was not intentional, but more a case of withdrawal against the mounting clamour of confusion and self-made isolation. Dealing with the reality of Edith's case took the whole family away from every normal activity they had known. Interviews, police courts, visiting solicitors, Holloway prison and dealing with the growing interest from the press, each activity took them away from friends, and their usual mundane lifestyle. Mary and Caddie attempted to keep in contact, but it quickly became clear that the Pages could only support them from a distance.

Mother and daughter also felt that there was a demonstrable amount of humiliation and shame rapidly developing, as shown on one of the last days at work before Avis took her extended leave. Conversation between them had already been restricted to non-Edith matters because Avis had for some days, refused to talk about her whenever Mary asked how things were, or if there were any developments. This was about the time when the case in its entirety was transferred to the Old Bailey.

Therefore, it was a period when reality and the wild imaginations of real punishment became a possibility. Even at that stage, however ludicrous it was to imagine, the family had become aware of the gallows, its hideous ancient blackened silhouette appearing on the horizon of their consciousness, now somehow connecting the ordinariness of the East-End family to the spectre of sudden and undignified death.

After Avis' first day back at work, Caddie fussed about as usual preparing supper, and she was already dressed to go out. Caught up in the pandemonium of another family, Avis managed to set aside her morbid thoughts for a short while, and became semi-animated once more, much to the delight of Mary who dragged her into their best front room, and gave her a demonstration of the family's new gramophone, and the set of ten records with which it had arrived.

Avis was very much impressed by the machine and how it worked. She was told that half of the cost of it was supplied by the kind and entertaining Mr Banks, which drew a raised eyebrow from Avis, as she immediately wondered what Mary's mother had done to deserve such an impressively loud machine.

After the fourth record ended, a sudden thumping on the wall signified that Mr Strong, one of their elderly long-suffering neighbours had had enough musical joy in his life. At the same time, Caddie popped her now, fully made up face around the door, and asked her daughter to put everything away as it was getting late.

It was a therefore a perfect time for Avis to take her leave, and a few minutes later, she began the three-minute walk to her house. A dark and toe-freezing icy white fog accompanied by a moderate breeze, had descended upon the area, much of it rolling off Wanstead flats, and it caused the normally boisterous area to become quiet, ghostly and strange as the streets emptied, and people disappeared into the warmth of their homes. Only a few solitary hardy ones could be seen, heads down against the wetness of the dark evening.

Avis' Bar shoes echoed on the cold paving slabs as she hurried along. In the very far distance she heard the sad hooting of tugboats working on the Thames, a lonely sound drifting through the dense fog, as if the atmospheric conditions were funnelling the sounds directly to her. Closer, she became aware of the shuffling steaming trains of the many railway lines, which surrounded and crisscrossed the area. The isolation of the sounds made her feel uneasy. There was no comfort to be had from them. Unlike as in earlier times, when she and Edith were children, and they used to lie in bed and listen to them.

Ethel had not made that much of an effort to celebrate her husband and her's return to work, and some form of normality. Just a steak and kidney pie, potatoes and vegetables followed by Spotted Dick and custard. However, the meal was up to her usual high standard. That was just one of the many reasons by which Ethel had originally impressed William when they had met at a Christmas work dance. Although not a man who ate a great deal, he did nevertheless, enjoy his food, and Ethel's cooking skills had flabbergasted him. A long time, it must be suggested, before they had become betrothed.

Dinner was a silent affair as all the asking about how the day had been had been discussed in the short time beforehand while Avis and her father had been washing their hands. Avis noticed that a new picture of Edith had been added to the small collection, which adorned the mantelpiece in the kitchen, and she made her approval known.

Her father had picked it up from the photographers on his way home.

A prayer was said before eating. Grace of sorts, and for a moment, it was as if Edith had joined them again. When they closed their eyes, she was there. A giggle just permanently below her personality, no matter the occasion. Nevertheless, there was a distinct and real sadness over all three as they ate. Each knew this would be the last time the three of them would be together on their own. The three members of the family who had suffered the most. For the boys would be returning over the next few days, and however much they missed Edith, it would be impossible to maintain this level of grief with them constantly around. Perhaps it was time the house stopped having the inertia of a morgue.

Eight

Upon their return the next day, the three Graydon young men, aged between nineteen and twenty-five, did revert the household into some semblance of its former self soon after their arrival. What made everything more interesting was because two of them were dating. Perhaps not seriously, but passionately enough to occasionally bring their lady friends to tea.

Therefore, very soon, at intervals, the house became quite noisy and occasionally unruly, and it was all William could do to keep order between the good-natured heckling that occurred between the three of them, or the five, if their dates were included. Avis was not prone to get involved with her brothers and their girlfriends, although she did her best to help her mother with the cooking. But as this activity was not one of Avis' gifts, she was often relegated to principally laying the table, and being a host to her brother's young ladies, whom she used to take into their glasshouse in their garden where they could smoke without disapproval from Ethel and William.

It must be remembered, concerning the boys, that they were not bred to exhibit their emotions so easily as their sisters. Almost immediately though, Avis saw through their bravado, and discovered three hurt men, made worse by their inability to admit and display their fears. The oldest would find temporary solace in alcohol, and the others in the church.

If all this sounds as if the death of Edith were quickly forgotten, nothing could be further from the truth. In the boy's back bedroom, a picture of her enclosed in a white frame was placed on a wall, and there it would remain until the house was sold, some seventeen years in the future. It was just one of a series of reminders dotted about the house, which William and Ethel implemented to insure that the memory of their once effervescent eldest daughter would never be forgotten.

It is unknown whose idea it was to plant an ornamental elm to mark the celebration of Edith's life, but it grows there still. William brought it one Saturday soon after he had returned to work after he had already prepared the soil, and research at the local library on how to look after it. It was delivered quite quickly on the back of a lorry by three men. The tree itself was simply named Edith, and on a dry Sunday, one of those rare winter days marked by a clear blue sky accompanied by slight breeze, after church but before lunch, the six members of the family plus Mary and her mother, stood in a semicircle as William planted it reverently in the middle of their lawn. He had already cut away a circle of grass some three foot in diameter and dug a hole deep enough to accept it.

Upon shovelling the soil back and making it secure, whilst enjoying the weak yellow sunlight, he then proceeded to read Job 7, which everyone found both calming and releasing. After, there was a moment's silence so that they could commune with Edith in their own particular way and say goodbye. It was during this final part of the semi-improvised ceremony that Ethel began to weep again, and had to be comforted by Avis and Mary. Finally, William unwrapped a cardboard tube, which had remained hidden from the rest of the family, and extracted a small brass plaque upon which was engraved in solid black, EDITH THOMPSON 1893-1923 REST IN PEACE. IN LOVING MEMORY OF A MUCH LOVED DAUGHTER. NEVER FORGOTTEN.

This was placed on top of the small mound of earth, which supported the elm. William would affix it securely later. For the time being, all that remained was for William to offer each person a chance to sprinkle some decent manure around the base of the tree, and pour some water.

After, they retired to the front sitting room for Sunday lunch. But it was a quiet affair. Even the boys were subdued. In saying Grace before they ate, William added that he hoped that the memory of Edith, and what had been done to her would far outlast her achievements. And that what they had just done would please her, wherever she was. They had roast beef that Sunday, also as a celebration of one of Edith's favourite foods. A lemon meringue pie followed, which was so tasty and light that there were no seconds left for anyone.

Outside, as the sun lowered itself, and the afternoon came quickly, the ten foot high sapling looked fine and healthy. By a strange happenstance of fate, the virulent strain of disease, which was to reach England in four years time, and whose name would strike fear into the hearts of all conservationists and arborists, passed by this particular specimen. While elms of all ages were being devastated in local London parks, Edith remained upright and strong. William, who fed it once a week after work, made sure of that.

Some forty-four years later, a new, far more virulent strain arrived in Britain on a shipment of rock elm logs from North America, and this strain proved both highly contagious and lethal to all the European native elms. However Edith, now a proud twenty feet high, and daily providing shade in the summer for one Miss Varny, a retired ambulance driver, again, escaped the devastating ravages of the usually fatal fungus.

Miss Varny, somewhat surprisingly, given how many years had passed, was quite aware of the story of the tree, and of her origin and planting. A combination of local gossip and urban myth. Miss Varny was the third person to buy the house after the Graydons had left. Nevertheless, by planting daffodils one year soon after she had taken vacant possession, she had uncovered the brass plaque, which confirmed the stories about which she had heard. After it was cleaned, it was again mounted on an oblong of hard wood, and once again assumed its place under the shadow of the elm.

The original plague itself, as brought by William, had been lost for several years when Edith came to the end of its natural life some 212 years later. However, others had been etched containing exactly the same description, and remained fastened to it though. After so much time had elapsed, many locals came to believe that Edith was buried beneath her.

In that future time, she was then surrounded by a quiet and contented area of growing woodland. A place for lovers and dog walkers. An area of gently sloping landscaping, where flowers grew all year round, and with not a house to be entered within twenty minutes walking distance. Edith had lasted well. By then, it had become somewhat celebrated in its own right, a tree people came to especially view.

A strong local monument with an eighteen-foot circumference, and a ninety-two foot crown spread reaching almost one hundred and twenty feet in height. The decision to end its life was made as its internal structure was no longer able to push nutrients to its furthest branches. It was by that time certainly celebrated, and its destruction was reported with a great deal of sympathy, but everybody knew it had to take place as the old thing was dying.

It took six workers, seven days to remove her, and the borough set up a committee to decide what was to be done with the wood. Eventually, it was decided to turn it into three uses. One was for pens for the children of the parish, the second provided small frames which was sold for charity, and the third was to make free walking sticks for the elderly. Nevertheless, a decision had to be made about what to do with the plague. And so, some 213 years after William stamped down the earth around the tree, a previous cutting from Edith, which had been nourished and cared for in a hot house, was planted in exactly the same spot and the plague attached to it.

William's Elm was not the only memorial to Edith. In a corner of the front room, that very same room where they had huddled together at nine o'clock in the morning on the day and hour of her daughter's death, Ethel had earlier in the week constructed a shrine. Perhaps constructed is too grand a word. For it consisted of little else, but a collection of her favourite photographs of her daughter, all mounted in especially brought new silver frames.

Along with a picture of Edith's favourite flowers, lilies and two candles mounted on brass candlesticks, there was a short list of plays that she knew she had particularly enjoyed, and a cover page of the catalogue she most used. When William had come home after work one evening and saw it, his first impression was that Ethel had become soft in the head. But compassion came to his aid, and after he thought about it, and reasoned that it was better than never placing actual flowers on a real grave, he nodded just slightly enthusiastically when she told him what she had done.

The absence of a real grave was secondary to the thoughts of everyone in the family, and those who knew Edith. That was an extra and unnecessary blow. It was not enough that anonymous people took their daughter away. That was her comeuppance. As unjustified as that was. But to prevent the family from exhibiting their grief by not allowing visitors to her grave? That was their punishment. And far from deserved.

Within two weeks of returning to work, William had drafted a letter addressed to Doctor Morton, the governor of Holloway prison asking for permission to visit the grave, but had received an official letter back almost by return mail abruptly apologising, but stating that the request was contrary to prison regulations. Whereupon, William continued this line of questioning, and appealed directly to the Home Office.

Who thought so little of his letter that it did not warrant a reply. However William was not a man to be dismissed so quickly, and he wrote again. And again. It was only after his third letter, that he, one Wednesday morning during breakfast, tore open a sharp white envelope, which could have only come from an official government department. He was silent while he took in its contents while Ethel and Avis glanced hopefully in his direction.

Emotionless, after a few moments, he offered the letter to Ethel while briefly shaking his head in his daughter's direction after catching her eye before buttering another round of toast. It was a letter designed to intimidate and reinforce the sentence of law and was brief, inexplicably hard and heartless, mentioning The Anatomy Act of 1832 and The Capital Punishment Amendment Act of 1868. As if those were enough. In short, they were not allowed to visit the place of burial because of an act of parliament. That implied also if they wanted to remove her body to another location. There was no alternative unless the law was changed. No further explanation was offered.

The thin paper on which the words were typed could have been an insurmountable metal wall a thousand miles high, wide and thick for all the hope it inspired in the Graydons. Edith was locked away from them. The notion that they would never be able to pay their respects at her graveside at all hardly sank into their consciousnesses. It would take many, many years before that occurred.

This ongoing torment flung a slightly recovering family back onto themselves and, once the boys were told, all six were forced to deal with the situation individually. Each felt immediately that they now had become the punished. That they were doing penance for the former childish actions of Edith and Freddy's murderous one. If albeit, in an indirect manner. It was a time of unreasonable paranoia and, as expected, the males reacted with expressed rage, while the mother and daughter felt quietly aggrieved.

Ethel, in turn, had not received the support she had imagined she would receive from the newspapers and politicians as so many of her letters also were not answered. Some were deemed important enough to reach the letters segment, but no further action was taken. They instigated no passion, no collection of names, and no action. As the days passed, the rest of the family who lived permanently at 231 fell, as a collective unit, into a form of impotent depression.

Avis was perhaps the most timid along with her mother, but later, below their sadness, plans surfaced to ruffle the feathers of the establishment. And she and her mother did it with Edith's favourite flowers, lilies one Friday morning not less than one week after William received that crisp white envelope. Their demonstration was twofold, and required two journeys. The first, by train once again, to Holloway prison. The weather wasn't promising, it being cloudy with the clean smell of snow on the wind. Which was picking up and tending to gust.

Ethel's sense of incredulity grew over the long months of waiting, and then the trial. For she had not realised that, should the worse happen, she would never be able to visit her daughter's grave. It just did not occur to her. Therefore it was at the end of the trial that she became sharply angry. And it was her fury that drove her to do what she did.

She and Avis had deliberately chosen to arrive early at eight o'clock in the morning at a time they knew the nightshift finished, and the dayshift began. Consequentially, the outside of the Porter's lodge would be a veritable throng with officers arriving and departing by car and walking. On the main gate itself, there was no police presence at the time, so it was easy for mother and daughter, arm in arm with fixed expressions, and with Avis carrying the lilies, to walk sedately on the cobbled stones between the Governor's house and the old Chaplin's house to the Porter's lodge whereupon they laid the bouquet under the white Rules and Regulations sign.

The sight of the two women, both dressed in dark plain clothes, obviously nowhere near the proper visiting times, caused many of the teeming officers to stop and stare. Some even to glare. Their interest as they watched Ethel and Avis delicately kneel before the flowers, was communicated immediately to the Chief porter. Whereupon Mr Flowers, a man of pyknic appearance accompanied by a cup of tea and a bacon sandwich, came out to see what was happening outside his window.

Naturally, his first intention was to remonstrate, and this he did unkindly. However, for expressing his ideas and thoughts loudly against the rising wind, he received nothing as Ethel and Avis ignored him completely. Avis had in the meantime, brought out her small King Esequiel bible, and had opened it in order to read the First Epistle of Peter.

Of course Mr Flowers and his deputy recognised them, and each viewed the moving scene with disapproval. When Ethel and Avis refused to remove themselves, a policeman was summoned, and they were threatened with arrest. Avis' response to this threat was to lift herself up, move across to the back garden of the Governor's house where she had spied a brick, and brought it back whereupon she laid it down upon the stalks of the lilies to stabilise them from the wind which was in danger of sweeping them away.

Mr Flowers, now accompanied by two deputies, made more threatening gestures with much use of strong language. Which was again ignored until he turned on his heels and went back inside to phone the Governor.

At which point, a young female officer, no more than in her mid twenties, approached the still kneeling martyrs, and knelt down on one knee beside them. She mentioned that she recognised them, and had been responsible for, on three occasions, escorting them through the building on the occasions when they had visited before. She was, as was the Porter, ignored until she mentioned that Edith let her personally know how kind she thought the officer was.

Therefore, upon mentioning this, a connection was made. A thin entrance against the high castle of impenetrable stone. Ethel caught her eye, and told her why they were there, and the young woman's face softened and understood. She told them gently that they would not be allowed in, and fully agreed that it was a disgrace, but if they were to remain where they were, they would certainly be arrested, charged and perhaps even may have to spend a week or two within the prison itself perhaps charged with trespassing.

With this, the officer touched Ethel's shoulder, and implored them to get to their feet and go to where their argument could best be put to use, on the shoulders of those who had the power to change the law. One of the other officers, a much older woman who was about to depart for the front gate, called out for her colleague not to get involved, but she was ignored.

Ethel and Avis glanced at each other, and both laid a single hand on the lilies, with a tenderness as if they were touching Edith herself, and Ethel nodded. Both the officer and Avis then helped Ethel to her feet, and they left the scene as rain arrived.

Mr Flowers and his two deputies also returned, and seeing the three women walking back to the main gate, pathetically shouted after them the equivalent not to return. Mr Flowers, despite the beauty of his name, was a bull of a man, as most pyknic's tend to be, not particularly intelligent, and positively insensitive. Writing a letter about the incident the next day to Doctor Morton about the injurious and verbal manner Ethel and her daughter had been treated, although she received a strongly worded warning that their prank would not be tolerated again, the governor informed her that Mr Flowers, the officer in charge of the Porter's lodge had been removed from his position and returned to normal duties.

Ethel objected highly to the word prank, informing him in another colourful exchange of letters, but however, had no intention of submitting herself to imprisonment, and had already decided that if she was going to do anything like that again, Avis would definitely not be invited. She did however decide on another round of campaigning by letter. The second part of her demonstration that day, because of the reception and threats received, she decided to cancel. She also didn't like the way the weather had turned, and she was a sensitive enough mother that she didn't want her daughter out in it for any prolonged length of time so soon after undergoing such a life-changing shock.

Therefore, once outside the prison gate, and in the Parkhurst Road, she thanked the young officer and moved to hail a cab. But the young woman officer again, touched her shoulder, and reminded her that she had known her daughter. At least up to four days before…at this, she trailed away with some embarrassment, and glanced away to the prison feeling that someone of importance might be spying on her. This caused Ethel to ask her one question. If she might be allowed to buy her a cup of coffee.

The World Tea Rooms in Holloway Road saw the three women, some twenty minutes later, huddled around a pot of coffee, and three rounds of cheese sandwiches, all paid for by the woman who had introduced herself as Miss

Baker. Unlike many women of her age, she wore her hair long, most probably in the same style as when she had been a child; straight and allowing it to fall across her shoulders and down her back. It was held away from her kind, but not very pretty face with a plethora of metal clips. She possessed almost painfully thin arms, and she fidgeted constantly. Ethel fired an immediate question at her. One entirely understandable for she wanted to know if her daughter had suffered.

Whereupon a dark expression of some despair fled over the young woman's face, and she was forced to explain that her duties as a prison officer completely forbad her discussing any part or aspect of her work. It was clear though, having felt a need to defend her professional position, there were things to which she wanted to admit. Nevertheless, she continued, my conscience is troubled. Then her lower lip began trembling, and she drank coffee while Ethel and Avis waited.

The rooms, holding some twenty tables were comparatively full and busy, it being nearly lunchtime, and the normal restaurant raucous ensured, which gave them the privacy they had desired. To maximise this, they had chosen a corner table where they could whisper, and not be overheard. The luxury of giant potted plants also surrounded them, as they did the entire place.

Taking a nibble of her sandwich, Miss Baker then began to offer an approximate and brief explanation on how the prison rotas were organised, and how it happened to be sheer coincidence (because she had followed the case from the beginning and believed wholeheartedly that Edith was innocent) that her shifts coincided with the wing where Edith had been held.

She explained that staff were routinely moved from wing to wing, and from floor to floor to maximise performance and efficiency. This miracle of organisation was performed biweekly by Doctor Morton's secretary's assistant, a Miss Bright. Therefore, she not only met Edith on a daily basis, but also over the time of her confinement, came to know her as well as anyone could given the circumstances.

Accordingly, she was able to pacify Ethel and Avis' almost aggressive line of enquiry, and told them that for much of the time, Edith had behaved in an upright and dignified manner. The other prisoners thought a great deal of her, and quite often a little positive word from Edith changed and cheered up another prisoner. That was when she had been allowed to mix with them. Of course, she told them, after she was convicted, all association with the others ceased, and she even had her own room in the hospital wing which is where she was placed following her final day in court.

Although given limited contact with the rest of the wo-men, many of whom were being incarcerated for extremely minor crimes such as drunk in public and serving, only days or weeks, Edith, she told them, became a popular in-mate. There was no doubt that she was the prison's most famous resident.

Miss Baker continued. She spent much of her time read-ing exhaustively, requesting books from the prison library, and then sending them back them the next morning after breakfast equally as fast. Miss Baker told them that she ac-cepted her confinement, if not willingly, then stoically, al-ways believing that right and justice would always prevail, and that what happened was a ghastly and unutterable mess. As to her dead husband, some would criticise her for her lack of pity and grief. But there were many, officers and prisoners alike, who sided with her own thoughts on the matter, which was, she was simply concern for her own neck. There was no time to grieve, and it was not the right place anyway. Miss Baker was clear to point out that those were the words Edith herself used.

The other use of her time was of course spent writing those items which had convicted her; her endless letters. Each of which had to go through the process of examina-tion, which depressed her more than anything else. It was not enough, she said, that they confine me here for no reason, but to invade my privacy was too much.

'But then,' Miss Baker muttered, lowering her voice even further, 'when she was found guilty, she was moved out of my sphere into another wing where there was several far more secure and sparser cells. However, news about her condition still filtered back to me. Edith's personality changed from that moment in time,' she emphasised.

'From the moment the governor spoke to her that evening, two days before, on the seventh, and told her that the law was to take its course, your daughter became sullen and dull requiring extra medication. Her book reading fell away considerably as she attempted to take in what was going to happen to her.'

At this point, Miss Baker took out a handkerchief, and blew her nose powerfully before taking another gulp of her coffee.

'An internal message was posted asking for volunteers to make up a shift rota especially for prisoner 9641, and although I knew how testing and dreadful that time might be, I put my name down immediately. Being forced to be on the deathwatch was not expected of us.'

She was then interrupted and pre-empted by Ethel.

'Were you successful?'

Miss Baker shook her head mutely.

'I had spoken with my immediate superior who had decided that I was too young and inexperienced, and had therefore blocked my request. So that appeared to be that.'

'However,' she continued, 'with one week to go, and the rota filled, illness — common opinion among the staff thought that it wasn't illness, but fear — forced one of the officers to drop out, and rather than go through the lengthy procedure again of recruitment, my name was reenlisted, and I took my place on the watch. Unknown to us sixteen women at the time, a second shorter list was being prepared by the governor who had enlisted the help of a senior officer from Pentonville. This list was about which officers were to accompany the prisoner on the actual morning of her...,' Here Miss Baker was obliged to blow her nose again, and as Ethel and Avis were beginning to reel at the intimate knowledge of what had happened to their daughter and sister around that time, they appeared stunned, their coffee and food untouched.

Miss Baker's eyes wondered over to the counter, and searched for their waitress who swiftly came across. More coffee was ordered, another three cups. The three of them were now almost oblivious to the surrounding level of noise and chatter. A tray was dropped, but it was ignored. Eventually, somewhat settled, Miss Baker put away her handkerchief again and continued.

'This second list was highly confidential, and most people might imagine that it's just bad luck who gets to be with the prisoner on the...morning, and in the days running up to it. But it's not. They wanted the most mature and responsible women, and it is very important that the right choice is made. As you can imagine, a woman needs to have a special attitude to perform fulfil such a position.'

'It's monstrous!' Ethel's small voice shook with rage.

'I was told all this after by the way from one of those women who was chosen. I can tell you now that I was not placed on that second rota. There was just no person in Holloway who had the experience to deal with this sort of thing being that the last person to be executed there was twenty years ago back in 1903, so assistance had to be brought in. It was a terribly anxious time.'

Ethel ignored the remark, which just seemed to call for ridicule, and Miss Baker continued. 'As I mentioned, I last saw your daughter just four days before she died. I'm glad to tell you that at the time, she was happy, and in the process of writing another letter. She was all right because she was convinced that she was going to be reprieved. She was so convinced of it. And to tell you the truth, so was I.

The new rota began four days before, and I was returned to my former position. But I wanted to tell you that in the sixteen days I spent with her, both mornings and night, I

never spent better time with such a charming and intelligent lady. When I last saw her, at the end of my shift on the
fifth, I truly expected to visit her later on after the reprieve
had been granted. I don't think there was one person in the
whole prison who truly believed that the sentence would be
carried out on this clever and bright young woman.

On his daily rounds, I saw Governor Morton each morning, and as the ninth came closer, he looked more haggard
and older each day. I believe he was undergoing a terrible
personal crises of his own. Mrs Graydon, Miss Graydon, I
feel as if it's my duty to let you know how much Edith's
death concerned and upset everyone involved. You won't
hear this from any other source, but on that morning some
time before nine o'clock, the prison became completely
quite, and everyone either stood still, or stopped working,
or doing whatever they were doing.

Of course, it was common knowledge what old man Ellis was there to do, and he had arrived on the eighth. An
unofficial prayer meeting had taken place in the chapel the
evening before, and it was those women, mostly based in C
Wing, who led the singing of Nearer My God To Thee.

And I tell you Mrs Graydon, Miss Graydon, their voices
sounded right throughout the centre, and not one officer
dared to try and stop them. Those who were not weeping
just stood still, their head bowed. It was a shameful mo-

ment, but one that brought the prison together if you know what I mean.'

Ethel and Avis, who were close to tears, said nothing, but Ethel's mouth was tight with grimness. Miss Baker continued.

'What I wanted to say Mrs Graydon was that the passing of your daughter was accompanied not by brutality, but with such companionship. I realise this is of little consolation to you, but please take some comfort in the knowledge that she was looked after with the utmost care until the end.'

The coffee arrived, and the waitress decided that there was a change in the aura surrounding the table seeing the uneaten food, and naturally and falsely assumed it was the restaurant's fault. She asked if there was anything more that she could get them, and all three shook their heads whereupon she turned slowly and walked away, with some part of her memory digging at her, now that she had concentrated a little more on the customers.

Ethel touched Miss Baker's hand and spoke.

'You mustn't think me ungrateful Miss Baker. I'm under no illusions how quickly you would be dismissed from your position should the authorities ever find out what you have told us. Fear not by the way, as we shall not utter a word. I...we...are much gratified by your courage to let me know what happened to my daughter and yes, although I admit, my grief is still to strong to allow me any forgiving thoughts about the last and final days and hours of my daughter concerning the prison, I do take some measure of cheer that she was surrounded by God's love if you take my meaning.'

Now Miss Baker's eyes seem to well up, and she took her coffee in silence. Ethel's eyes seemed to bore into her, and the silence made her look up again until she met them.

'I would like to ask you about the painful circumstances of Edith's death though,' Ethel continued, 'and if you are aware of what happened? No doubt you have heard something?'

Now Miss Baker looked a little panicky. As if she had entered the lion's den with confidence, but then discovered the lion was roaring louder than she had anticipated, and what's more, that the beast wasn't chained. Thus, she shook her head. But perhaps just a little too vehemently. Avis began speaking too.

'We have heard the most terrible rumours Miss Baker. Can you confirm or deny them?' There was silence...at their table anyway as the atmosphere continued to increase in volume as lunchtime continued. Miss Baker's mouth, at least the side of it began to twitch, as if she were chewing her gum. But then she broke her silence.

'It's just a fabrication you understand,' she almost mouthed the words, 'we have no idea how the papers got hold of that horrid story.'

'In my experience Miss Baker, I am fond of that old saying that there is no smoke without fire.'

'I cannot help you because I don't know anything. You must realise that that part of the system is entirely unknown to me, and I took no part in it. Your needs are with the coroner not I.'

'Miss Baker,' asked Avis, 'forgive me, but you and I are about the same age are we not? Have you not spoken to those who were with my dear sister at the end?'

'I have not Miss Graydon'. Then she noticed the mother and daughter's eyes, hungry like wild animals, but in this occasion, not for food, but for information.

'At least not in any professional capacity which I would have no occasion to do anyway...'

'Tell me my dear,' spoke Ethel quietly, 'what did you hear?'

Miss Baker again bowed her head, and her shoulders dropped appreciably.

'Hearsay says that her slip had to be burnt, and her dress hastily washed. That is before you and your family could see her. Beyond that I really don't know. And now I really must be going.'

Something in her voice told the mother and daughter that nothing more would be gained from questioning this woman anymore. The subject matter had become too deep and disturbing, and the implications were becoming obvious. Therefore Ethel touched her gently on her arm again, before offering her the best smile she could given the circumstances.

'I do understand Miss Baker, and I and my daughter thank you from the bottom of our hearts for having the courage to speak to us today. It couldn't of been easy, and we understand. We also, I think, comprehend how you may have put your position in jeopardy as well. However, please would you do me the courtesy of taking this please?' And Ethel held out a scrap of paper on which she had been scribbling her address.

'Should anything else come to light, perhaps you can write? Completely anonymously of course.'

'It has been a pleasure to meet you Mrs Graydon, Miss Graydon. I hope I have been of some service, and I do ask you again to mention to no one that we ever met.'

With this assurance, the three of them stood and made their way to the till where Ethel paid for the second round of coffees, and the three of them walked to the entranceway. But suddenly, given a wink from the waitress that had served them, a man in a dark and close-fitting suit rapidly approached them when they reached the outside, and within a second, a camera appeared in his hands, and he had taken a snap of them before anyone realised what was happening.

Automatically, the three women scattered, Mother pulled daughter in one direction, and Miss Baker in another. What happened to her next is unrecorded, but Ethel and Avis ran speedily up Holloway Road until they felt they were not being followed. They then boarded the first tram that came along, and this rattled them to the nearest railway station.

Nine

The newspapers had not been kind about the execution of Edith. Invention and lies abounded, but no one of any importance put in an appeared to state the truth. One thing had changed though. Whereas before the deaths, there was a clamour for Edith's destruction, a hated woman, a grisette, a virtual pillorying conducted by the broadsheets of the day, public opinion weighing heavily on the side of Freddy, the younger of the two; leading up to the event and after, there was generated much sympathy for Edith. A remarkable and perhaps unparalleled turnaround of sensitivity.

To millions of daily and avid readers of the case, it had seemed impossible that a young, bright and vivacious woman had been done to death in such modern and enlightened times, and a powerful wave of abhorrence against the hanging of women swept throughout the width and breadth of the land. People wrote of the so-called civilisation in which they lived, proclaiming that England was no better than foreign lands. Letters were written by the thousands, and published by the hundreds proclaiming that her punishment had been too harsh. Many emphasised her innocence in the actual murder. A case was even put forward in The Times for the resignation of Bridgeman the Home Secretary.

Punch ran a cartoon lampooning Andrew Bonar Law, the Prime Minister as having no control over the members of his cabinet. He was portrayed as a mad, moustached, long-haired coachmen cracking a whip across the backs of six horses over whom he had lost control. Each horse's face looking remarkably similar to six of the top members of his cabinet.

The executioner, Ellis was portrayed as a cowering and shockingly dreadful monster who enjoyed murdering innocent women. In one newspaper, he was portrayed as a tall Victorian skeletal man with dark and deep-sunken eyes, wearing a belt of nooses. And while he held a white hood in a crooked left hand, in his equally deformed right, he grasped a sheet of dark-stained paper upon which was written a list of women. At his feet and on her knees, Edith Thompson, thin as bone, and half way towards swooning, herself tugged for mercy at his trousers while he looked dissuasively away. The press had especially hounded the executioner mercilessly on his journey home to Rochdale causing near havoc at London's Euston train station.

Eventually, questions were even raised in the House of Commons. Nevertheless, even though the arguments and the fury rumbled on for several weeks, a position of which the newspapers took obvious advantage, the Prime Minister refused to speak against the emotional avalanche except to issue one short pithy statement which maintained that he believed the Home Secretary was correct, and that he stood firmly behind his decision.

The Graydon family, barely coming to terms with the death and loss of Edith, during this time learnt that the only possible way to deal with this emotionally crushing public spectacle was to avoid all references to it. However, not even they were immune to the caustic effects of the unkind press, as they occasionally heard of the rumours of how Edith collapsed as a human being, how her insides fell out, and how she was eventually carried like a dead weight parcel to the gallows, so frightened that she kept fainting.

Out of respect at his work, newspapers were kept away from William on the factory floor, and most were careful in what they talked about when within hearing distance, but Avis was not so fortunate. Working with so many women, most of whom had a tendency to gossip and even, with some of the older and more forthright women, belittle, it was inevitable that occasionally she would overhear some revolting piece of information.

There were no confrontations as such. Avis was not that sort of person. Mary was the more demonstrative woman, and unknown to her friend at the time, she even had strong words at the back of the building one Wednesday afternoon, soon after the hanging, with a particularly nasty woman in her mid twenties of German extraction who previously had made Avis very uncomfortable in her opinion of Edith's sentence.

At the time, Mary was accompanied by two friends, and all four were enjoying a cigarette break. After two minutes of hard arguing, Mary's friends had pulled her away as the encounter had showed signs of escalating beyond what was socially acceptable. Eventually, names were called, appearances and countries were insulted, and the two women never spoke again. Mary, it turned out, was a demon at confrontation.

Avis, although strong, and perhaps a little wilful internally, had never enjoyed angry engagements and had, upon returning to work, immediately noticed some tension. The women, to a greater extent, were pleasant enough, although most had the problem of what to say, and how to say it, and what subject to avoid. Most showed distress, although some were not so expert at hiding their feelings, and showed discountenance.

There was a sense therefore of rigidity in her workplace, and that continued for a few months until the exposure that the case had warranted, diminished. Over time, new employees arrived, and less was mentioned about the sister of the executed woman who sat, mostly during the day shift, at position twenty-nine. Avis though, noticed no real sense of tenderness for her sister, or for her loss except from a few close friends such as Mary.

She was not, for instance, invited to any more social situations than would have been usual. Sympathy as a motivation did not appear to play any part in asking if she wanted to go to a dance, see a lecture, enjoy shopping, or to see a band, or any other activity that the young women of that time enjoyed, and for this, she was immensely grateful. The very last thing Avis needed or desired was to have a fuss made over her.

She made it through the first month, and then, as if she had broken a particularly nasty curse or spell, felt a great deal better. It was of course natural for her personality to change. Mary, wise beyond her years, had predicted it. She had stated the obvious from the time they had been thrown together again, that no one could accumulate such grief and remain alive without it being expunged by some method, real or just over time.

Her religion, Anglican, continued to offer her a great measure of comfort, and she, her mother, father and the boys if they were home, never missed matins or evensong on a Sunday although occasionally it was difficult to get the boys involved. Perhaps because it was their sex, but Newenham, William and Harold seemed to recover quicker from the family ordeal than Avis. Or perhaps it was because the remaining daughter still lived at home, and therefore felt the continuing dull and sad effects from her parents as well as her own grief. The effect on their children was an important issue Ethel noticed, and she spoke to William about it on more than one occasion.

He though, dismissed her fears and objections, telling her that his boys were grieving just as deeply. But being men, they just did not show it. However, Harold, the youngest and certainly the most sensitive of the boys, did undergo a powerful transformation after months of crying when he was alone, for he missed his big sister dreadfully. His very earliest memories were of her playing games with him, specifically tossing a red and yellow ball, and for those he remained grateful for the rest of his life. In his very young eyes, she was the most beautiful girl in the world even surpassing his mother because she showed him so much kindness.

Although just nine years between them, Edith used to act as if he were her own child, and had always looked after him in her childish way whenever the family was out. It was imagined Harold's personality became inflexible because he never grieved properly, but it was the reverse that was true. Only he was aware of this until much later on in his life.

The family's parish priest, the Reverend Father Esequiel Vega had been a constant visitor to the Graydon's house before, during and after the execution. Although Ethel and Avis thought it prudent to allow him access while the trial was taking place, William took no interest in the comings and goings of the man apart from being momentarily convivial as he passed him in the hall or opened the door. It was only after the verdict, and then the last negative communication by the Home Secretary, when William understood there was a chance that his daughter may actually die, that he paid attention to his visits.

Reverend Vega was a kindly soul of the first order. He had risen to become an ordained minister in 1890 at the late age of 29, and, after presiding over two small country parishes, one in deepest Essex and one in Sussex, he was finally awarded the duties of the large parish of St. Barnabas Church, Manor Park where he quickly gained the trust and loyalty of the parishioners due to his maturity, the basis of which was kindness, and a tendency for his sermons to be brief.

He became known as what his parishioners affectionately called, 'A fine old foreign gent'. A thoroughbred bachelor and moreover, one who exhibited all the characteristics and slight eccentricities that accompany that station. For example, he was known to fiddle with, and occasionally wave his old pipe around even as he spoke in the pulpit during Evensong. Although it was never lit at the time, it did appear odd, and little granules of tobacco were sometimes to be seen floated down like dark confetti.

His only constant, and perhaps unsettling companion, until the parishioners became familiar with her, was a young to middle-aged mute, and facially disfigured charlady who went by the solitary name of Nellie, and who had arrived with him when he took up his duties. Her injuries were somewhat appalling when first viewed, and the inevitable local gossip eventually came to the conclusion that they had been caused by acid, although whether they, and the mute part of her personality had any basis in common, they were not able to establish.

Reverend Vega's most striking feature was his baldness. He wore it like a scar. Without any pretence whatsoever. He had a fine circle-like dome with, luckily, no blemishes whatsoever. Being over six feet four inches in height, and slightly undernourished, he gave the appearance, from a far distance, of a swiftly animated tall and blunt pencil. His clerical collar was normally the first part of his attire people recognised for he had a tendency to wear dark clothes. This was because of his rather swarthy complexion, a consequence of being Spanish, his habit of wearing dark gloves all year round when outside, and the busy moustache which entirely covered his top lip.

He had begun to lose his hair when he had reached puberty, which in his case was thirteen. Looking at the few family photographs he possessed, he had long ago noticed how his mother's hairline was high, and therefore assumed his own appearance was based on her. By the time he was seventeen he had the tonsorial appearance of a man of seventy. It was this particular quirk of genes that sapped his early confidence, and placed him on a path of depression which led eventually to aloneness and bachelorhood. Much of the reason why he rediscovered Christianity so late in life.

His parents had not been churchgoing people, and they had encouraged no such behaviour in their little son. However, by the time he was twenty-three, his mercurial, polymath mind had left the family's apple-growing business, some six miles south of Sevilla, and settled in England, where his quick and versatile brain learnt the basis of the English language in under three months, and was fluent in it in under a year. However, he retained his Spanish southern accent for the rest of his life. When mixed with the earthy roughness of the East End, the result was a broad, hard sound...perfect for sermons in large open Victorian churches.

His once dark moustache, in the Hungarian style, was now showing definite signs of whiteness, and it had occurred to him that perhaps he could find some way to inhibit the process. Although, as he thought about it, his ecclesiastical thinking, particularly the part about vanity came to the fore and, with a sigh, accepted the fact that he was getting older. The white hairs alas extended also to his eyebrows and certainly to other parts of his body that no one but he would ever see. He appreciated that he was getting on.

Reverend Vega was also the priest who married Edith Graydon and Percy Thompson in January 1916. Although it was one of a number he conducted that month, he never saw a more splendid and radiant bride as Edith. Her tall slim figure as she walked down the lines of invited guests, her new wedding dress flowing gently, cut such a beautiful figure that he could hardly believe he was in East London. Amongst all the brides he married, it was Edith which, in his memory, he remembered.

It was not so much the altar sited at the East end of the nave which interested the Graydon family since Edith had died. Instead Reverend Vega later used his vestry to council them. And had been doing so since the execution. At first, he thought it best that the entire family were present, but as time went on, and they became ever more comfortable in his presence, they begun to arrive individually although Ethel and William still always arrived together even after a month or two.

The counselling, if what he did could be named as such, began after he was told that a family in his parish were undergoing, and were caught up in a great deal of trouble. When he realised the full extent of who that family was, and remembered the beauty of the bride from almost seven years previously, and what a dreadful predicament she was in, he made it his business to walk around to their house one late afternoon. Only to find it quite empty.

As it happens, William, Ethel and Avis were at that very moment on a train having been discharged after the third day of the trial at the Old Bailey. It was Ethel who had picked up a note from the priest left on the front carpet, and had thought it a good idea to take him up on his offer of assistance. To which William's immediate reply was negative to say the least, saying that the less the surrounding area knew of their business, the better it would be for all concern.

However, the press soon put paid to that as within a day, a problematic series of reporters had come knocking demanding attention and offering William some reasonable sums of cash for more information concerning his daughter's story. It would be quite true to write that the force of this monstrous effort quite overcame the innocent and naïve East-End family, and it was this that eventually sent them into the embrace of the church. Not as a group who attended the usual services, but as a family requiring help, protection and love.

The situation that now presented itself was in severity a little beyond the type of situations Reverend Vega had counselled before. Former problems amounting to bereavements, loss of faith, high-spirited youngsters, runaway family members and the occasional unwanted baby were understood and known to him. Murder and execution was of a different order. By several magnitudes.

After the trial, and with Edith awaiting execution, it required an entirely different approach to the family who, in the case of the mother and father, were not particularly keen churchgoers at that time. Along with many other families, the parents sent their children to Sunday school, but more for the peace it offered them for an hour or two rather than for their spiritual salvation. Therefore, in the beginning, Reverend Vega had decided to dispense with the comfort, and the surroundings of his church, and conducted the sessions in the privacy and comfort of their own home.

It was therefore on his second visit to 231 Shakespeare Crescent, just two days after the judge had condemned Edith to death, that he was welcomed into their front room, and offered a strong cup of tea and a triangular piece of Dundee cake. Ethel, William, Harold and Avis were present, who were understandably still disturbed from the sentence.

William, although there at the request of Ethel, in the beginning displayed his irrelevance by tapping his foot while Reverend Vega began by stating how sorry he was. He followed this by assuring them that the final decision had not been made, and that there was the appeal, and then possibly a last minute reprieve. He had made it his business to know these things, by making enquires at the local police station. He informed them that no woman had been executed in Britain for fifteen years, and so that was all a thing of the past. He did all he could to make them feel positive about the shocking and distressing situation in which they now found themselves.

His manner, position, knowledge and his particularly insightful foreign voice helped immeasurably that first evening, and besides Harold excusing himself on the flimsy indulgence that he had something in his eye, the evening finished with the others feeling much relieved, and with Reverend Vega promising to return in a few days. To close the evening, he recommended that they joined hands in prayer which he led.

The family's faces as he left, told him that what had happened that evening was a positive beginning. Reverend Vega called out to Harold as he stood in the hallway, but received no answer from upstairs. Ethel made a face apologising for him, and the Reverend left soon after, walking back to the church accompanied by a dark fog which again had blown in from the dark grassy mass of Wanstead flats as it often did. With only tiny pools of light spilling out from the lampposts, he spent the time brooding on the family as he walked. Very few people were about. To his distress and a little shame, he could not get the image of Edith in her dramatic and beautiful wedding dress walking towards him down the aisle of his own church out of his mind. It was that vision that made him declare to himself that he would do as much as possible to help the family.

Ten

Leading up to and surpassing the day of the execution, the telegrams and letters overwhelmed the family. To the extent that hundreds were arriving each week, and the postman's knock became a dreaded sound. They really did not know what to do with them. Apart from an extremely small percentage, less than one in a thousand, all were thankfully supportive.

Which provided a conundrum for the Graydons as, to be sure it was gracious of strangers to write showing their support, and generous, but to receive so many was overwhelming, and William had decided when they began to arrive, that everyone ought to be answered. Nevertheless, leading up to the date of the execution, this was a task which became impossible. Therefore each letter was stored by date received, and placed in a cardboard box. As that box filled, they began another. Eventually, even the boxes mounted in number, and became a dark assemblage lying in wait in a corner of their small front room.

The moment the Home Secretary failed to reprieve Edith, the headlines wrote of her demise, mentioning unnecessarily cruelly, and incorrectly that she had struggled hard as she had taken her last breath. As a consequence, the Graydon's post-bag increased dramatically until they felt they were being crushed. Cardboard boxes were no longer sufficient.

It was Reverend Vega who came to their rescue again. He and the 12th of East-Ham scout group volunteered their time to remove and store the overwhelming mass of written support. William continually wondered how they knew where they lived. All those strangers he used to say. Many of them were just addressed to The Family Graydon, East Ham. Despite the huge numbers still arriving each day, the family read a few, and nearly all were written in the same manner, and with the same comforting message.

It was suggested to the post office that all letters be delivered straight to the scout's club house in Browning Road, but the GPO refused, stating that it was their legal obligation to deliver post to the named recipient. When it was pointed out that many carried no address just a name, the little official in East Ham's main sorting office seemed not to care, and told William and Reverend Vega who were visiting that he was doing his duty as prescribed by law.

They could see he was not going to change his mind. At the time, Reverend Vega caught William's eye as they both recognised that here was a system as inflexible as the one that had executed Edith. Here was an autonomous arrangement, a detached and dispassionate set of rules, which no one wished to break or ignore. As with the Home Office, there was a distinct lack of compassion. For a brief moment, William's fist tightened, and there was a stand-off which the little official did his best to disregard as he pretended to shuffle papers on his desk, hoping the two men would leave quickly.

Reverend Vega touched William's arm, and shook his head. Clearly he imagined he knew William's dark thoughts. And clearly he was correct by the way William slammed the little official's door, and steamed silently on the walk home through the endless and breathlessly cold and foggy winter streets. When they were out of hearing, the little official muttered under his breath.

'Like father like daughter.'

Reverend Vega had the shrewdness not to talk as they made their way back home. A little near 231, William thanked the priest for his assistance, but told him he had decided to go for a drink. Therefore, the two men, shook hands, and each went their separate ways. Reverend Vega continued to 231 to inform Ethel of their disappointing news, and William headed to the Fox and Hounds in the Romford Road.

This was ten days after Edith's execution, and although the amount of letters had slowed, and the scouts had taken boxes and boxes of sealed letters away to be stored at their hut, the household was still left with the task of sifting those that arrived daily to extract any genuine non-Edith related items of post.

The geographic diversity of the mail astonished the family, some arriving from as distant as the United States of America and even Australia. Although the letters continued to take up almost all their time, because so many offered their sympathy and deep respect for their loss, the Graydon family found a great deal of comfort in them.

Enough for Ethel to believe that without them, the family's ordeal would have been a great deal harder to bare. Knowing that streams of unknown people from across the globe were actively praying and showing them how much they cared, in this, she found a great sense of warmth. There were occasions when she imagined that not one letter had arrived, and the atmosphere of the household would have been so different. Bare, cold and unloved. It would have been unbearable. It was certainly the outpouring of indignant people of many nations that helped them through those early and unimaginable times.

Ethel wrote too. Just as she planned. With the assistance of the Reverend Vega and Edith's solicitor, she was able to craft letters of poignancy which were duly dispatched to those major participance's who had taken part in Edith's execution. It did not take William much persuasion to indulge in letter-writing as well. Many of them were typed and sent on to Ethel's sisters according to Ethel's previous agreement despite her earlier failed efforts.

The Weekly Despatch, Doctor J. Morton, The Stratford Express, Judge Montague Shearman, The home Office, The prime Minister's Office, almost all the broadsheets and local papers, and even His Majesty the King, were only a few recipients of the family's feelings, both thankful and critical.

Ethel knew when her husband's heart had been truly broken when one morning, no less than fifteen days after Edith's execution, she awoke to find their handsome glass-framed portrait of George V had been removed from over the fireplace in the back room. At the time of this discovery, she did not know which shocked her more. The absence of the framed print, or the brown vertical oblong of smudge where it used to hang. Clearly, the room needed decorating.

She found it most disorienting to stand in front of the mantelpiece, and not see the familiar face and stance of her King. Only the day before had she allowed the curtains of the house to be opened, and the weak winter sunlight illuminated the dull, flower-patterned wallpaper pitifully. Clearly, William had removed it before he left for work. But he had mentioned nothing.

With a little searching, Ethel found it in the back garden shed which is where William (it looked as if it had been thrown, for it was on its side) had taken it. It did not take a woman's intuition to understand why he had done what he did, and she felt her own eyes begin to sting again. Writing to the King, before the execution had been a last resort for William, and in it he had pleaded with a desperation unknown for him for His Majesty to spare his daughter's life. He had made the child, and now he was pleading for her continuance.

He and Ethel had had no idea if George V had even read the moving letter, but by 9 January, they knew for certain it did not have any effect. They received a standard reply two days after Edith had breathed her last, and it wasn't from the King, but from his private secretary. Or to be precise, one of *his* secretaries. Who stated succinctly that it was the policy of His Majesty's Office to refrain from intervening in legal proceedings. When William had read that, he could not ever remember being so mad.

Ethel, at the time, had taken the crisp paper from him after he had let his hand drop to the floor, and they were both silent for a good while. She could not describe herself as a Royalist. She remembered clearly when she had been a child, her mother more than once criticising Queen Victoria, and for some unknown reason, her mother's displeasure had stuck with her. Therefore it had coloured her life, and made her ambivalent of the monarchy.

Unlike William who, like many in the East End, was extremely proud to be British, and who flew the Union Jack at every opportunity. At the beginning of the 1914-1918 campaign, when he was forty-seven, and far too old to fight for his country, he could be seen waving and cheering the young men in their bright new uniforms, five abreast marching along the Barking Road as they headed off to the front in France.

With the help of his children, he had organised drives in his spare time, Paper, tin and rags...anything to help raise cash for the troops. Other drives were socks, scarves and jumpers for our brave boys. He wholeheartedly supported the war throughout its term even when the carnage began. Although he read of the terrible death toil during and after England had won, he still considered the entire affair worthy, *if we are to keep the Empire.'* By the end of it, his two daughters used to gently, as much as they dare, ridicule him about his fervent enthusiasm. But it was all done in the best humour, although William used to pretend he was annoyed, and make a show of wishing he had had all boys.

Therefore the removal of George V's picture, and relegating it to the outside shed where the wood and the coal for the fires was kept, was a serious indication that something grave and formidable had occurred in his thinking. Ethel tried her hardest not to think about the event during the day while she did what little chores she set herself, but when Avis came home, and she was shown the dirty shape on the wall, her daughter's face confirmed her own fears. Which was, her husband had no immediate plans to live and let be. Avis also added something normal.

'We need to decorate mum.'

William that night had decided to pay one of his usual visits to the pub on the way home from work. Within the short space of time since Edith's death, and his returning to work, William had been to his favourite haunt more than a few times, and arrived home, if not drunk, then definitely the worse for wear. Perhaps even occasionally slurring. Drunk enough for him to refuse his supper.

After a brief chat with her younger sister Edith, who was most definitely in favour of putting a halt to William's drinking before it got out of hand, Ethel decided to bring her fears to his attention, and therefore one night she and William had the worse argument that Avis had ever heard them have.

Ethel, screaming and crying from half way into the garden, called him an arse-hole, and made it plain that if he was to continue getting drunk time after time then he would come home one day to find the door locked, and his things in the street because she was not going to put up with that behaviour. Her normal timidness fleeing for that moment, she laid down the law.

His response was naturally opposite to hers, and that was to turn and walk upstairs with the aim of going to sleep. However, after Ethel had furiously trotted after him and swung him around by his arm, he let loose with the sort of words about which Avis knew, but certainly never expected to hear in her own home, and out of her father's mouth. Shocked and mesmerised, she sat in their kitchen while Ethel, in turn, raged at him.

After a moment though, Avis became aware that here was a situation in which she ought not to be included. Her parents sometimes traded angry words, but then again, so did most families. When such times occurred, she and the boys, and Edith too when she was alive, would have rolled their eyes, and escaped to another room until their parent's rage had dissipated. It was normally over money anyway, or the lack of it to be precise, and in which way it ought to be spent. Nothing else really, for both were true to each other and, before Edith's death, William didn't drink that much, and Ethel remained too much of a mouse to cause him any trouble.

But that early evening was very different. They were not listening to each other at all, and a kind of spiteful rage had quickly developed making it clear to any listener or listeners, of which there were two families, one on each side of 231, that their row was really not about William's drinking. Avis therefore retired to the front room as she could not get to the emotional safety of her own bedroom. After a while, as her parent's moved upstairs, she fled back to the kitchen. There she boiled water for hot chocolate, and distractedly listened to the increased and frenetic screaming sounding from above with growing concern.

She could hear her father banging his fist repeatedly against the wooden balustrade and walls of the landing, her mother's decent into agonising tears, and the terrible short silences when they stopped for breath. Their words were muffled for the most part, but it was clear, that after two minutes, drinking alcohol or arriving home late from work was not the subjects anymore.

It was also obvious that neither of her parents were shouting out of a sense of wanting to be right. There was no accusing, no blame by either. Simply an onslaught of venom. An attempt to expunge every memory. A way to safeguard their sanity. Avis sat in the kitchen in her father's chair by the glowing and grustling fire, and allowed a trickle of a tear to fall down her cheek. She made no attempt to wipe it away. Here was another powerless situation against which she could do nothing. Her family were on fire. They would burn until there would be nothing left.

There was a longer silence, and then several deep coughs before her mother's light footsteps pattered down the stairs, came along the short corridor and entered the kitchen where she made for the sink and banged crockery about pretending to wash up. Her not so young face looked a terrible mess. Twisted, ugly and crying, and she stopped momentarily and hung her head.

It was all too much for Avis who rushed foreword and held her tight, whereupon mother and daughter descended into crying together. A moment later, William appeared at the doorway, a subdued tall man, his face as white and as gaunt as Avis had ever seen. The row was over. Ethel, her arms tightly entwined about Avis' shoulders, motioned him to come and join them, and silently he did, wrapping himself around them both as all three stood by the sink.

'Please don't argue. She wouldn't have wanted you to.'

William wanted to offer his daughter some sort of apology, but he felt that if he were to speak, he would begin to cry himself. So he did nothing, but stroke her long brown hair and aimlessly play with one of her earrings, his chin resting on the top of her head while Ethel's head lay against his rapidly breathing chest. But his mouth did crumple, and his tears fell nevertheless.

It was Ethel who eventually pulled away.

'There are no words, and there is nothing we can do.' She sat in her own comfortable rocking chair by the fire, opposite William's. 'We have to trust that wherever she is, she is being looked after.'

She looked up pleadingly at William. 'We have to let her go Will. We have to find a way to carry on without her.'

Avis returned to her hot drink, and sat at the table, while William too, sat in his chair. After a moment, he reached out his hand and Ethel took it.

'I can't talk to anyone but you Eth.'

'We're manage Will.' She looked at Avis. 'Won't we darling?'

'Yes, mum, we will. She would have wanted us to carry on. Please don't row like that again. You scared me.'

Rather sheepishly, William and Ethel looked down as if they had been told off.

'Won't happen again luv. And Eth? I'll stop going to the Fox and H. Yes, I see it now.'

'I don't want you to stop seeing your pals luv...'

'I know, I know. But perhaps I won't need to see them so much there. It's all been too much Eth, and I'm sorry.'

'I think I'll go upstairs if you don't mind. I've a book to finish before I have to take it back to the library tomorrow.'

'All right Avis, and we're sorry for scaring you. I'll come up and pop my head in before I go to bed.'

'It's okay mum. I'm sorry too. Night dad.'

She offered him a kiss on his cheek which made him feel more humble than he could ever remember. What a couple of glorious daughters he had raised. As Avis left, he released his wife's hand, and fell back more comfortably into his deep fireside chair whereupon he closed his eyes sensing the last remains of the five pints of ale that he had drunk at the Fox and Hounds.

Ethel meanwhile, made them both a pot of tea, and after settling into her own chair again, picked up a heap of letters which had not yet been sorted. Almost absentmindedly, she began to read and examine each of them, sorting them into piles.

There could be no question that Ethel loved her daughter Avis. Just a little under two years younger than Edith, she was perhaps a little less spoiled than her first child, although that is a matter neither parent would have admitted. Although raised the same, Avis did not have the gregariousness that had accompanied Edith wherever she went. It could easily be mentioned that whereas Edith's personality was outgoing, Avis' was the opposite. Indeed, to the point of being diffident.

Whereupon Edith's birth could have been regarded as trouble-free, her confinement with Avis', as she remembered it, was not so. She was physically sick during the early stages of both pregnancies, which of course was natural, but with Avis her morning sickness lasted a great deal longer. In fact, well into the twentieth week. Whether that had any influence on the baby's eventual personality, only her mother had an idea.

Outgoing or not though, both babies were charming little individuals, and showed no sign of what tragedy the eldest would eventually bring upon herself and her family. They had been good children with, particularly Edith, not a trace of unruly behaviour as had been so often misrepresented in the newspapers. Both shone at many different subjects at school, both Primary and Secondary, and Avis was especially fond of geography. On the wall above her bed, she still had pinned to it, a map of the world that her father had brought for her when she was aged twelve.

Covered in pencil lines and curves, illustrating the many journeys she would one day undertake, it was rather tattered now at the edges, but sentimentality even at the age of twenty-seven, meant that she refused to take it down. She realised that those many lines now were pure fantasy. For she knew that she would in all likelihood, never make any of those journeys. She no longer was sad though, and geography, like the capital cities she had once committed to memory, faded from her mind as a main interest.

Taking after their father, who was a ballroom dancing instructor in his spare time, both girls had learnt early, and both had taken to it passionately. However, no one had danced in the Graydon family since October 1922, and the parents would not for many years. This one activity not now available to her, Avis, post Edith, turned her attention to more mundane, family oriented, and old fashion pursuits such as knitting and crocheting. And one other which was not at all normal...

*

An instance, associated with Edith, had seared itself into her memory, and it particularly haunted her. This was the day of Edith's execution when she and her parents accompanied by Ethel Vernon, were allowed to pay their last respects, although, for prison purposes only, it was so that William could identify the body. Of course it was winter and bitterly cold. That day, a northerly wind blew across the building, and after the family had been identified by Mr Flowers, and stepped passed his lodge and into the inner yard, instead of being taken into the horrendously oppressive main building, they were escorted across to the morgue which was one of the smaller buildings to their left.

What the family saw on the way, although she impressed herself on Avis more than her parents, was a small woman between twenty and thirty. It was difficult to put a correct age to her for her face was smudged with dirt and coal dust. However, there was one thing about which Avis was sure; she was bone cold. She wore the usual prison garb, the same as Edith had worn when last they saw her alive. A loose, straw-coloured dress on which was printed the ubiquitous upward-pointing black arrows. Over that, she wore a filthy dark coat which barely covered her knees. One large black button prevented it from flying open. Her cut-down, black hobnail boots were marginal and scuffed, the soles being worn almost away.

She wore no scarf, hat or gloves of any kind, and she looked as miserable a specimen of human being as Avis had ever unfortunately witnessed. Her hair was wild and loose, and she was energetically shovelling coal, moving it from a fifteen-foot high shiny black heap into a large steel-reinforced wooden cart. Moreover, she looked exhausted.

As if this impression of modern punishment were not enough, it paled besides, what Avis then noticed, for what she saw sent the scene back into the Victorian age, or perhaps even Georgian. For connected around the woman's right ankle, was an iron buckle which was itself attached to a fairly weighty black chain which was fastened to a brick wall. A female warder stood close by, out of the wind, and protected from it by a heavy dark coat. It was shocking enough for Avis to nudge her mother's arm, which she was clutching at the time, whereby she drew her attention to the poor woman's plight.

However, Ethel was far more concerned with the reason she was there, and apart from giving the woman a preliminary cursorily glance, looked straight ahead again, and followed the tall figure of William who in turn was following the coroner's assistant, and a wardress who was escorting them across the yard.

As preoccupied as she was with why they were there, Avis could not stop herself staring at the poor woman as they got close and passed by. The woman in turn noticed them, and looked palpably embarrassed. Enough for her to stop shovelling for a brief moment. It was the halting of that sound which caused the wardress to bark at the prisoner.

'Get cracking Brown. Eleven more loads. I don't want to be stuck out here all day in this wind.'

Brown did not answer, but managed to catch Avis' eye before she turned back to her drudgery. To mention that Avis was shocked does not do her emotions justice. In the few times she had visited Edith in Holloway, she had not seen or encountered many prisoners. The few she had glimpsed had been well-dressed and clean, and now that she thought about it, they were probably the well-behaved ones allowed special privileges of the sort currently un-dreamed of by the poor creature who looked so miserable.

The beggarly woman that was undergoing punishment, had a considerable and unexpected effect on Avis, and in just the few seconds it took to pass her, now a great pity rose up within her breast, and this she expressed by means of a friendly and sympathetic pitiful grimace, which was re-ceived with gratitude. If only for a second. This sorrowful communication however, was quickly forgotten when they entered the morgue which seemed to be even colder than outside. Besides the governor, the under-sheriff, the doctor, the coroner, and three other representatives of the prison service and the Home Office, there was only one wooden object in the room and in it lay her dead sister.

They stood in that cold, white-tiled room for just over thirty minutes, and were not allowed any private time with the body at all. The family felt as if the Home Office still wanted total control over Edith's body, even in death. Which was true, as very soon they would bury her in the manner and the place of their choosing. Their final act of in-dignity. Avis was sobbing deeply into her handkerchief when she left the building leaning heavily on Miss Ethel Vernon. Having all kissed Edith on the cheek, William, after recovering himself, thanked Doctor Morton, briefly shook his hand, and the family was escorted back to the Porter's lodge, naturally passing the shovelling woman again.

However, this time she saw them coming, and realising now who they were, and why they had visited the morgue, she deliberately stopped work, laid down her shovel quietly, came to attention and bowed her head as the Graydon's passed by. The wardress barked at her to carry on with her work in the same tone as she did previously, but this time the waif didn't continue until the family had disappeared into the Porter's lodge. A matter of moments. Avis later wondered if *her* act of compassion had got her into even more trouble, but she gave her no more thought until a few days later.

The family's emptiness, after the stern castle-like building had discharged them into Parkhurst Road, was palpable. Each were magnetically drawn to remain where they were because the body of their child and sister was beyond those high walls. Now that they had left her behind, a natural sense of paranoia wondered just what they were going to do with her, and how she was going to be treated.

The wind had been bitterly cold and dusk was approaching. The huge crowds, which had accumulated, and had been waiting since before sunrise, had almost disappeared, but there remained a few reporters, and one photographer recognised them instantly, and took advantage of his luck.

To prevent his family being harassed by the press, William hailed down a cab, and they gratefully entered it whilst shielding their faces as much as they could. It took an hour before they reached the sanctuary of 231. By that time it was getting dark, and as the three hundred or so prisoners were enjoying their supper inside the bulk of Holloway prison, a small guard of men, under torch-light and in extreme secrecy, were conducting their clandestine business in the south-east corner of the prison next to the thirty foot high wall. An unimportant, unmarked and designated area unknown to all but the Home Office, the prison Governor and his immediate staff.

There were two bodies, buried at a depth of ten feet already at the conspiratorial co-ordinates, and they had been interred there in 1903. The, so-called, baby farmers, the consequence of a double hanging. It was not the most pleasant of places in which to be eternally laid to rest. The area of waste-ground was adjacent to a transformer housing, wood storage and dustbins, and the ground was as hard as iron. Broken and powdery cracked concrete vied for supremacy against an eternally growing shield of perennial tough weeds. Eventually, five woman's bodies would be under bindweed, ground-elder, creeping buttercup, chickweed, thale cress and hairy bittercress.

It was late in the evening when the hole, at a depth of nine feet, had been dug and a thick layer of lime was tossed over Edith's young and still pretty but now, very white face and body, and the coffin sealed and lowered. No priest attended, no prayer was spoken, no funeral litany offered. Doctor Morton observed the proceedings for his records. An hour later, the two grave diggers, brought in from outside, patted down the last of the earth, and they and the single male officer who had been assigned to oversee their work, left for a well-deserved hot drink in the Porter's Lodge. By then the ground was soaking from a downpour. But not before the eldest of the grave diggers, knelt down and marked out the sign of the cross on top of the heap of earth.

He could not answer why he suddenly felt compelled to contravene known orders. He was not authorised to administer such a compassionate act. However he knew who he had buried. And knew also that not a trace of a mark was allowed to show where she was. Even though it would be gone within a day he imagined. The shame of the legal system was complete. Nevertheless, he was a Christian and, privately quite disgusted at the secrecy surrounding the way Edith Thompson's body had been treated, Mr Kitson felt he needed to do something.

His assistant, a boy aged no more than seventeen, had watched him with disinterest for all he wanted to do was get home. However, the guard showed clear signs of dissatisfaction through his expression, although he said nothing as they returned to the hub of the prison. The promised hot drink was taken in silence in the little upper room in the lodge, and both men warmed themselves by a roaring fire. With fifteen minutes, they were heading off home themselves.

It was five days later that Mr Kitson received a letter from the Home Office informing him that his company and his services would not be required any longer, and that Kitson and Sons were to be taken off the Home Office's official lists of contractors. No explanation was given, and Mr Kitson required none as he knew exactly why. Bound by the Secrecy Act, which he had signed eleven years previously, he had no recourse but to accept the judgement. However, he had not a day's regret for what he had done.

Two weeks passed before Avis remembered the frail woman prisoner, and it was over lunch at work, picking over the remains of a friend's Daily Sketch, that the memory of her flooded back. Her defiance and her mercy far stronger she imagined than even the thick walls of Holloway. In those early days, the newspapers were still writing about her sister, and although she blocked most of the lies out, those that reached her became agony.

Nevertheless the woman prisoner returned to her memory again and again, and soon, she even remembered her name; Brown. Having the emotional need to be as close to the prison as possible, Avis, after a suitable time had elapsed after the lily placing incident, underwent a form of transformation. She begged her hairdresser to cut her hair, and a Bob was her new look, which her father did not approve of in the least. It altered her appearance to a remarkable degree. It was also about this time that she began her lifetime habit of keeping a daily diary.

However, despite this experimenting with her appearance, she had no need to change her wardrobe, and she had no great reserve of cash had she so wished to do so. But she experimented with changing her day makeup, and this suited her new hairstyle. Ethel's eyes popped when she saw it, and her father, repeatedly, couldn't understand why his daughter wished to remove what many regarded as a woman's glory. He made an unadvisedly poor joke about now having lost a daughter and gained a son, which was not welcomed at all.

Avis' parents were already gravely concerned that she was not married and, with no suitor within her gunsight either. The one or two boyfriends, about which she had mentioned, had finished quietly, while the most promising one of all, young Freddy Bywaters, now lay ten feet beneath the earth in a waste of land similar in appearance to that which covered Edith not one mile away. The only difference being that he had many more neighbours.

In their quieter and more desolate moments, William and Ethel grieved privately over what was to become of their daughter. Already known as a bit of a wallflower, and now dominated and defeated by national events beyond her control, she, on the one hand became closer and supportive to her parents, but on the other, they felt her anger and distance.

About their sons, they had no fears. For the three of them somehow, as days turned into weeks, and weeks rolled into months, got on with the business of work, meeting wives and doing what regular people did. Which consisted of, for them, an everlasting round of concerts, the theatre and parties.

Not Avis though. Being a woman, and sister to her best friend, her loss remained the most terrible blow she ever had to undergo. She would love Edith, and the memory of her for the rest of her life. In reality though, a few weeks after the execution, Avis awoke from a dream in which

Edith was present. Or at least she thought it was a dream unless her sister herself had spiritually visited her.

It was a Sunday morning so a lay-in was allowed. This was not an activity to which Avis was used, but it had been an especially tiring week at work due to one thing or another. Her routine on the Lord's day was to give her mother a well-deserved rest, and bring both her and her father a pot of tea as a treat. On that day though, Avis awoke earlier, and noting the time as just turned six o'clock, snuggled in for another half an hour when, within a few seconds, she heard her bedroom door open with its characteristic squeak.

Turning over slowly, she expected to see her mother for she couldn't imagine anyone else entering her room at that hour. Yet, deciding this, Avis felt nothing but calm. However it was not Ethel who stood before her by the grey light of the early morning, but Edith, her sister. And she, moreover was smiling as she placed a cup of tea down on the little occasional table between the beds, one of which had once been Edith's before she had left the family home to get married. Then with no noise whatsoever, which was unnerving in itself, she turned slightly and sat on her own bed. She was now not looking at Avis, and not smiling anymore. She had become quite sombre.

Avis, still half asleep, sat up gently, and gazed at the apparition, staring, softly taking in all the details. Edith wore a dress with which Avis was familiar, and she appeared bright and clear, a far study from when Avis last saw her alive, when she was drugged and pleading to her father to take her home.

Avis's emotions were inexpressible. She could not, dare not speak, and she noticed the atmosphere had become appreciably sad. This induced a tear, and it was only then the image of Edith turned to her, and pleaded with her not to cry anymore. Her voice was the same; warm, friendly and light in tone. As she had been in life. But her face was unemotional. Avis, her nose beginning to run, looked down swiftly to search for a handkerchief, which she kept under her pillow, but when she looked up, the vision had vanished. So had the cup and saucer.

Coming to her wits, she quickly pulled herself out of bed, and waved her arm over the place where the vision had been. But nothing but cold air ran over her arm. Next she did the most normal thing anyone would do if they had been visited by the dead. She burst into tears, and buried her face in her hands while repeating Edith's name over and over.

Her grief swiftly turned to anger, and she ended up banging her fists into her pillow only stopping when her mother entered in response to all her noise. Avis told her exactly what happened naturally, and was passionately believed as she was not adversed to believing in an afterlife. Although, she then, was convinced, Avis was not. She guessed it was a dream. They did not mention the experience to William as his staunch Christian upbringing was against believing in such things. As far as he was concerned, Edith was with God and that was that.

Yet Avis' short bout of anger opened a wider door for her, and it was about that specific time that she began to feel genuinely angry with her sister. For leaving her, for exposing her to ridicule and excess. For allowing her to be humiliated, for destroying her family's reputation and honour. For making the rest of their lives untenable. For bringing disgrace onto everybody she knew.

Once began, this floodgate would not close, and in her righteous despair, Avis found the only person she could mention it to was Reverend Vega when she visited him in his vestry. Hence her painful education in the process of grief began, and it was to be many months before she reigned in her negative emotions, now compounded by terrible guilt for thinking about her one and only sweet sister in the way she did.

It was while walking back from Reverend Vega's church, one Saturday afternoon some two months after Edith had been executed, that she was again reminded of the poor shovelling woman and of her name; Brown. It would be untrue to say Avis had truly forgotten about her. After that last tragic day, she seemed to be the only earthly link between herself and her sister. A go-between although she could not explain why. Apart from the fact that Edith and her once shared the same living conditions. However, the more she thought about the prisoner, and her own guilt and grief, the issues became merged in her slightly confused mind and Avis, on a whim just before she slept one night, decided that she would try to make contact with her.

This she did in secret, and told not one soul, not even Mary, and certainly not her parents who would have been appalled if they had known that their daughter was returning to Holloway on a personal basis. Nevertheless, using the lie that she was visiting an old friend in Stratford, one Saturday afternoon, Avis again took the North London line to Holloway, and this time, as it was a pleasant and bright day, walked until she came again face to face with her sister's place of death.

She had chosen a Saturday because she knew that was visiting day. However, she had little joy getting in the heavily guarded and protected building whatsoever, now that she had no business there. Although she was allowed past the Porter's Lodge to speak to an officer, she was immediately recognised, despite her new appearance, and when that was confirmed by giving her name, she was told to leave.

But leave the plucky Avis did not, and a little outraged, put forward her wish that she believed it was her right to visit a prisoner. One of Mr Flower's deputies was therefore dispatched, and expeditiously, a tall woman wardress with an idiotic lopsided smile and a speech impediment, informed her that that particular prisoner was allowed to receive a visitor only once every three months. Avis therefore, not caring for the attitude of the woman at all, demanded to know the next date, whereupon the smile disappeared, and she was reluctantly given a date four weeks hence. Astonished at her arrogance, Avis turned on her heels, and barked over her shoulder as she walked back to the entranceway that she would therefore return on that date.

Consequently, at exactly the same time, four weeks to the day, and with the weather having taken a turn for the worse, and armed with a copy of the prison visitor's manual, to help should she receive any more discouragement, and which she had read thoroughly in preparation for any hindrance to her cause, she signed the visitor's ledger, a huge brown tome which rested on one of the heavy wooden tables in the Porter's Lodge along with twenty or so others, mostly men and, when ready, were escorted into the inner yard, and foreword under the watching eyes of the two stone-carved griffins, and henceforth up the wide white sweeping staircase to the visitor's clean, glass-panelled room.

The visitors were instructed to sit at three long heavy Victorian tables, and as Avis chose a seat, she took sideways glances at the six men of various ages to her side, each she imagined, of dubious character judging by their appearance. There was also on her table one very nervous young woman who spent the whole time clutching her handbag. Two tough-looking and sharp-sounding wardress' stood close by, their dark uniforms absolutely identical and spotless. The sterile room was bare with not a trace of comfort or emotional support except for an old clock.

Shortly the eldest one recited from a card what they could and could not do. Touching a prisoner in any way, and under any circumstances was forbidden. Raising their voice, meaning, either prisoner or visitor, was not allowed, Cursing was not allowed. Smoking was not allowed. Offering gifts of any sort was not allowed. Offering medicine was not allowed. Any mention, or anything to do with their case, if pending, was not allowed. Once the prisoner had entered the room and sat, they had twelve minutes and no longer.

Avis had no idea whatsoever why the period of twelve minutes was paramount. She understood that a time period had to be observed, but the length remained a puzzle. The room was extremely chilly as there was no heating of any description. Snow was in the air, and outside a north wind blew in gusts. Also, she could hear distant traffic, and the moaning of a great mass of women, and wondered if this was how it had been for Edith. She shivered, partly from the cold, and partly from fear as she received a diluted experience of what Edith must have undergone.

On trial for murder, and in a place so hard, alien and queer from her everyday routine and family. From her furs and theatre lunches, her love of fine food, and devoted friends, her trips abroad, her freedom, her lavish (for her) expense account...how she must have suffered. Locked in a small cell, her personal life, her deepest secrets now exposed to the judgement of the world, and surrounded and ordered about by these hard and vicious-faced women. These were the imaginings of Avis as she sat patiently waiting for the prisoners to enter. At one end of the plain large room, a mid Victorian clock, part of the original fixtures and fittings, loudly ticked away the seconds. It seemed worse than a dentist's waiting room. All visitors were unusually quiet, and Avis felt a sense of shame permeating throughout the room.

A previously unseen and older officer entered, and moved to a cabinet on one of the walls from which she pulled out a set of white cards. She then proceeded to place one before each visitor on the table. On each card was printed in large type, a number. Avis was designated as number six. A similar-sized card with the same number was then placed opposite each of them, and all were aligned precisely with the edge of the table. This activity was performed in complete silence. Avis desperately wanted to blow her nose, for the chilliness had given her the sniffles, but she was hesitant to reach into her bag least she be shouted at, or worse, told to leave. The atmosphere was overwhelmingly oppressive. Avis did not have the creativity to imagine how strict daily life was for the prisoners, if this was how they treated their visitors. Eventually she had no choice, but to discreetly and briefly wipe her nose with the back of her forefinger whilst staring straight ahead.

In the background, she had become aware, since sitting, of the endless clatter of keys turning accompanied by a moderate amount of shouting, but soon everything grew louder. Loud enough to recognise that the clamourous racket was coming from her right. From beyond an impenetrable metal door. A door with no window. The disorderly and vulgar sounds grew louder and then, with a squeak and a groan, the door was pulled open from the other side, and another officer entered flourishing a set of keys. Orders were barked and sheets of paper on clipboards were marked as a line of similarly dressed women of all ages filed into the room, all eagerly scanning the table for the number to which they had been assigned. In a fraction of a second, they identified them and noisily sat opposite their visitor.

Avis' prisoner had hesitated for a moment, but had then sat, her hands resting lightly on the table in just the manner of the other prisoners. Avis wondered if she too were supposed to put her hands in the same position, but taking a brief glance at her immediate neighbours, she noticed that that was not necessary. Therefore she turned her attention to the young woman who now sat across from her, and wondered briefly why she had decided to embark on this, quite dotty adventure in this unknown place. However, her selfish thought was cut short when the woman spoke immediately. She had a strong Newcastle accent, and a stimulating impertinence, which threw Avis momentarily.

'Did 'arry send you?'

'I don't know who Harry is. We've never met. That is, you and I.'

'Well, who are you then man?'

'I saw you...a while ago. You were in the yard? Shovelling coal? I was passing with my family...'

'Why aye! It's you. The Thompson family.'

'Yes...'

'What you doing here man?'

'I've brought some cigarettes for you. If you smoke...'

'Aye. Thanks. But why yah visiting?'

'Well, truth is, after you did what you did. You know, laid down your shovel and that...I was really touched as it was the only time anyone in this place had shown my family any kindness.'

'Ney botha man. What happened to the sharon was the worst. Tore this place up it did. Should never 'ave 'appened. You the sister then?'

Avis nodded.

'Sympathies man. I canna imagine losing mine.'

'You have family then?'

'Oh aye. Back home.'

'Do you mind me asking how long you've been here?'

'Coming up to six months. Two and a half to go.'

'What...years?'

'Aye man, but it's ney bother.'

'I guess you get used to it?'

'You jesting? Ney, never. Just do it don't yeh. What's your name?'

'Avis...your's?'

'Ruth. How did you know me?'

'I heard the guard call out your name.'

'Well now, so you're a pretty one. What do you want with the likes of me?'

Avis, now that she had a first name to attach to the interesting face, managed a short smile, and was able to observe her better. She was certainly in a better condition than when she was scraping about that pile of coal. Ruth's expression was not smiling though. She was as plain as flour, as her mother was fond of saying, with no pleasantries about her whatsoever. Her dark eyes were lined and hard, her skin puckered, her cheeks pinched, her wide mouth severe and her lips a light shade of brown. Her loose, fawn-coloured dry hair was pinned back and entangled with a faded red and white polkadot scarf, which was tied around her small head. Her uniform, the ubiquitous brown dress, was open at the neck, and her exposed red skin on her chest and on her hands told Avis much about the way she was being forced to live. Her nails were bitten down to the quick, and were even redder than her chest. Her teeth were crooked, and dark. Yet somehow, beyond the reach of her scavenger-like appearance, Avis sensed some sensitivity. She felt an impression of sympathy rise, but found the means to control it.

'Since I lost my sister, I've not been the same. None of my family haven't. Our lives have been made thoroughly miserable by nearly everyone, and we wasn't even allowed that day when you saw us, to be with her as she was buried. It's all just been too much.'

'Why aye. I canna imagine.'

'Then you, and you was chained up at the time, like some beast of the field, did the only decent thing I can remember anyone doing for Edith, or us. I searched you out because I wanted to know why. You didn't know us, and I've a feeling that you gave yourself some trouble because of it. Why then?'

Ruth pressed her fingers together and then drew them apart several times before she answered although she kept her hands in the same place on the wooden table.

'Aye, I was chained, and I was on punishment. I'd tried to escape twice, but there's no escaping this dungeon. Built like a...,' here she lowered her voice to a whisper, 'a true southern shit house. I saw no food that evening for what I did. I missed me kipper! I saw you and your people walking, and I knew where you were going. 'Cause old Mary was taken there not two weeks ago. As I said man, what happened to the sharon was the worst. They say she was a real lady.'

'She was family.'

'Aye man...understand. What I did any Northerner worth her salt would have done to pay her respects. Do you not do that down here?'

'Perhaps not to folk we don't know.'

'Then I call you strange man. People is people and death is death no matter what they've done.'

'That's a noble attitude.'

'Don't know abut that man. It's just what we do. We Northerners may be piss poor and basic, and we may chaw a bit more than you lot, but when it comes to family, we know what's what and who's who.'

'I beg your pardon. But chaw?'

'Steal man, steal. Hoo man...have you never stolen?'

'I don't think so. No, I'm sure I haven't.'

Why aye then. You must come from a rich family.'

'We're not! But we get by without stealing. I must say, if you don't mind me saying, you've got a conflicting set of morals.'

'Aye, maybe we have, but not when it comes to death. Family we trust and God we trust.'

'You are religious then? But how can a thief be a Christian?'

'Hoo man! You live in a little world. You go away and think abut it. You Londoner! It's a tidy big place.'

'One minute.' A guard's voice cut the air.

'Did you get what you wanted from me? I wondered who it was a visiting.'

'I don't know. It's going to take a long time to get over my sister, but I wanted to thank you for what you did.'

'Will you see me again? Pop in again. I like your kindness.'

'I will, but its such a long time to wait.'

'I'll do me best to keep clean so you can visit again, and not make it so long.'

'I'd like that Ruth. But before I go, may I ask what it is you are in here for?'

'Will it make a difference to you visiting?'

'No, of course not!'

'Then see you next time.' She managed a smile. A supremely forlorn one.

Avis enquired from the Porter's lodge if she had to wait another three months before Ruth's next allowed visit, and was told with some relief that her punishment ended in three weeks time. Therefore, in another twenty-eight days, she would be allowed another visitor. Avis then gave the officer the hundred cigarettes for which she was given a receipt, and a promise that they would be delivered to the prisoner later that day after lock down.

Then Avis, after signing out, was escorted with the other visitors to the front gate, which was banged shut and locked firmly behind them. The wind by early evening had increased, and Avis locked her coat closely around her with four large buttons as she ran for a tram, which was to return her to Upper Holloway train Station.

Her thoughts of the journey home were original and peculiar. Ruth, had no doubt, been possibly the most interesting specimen of womanhood she had ever met. Beyond the rough and emotionally uneven exterior, she thought...no, she knew, because of her one selfish act, that here was a woman worth saving. If she wanted to be saved, she added reflectively.

*

Ruth was marched, although shuffled would be a more appropriate term, back to her cell where she spent an hour before supper, cleaning and polishing her bed, and repairing the thin mattress of its many tears. She was allowed to join the others on C Wing for supper, which consisted of soup, bread and tea before she was again locked away until the next morning at six.

Before the light faded, she continued with the only pastime that held any interest for her; a paste-book. This was where she would cut images from various magazines and paste them in a scrapbook, given to her by the Friends of Holloway Society. The magazines she obtained from any source she could. It was the one activity, which gave her pleasure.

However, at eight o'clock, the wardress' did their final rounds of the day to check on the condition of their charges, and to tell them to sleep. Whereupon, the image of Avis occurred to her, and wondered simultaneously what the future held. What she did in the yard that day, her mark of respect, was nothing less than she, and virtually everyone that she used to know would have done. It was her way, and she didn't understand at all Avis' opinion that courtesy or compassion was only for those you knew. It was just another pointer how strange the people in the South were.

Avis' homeward train rattled eastwards, and people boarded and left until only a handful remained. Three alighted at Woodgrange Park, whereupon East Ham proved to be as damp and miserable as North London. However, her moderately happy reverie was cut short when, upon stepping up into Romford Road, a paperboy swaggered by yelling that no reprieve had been granted for the Manchester born man George Perry, and he had only some fifty-two hours to live. Avis, upon hearing this dreadful piece of dirt, stiffened with fear, and moved herself next to a metal fence where she steadied herself. Due to her mother's insistence, she always carried a small bottle of ammonia of salts, and now she felt a need for a short sniff to ease her giddiness. She knew nothing of this business, and her paper, through which she had previously skipped, had reported no such event. Later she was to learn that he had been tried for killing his sister-in-law.

However, all she could think of was random and unpleasant thoughts about his family, and the gruesome way the state was intending to put him to death. She wondered about the crime, and what drove him to it. And even if he was guilty, or could it possibly be another miscarriage of justice about which she had heard. She found herself miserably sad for his situation, and the ordeal his family would have to undergo tomorrow after the execution. And then never knowing where he was buried...never being able to place flowers on her grave...

Avis admitted that she had worked herself up into too many unhealthy thoughts, and took a longer route home than was usual. Just to clear her head. As she walked, her short heels made a soft clatter on the wide paving stones, and she could not imagine the inability to not being able to walk more than six feet without stopping and turning. Just as she also imagined Mr Perry too walking back and forth in an unconscious, frantic and hopeless attempt to escape the hangman's rope on the Monday morning.

She also imagined Ruth lighting one of her free cigarettes, and hopefully thinking of her, but imagined that she wasn't. At Home, Ethel had made a thick rich stew with dumplings, and boiled potatoes, and Avis, her mother and father, Newenham and Harold who had also joined them for an hour or two, quickly, upon Avis joining them, sat down to enjoy it. Uncommon for the Graydon family, even given the faith of William, Grace was said by him. This was a recent habit into which they had fallen since the death of their daughter, and it seemed the right and correct thing to do.

Reverend Vega had suggested that they all, as part of coming to terms with Edith's death, begin to say Grace again as they did when the children were young. And always, he stressed, to include how grateful they were to God for what they had, and not to search their minds for the things they did not have. The prayer was comforting to Avis, and she enjoyed her father's words spoken at the beginning of each meal.

Unfortunately, Avis told lie after lie about where she had spent her afternoon. She kept remembering about Ruth's short opinion about family and felt doubly guilty. However she felt she had not done anything wrong. Indeed, she was attempting to protect her mother wasn't she? During the pudding, she thought she might reveal to her parent's at some time just where she had been. She was a grown woman anyway, and senior even to her three brothers, and she ought not to be afraid of their reaction.

Her brothers were extremely talkative that evening, and bombarded their parents of all the broad details of their lives, leaving out naturally certain circumstances, mostly to do with their current beaus. But Avis, due to the nature of her day, found their mindless chatter overwhelming, and she soon asked to be excused giving a slight headache as the reason.

She therefore went straight to her room, and lay on her bed, and continued to think about the events which had so overtaken her. Her only real concern in the matter of informing her parents where she had been, and where she intended to return was the press. Now that the initial hysteria was over, what the newspapers had described as an atrocious act, the hanging of a young and innocent woman, had diminished somewhat, now that it was March, it would be unconscionable for the affair to start up again, and Avis was quite aware that her mother's nerves might possibly snap if she were put under any more undue strain. Her migraines were now occurring on a weekly basis, and each time forced her to stay in bed for perhaps as long as two days.

During the last four months, Doctor Wallis had become a familiar visitor to number 231. Avis suspected that her father had not yet settled his account. However, the doctor was a kind and sympathetic man, and Avis imagined that he knew just how difficult, as much financially as emotionally, the tragedy had struck the family. She noted that he recorded every pill and powder he prescribed, but so far, had always waved William's attempt to pay. But at some point, she guessed there would be a reckoning.

Spring 1923, at least in the biological sense, came early to London, and when on another Saturday, Avis made the journey again to Holloway prison, daffodils and white crocus' were smothering the few weeds which had spouted in the garden of the Governor's house, and their heads nodded gently in her direction. The sweet odour of oak and lavender filled the nostrils of everyone who entered the building. The trip had been pleasant, the weather so contrary to how it had been before.

Avis had also done something she hadn't done for a long time; she had brought a tabloid and read it on the train. She noted with extreme satisfaction that there was not one mention of the Thompson and Bywater's case, and the surnames of all involved were absent as well. She happened to know through an acquaintance at work that the Bywater's family and the Thompson's had also suffered from the dirty fingers of the gutter press. This was extremely positive news as it meant some sort of normality could now endure.

However, as Avis filled out the visitor's ledger, she was nevertheless aware of an uncomfortable sensation, mostly caused by the high spirits of the attending officers, perhaps caused by the warmth of spring. As she waited, her newspaper, now rolled and poking out of her shopping bag, she had a few minutes to observe these men and women who had participated in the destruction of her sister.

Although the atmosphere was far from carnival, the officers were nevertheless, far more relaxed in manner and speech than they had been a month previously. But however, Avis could not see the arrogant Mr Flowers anywhere.

It was only when the visitors, as a group, were escorted beyond the lodge into the inner court yard, that Avis felt an old emotion; dread...and the coldness that accompanies it. She saw it in her mind's eye; a multiple vision of Edith laying in that wooden coffin, Edith crying and struggling, and pleading for her father to take her home, Edith drugged, and plummeting to her death trussed like an animal, now Edith in spirit, her undaunted soul watching over the place, watching over her... Somewhere, here she was, buried, and Avis glanced hopefully around, perhaps expecting to see a white painted Christian cross on a wall or something to illustrate what the law finally did with her.

The short walk into the prison certainly did not lead the group anywhere near the waste of land where now, weeds once again, were already covering the bare earth under the long shadow of the high perimeter wall.

All had to undergo and endure the same procedure as before, as if the prison service regarded the resident's visitors as having no sense or memory. Avis noticed that three of the visitors were (she was certain of it) the same as on her last visit. The young nervous woman had again chosen the same chair, and Avis guessed correctly that she was visiting her mother.

She looked a poor, bedraggled thin thing, probably aged no more than seventeen, and Avis glanced shyly at her as the only other women visitor present as the cards were laid out as before. The young woman kept her eyes firmly on the table as she clutched the same little brown handbag to her chest. Avis wondered how she was suffering; seeing her mother condemned to live in a place like this.

Ruth entered amid the clanging of oversized metal keys and locks, a cacophony Avis would never be able to forget, and with an expression of great sourness, sat. It was all she could do mutter a hello.

They exchanged pleasantries, but not without some forcefulness on Avis' part who attempted to cheer the prisoner up by telling her she had, this time, brought two hundred cigarettes. The conversation though was almost all one way this time, and the Newcastle woman did not once ask

Avis how she was or had been, or how she had been coping. Within five minutes, Avis felt uncomfortable as she attempted to spread what conversational material she had out to occupy the remaining seven minutes.

Ruth appeared about the same. Unhappy, thin and extremely depressed. She looked as if she hadn't washed or changed her prison garb since the last visit. However, Avis was able to eventually get out of her why she was so unhappy. Although not a punishment (because no visitors would have been allowed) she had recently been confined to K Wing, the hospital, for she had been seriously attacked with a home-made knife. Then scurrilous and untrue rumours had been spread that she had offered up a name, and now she was 'on watch'. Her reputation with the other inmates now cloudy and uncertain.

Close to the end of the twelve minutes, Ruth lifted up her sleeve and Avis saw with horror, a three-inch jagged red line on her right forearm just below the elbow. In the well-lit room, the wound looked puckered, fresh and dangerous, and Avis regarded it with some horror, her hand moving to her mouth. All she could stammer in return was how sorry she was, and repeated an earlier question about if she had received her earlier present of the cigarettes, to which Ruth nodded, her mouth tightening.

'I wrote my address on the inside of the box Ruth if ever you wish to write. Did you see it? I'll always be glad to read about what's happening here.'

The remark caused some sudden amusement, which caught Avis by surprise.

'I canna read or write man, so I'd have problems there.'

'Shall I write to you then? Will there be someone to read it for you?'

'Ney botha. Father will do it.'

'A priest?'

'Aye, he's good, and we smoke together.'

'You're Catholic then?'

'Aye.'

Avis apologised again, but affirmed that she would write. She then asked if her visiting was causing her pain or upsetting her in any way.

To which, in the one minute remaining, Ruth tried to squeeze out something positive, but it was hard-going. Her reply was simple.

'No', she replied, 'but you will come back again?'

Before she was escorted to her cell, Ruth never thanked her for anything Avis had brought or done, and that left her with an empty hard feeling that even the spring flowers and sweet warmth outside could not remove. There had been at least one thing different about Ruth though, although it was only as she shifted about in her hard chair that she had caught a glimpse of it. It was the sight of a St Christopher, something Avis would have sworn had not been around her neck before. And mentioning the priest, was the only part of their twelve minutes together that Ruth showed any sign of animation.

The Ordinary, (Holloway's resident priest) had indeed visited Ruth in hospital, and given it to her, for which she had first expressed antipathy, but later had been much amused by the pewter pendent. On her way out to the road, Avis briefly wondered if this had been the same cleric who had been present at Edith's death, but quickly saw no point in concentrating on that issue. At work she had been told of a newspaper article in which the priest concerned had now become an entirely different person on account of his experience of the 9 January, and apparently did all he could to speak out against the barbarity of the ancient procedure.

Naturally though, even though Avis had not read the article, the impression was extremely upsetting as it gave the impression that something untoward or even horrifying had happened. Avis had closed her ears and eyes to the woman telling her of it. The fact that he mentioned he would never again preside over a hanging indicated a great deal about what he had experienced that morning in January.

In the two weeks while Ruth had been recovering, for in truth she had lost a great deal of blood from the attack, and had endured neural shock, the priest had visited her daily and oddly, she found his presence comforting. Reverend Glanvill Murray was a quiet, well-spoken man with a long history for doing good at Holloway, and her hard northern personality, under the spectre of her own close shave with death, eventually softened. Therefore she had accepted his St Christopher, and even enjoyed his stories, vaguely taken from the Good Book. He by degree was immensely surprised to uncover that she had never been christened, and indeed, had never seen the inside of a church in her twenty-five years.

However, what positivism he had inspired in her, had most defiantly fled from her personality that day on Avis' second visit. Her return to the Fold, the priest knew it would take time naturally. She had almost appeared to him to be similar to a feral child, and in his quiet moments, he wondered what sort of society in these modern times, when the cruel Victorian within them all had been abandoned so long ago, was capable of breeding such a Godless creature. As with most of the inmates, he was not at all surprised she was incarcerated.

Religion occupied a great deal of Avis' time over the few weeks that followed her second visit, and she herself visited

Reverend Vega in his vestry several times. In one extremely potent dream, she was actually in Edith's cell as her sister was converting to the Catholic faith. Which of course never happened. However, in the aftermath of the dream, Avis' devotion to the Anglican church became tested over the following few weeks as she became convinced of how kind a certain Catholic priest had been to Edith during her last days. It was this confusion that peppered Avis' mind with doubts and questions, all of which she had no way of answering.

Ironically, it was Reverend Vega himself, through no fault of his own that turned Avis' inclination away from the Anglican Church after almost thirty years. It was over a very simple matter. Reverend Vega could not see her after she had finished work one evening. He was, at the time, busy comforting a newly bereaved widow while she, in a particularly vexatious state needed his council. She was informed by Nellie, by her usual manner of hand waving and pointing, of Reverend Vega's indisposition, but could not get out of her how long he would be.

That Friday was not particularly any more stressful at work than any other for Avis except the weather had disagreeably turned extremely cold, and coincided with the collapse of the three ancient hot water boilers at work whereby some electric heaters were issued, and the women were allowed to work in their coats. However, working for nine hours, with only half an hour break in such cold conditions did not improve her personality.

At work her initial unwelcome infamy had been much reduced, and she had, thankfully, become one of the girls. Nevertheless, she still had moments of great anxiety. Unaccountable times when the image of Edith, pathetically weeping and crying, and asking to be taken home on that last visit, would loom up particularly large before her eyes. Once there, the memories often took over her reason and concentration. As had happened that Friday. From experience, she now knew the only way to dissipate that anxiety was to describe the horrors. As she could not discharge her feelings onto Mary, or her parents or brothers, the counselling of Reverend Vega after work remained her only option. But not that evening.

Snow had even been promised, despite the lateness of the year, and had been threatened by the long range weather service for the last twenty-four hours. As the temperature plummeted, Avis could almost smell the snowflakes as she walked home from St Barnabas. Only a walk of five minutes against the cold with a light to moderate wind, it seemed longer. Her mind racing with unhappy thoughts, and deeply disappointed that she had not been able to speak with Reverend Vega, she walked lightly passed her home, and headed towards the Romford Road, and then Station Road, beyond which lay the dark expanse of Wanstead Flats once she had walked past Manor Park Railway Station.

Being extremely dark, it was not an attractive area at night. It was an expanse of open land with few trees, and had been so for almost a thousand years, the only things living on it, beside vegetation were cattle and sheep who had the protection of the king. To her right just by a short walk, lay the great expanse of the City of London cemetery. However tempting it was to walk on the Flats, Avis was sensible enough to stick to Capel Road where there were houses and some street lighting. She had heard of many unsavoury and nasty events going on under cover of darkness, round and about this particular stretch of ground, and she had no wish to get into any trouble or to add to the stories.

What Avis wished and needed was simply a walk to settle and clear her mind, and the flat, quiet area of scrubland provided plenty of silence usually. At least during the day. Avis proved to be no different to any other human being who had essentially, if unintentionally, been snubbed, and a minor rant raged a little silently within her, disregarding so easily the many hours the Reverend Vega had previously devoted to her.

He became, if not an unbearable clot, then certainly he took on the perspective of a man with whom she could no longer trust to look after her best interests. It was evident, to her, that he had become enervated of her family's difficulties, and now wanted to distance himself. At the very least, on a personal basis. After all, she reasoned, they had been under his guidance for some months, and it had to stop at some point.

However much this cerebral thinking satisfied her logic, emotionally, she was still agitated, and not just a little depressed. It was therefore, after she had accepted her resolution about Reverend Vega, and by one of those little coincidences which gives life such a pleasure to live, that she turned left into Woodford Road and, having reached the halfway position of her journey, just after she had passed Forest Gate Railway Station, the next station along the Tottenham & Forest Gate Railway line, noticed a number of people entering St Thomas' Catholic church.

Over three quarters of an hour into her walk, her eyes were beginning to ache with the cold and the very icy wind, and she imagined that instead of walking home, she might catch a tram. However, the strains of a well played organ fairly streamed out of the open doorway of the church, obviously, she imagined, as some prelude to a service.

It was probably not the holiest of reasons to enter a church, but no doubt, she imagined, there had been worse. Pulled in by the allure of the music, and the spiritual warmth the church offered, Avis, although she had never before visited that particular one, took a chance, and entered it where she was given a warm welcome by two smiling middle-aged ladies, one of whom offered a hymn book which she readily took.

The solid wooden pews were already mostly filled, so she naturally moved to the back, and pulled her coat closer around herself before crossing, firstly spiritually herself, and then physically her legs after she sat. Inside the hymn book was a four-page pamphlet describing the service that was about to begin. It was Holy Communion. A white marble statue of the Virgin Mary gazed down upon her comfortably from a little way away, and the music from the organ sounded beautiful, and induced a well-received sense of serenity. Arriving from the wicked cold of the outside to this heavenly warmth was a pleasure in itself, but Avis, from the moment she had sat and taken her first gaze at the ornate and decorative woodwork, felt that there was more to it than that mundane reason.

By straining, she could just see the organist who appeared to be a youngish man. A fellow with a mass of yellow hair, which was rather long for his important position.

He played finely, and with a delicate touch, Mozart she imagined, at the moment.

St Thomas the Apostle Roman Catholic church was not an old structure. It had been built along with the predominantly double fronted Victorian houses of the Woodgrange estate, which comprised the long streets of suburbia when expansion had arrived to the area in the late 1880s. It had been designed especially to serve the new residents, which it had been doing successfully for over twenty-five years. It was a permanent church, and was a brick building in the Perpendicular style, but the entrance front and tower was faced with stone. It consisted of an apsidal chancel, and an aisled and clerestoried nave, the aisle terminating in side chapels. It also had a baptistery and a west gallery. Avis was impressed with the cosmetic arrangement, and with the perfectly balanced symmetry between high spirituality and pleasing aesthetics. She noticed the many stained glass windows, and wondered how fine they probably looked in daylight.

With that thought, she made a mental note to come back during the day. The ceiling was of finely carved oak, and beams arched from side to side above the tall windows. The high altar, over which presided a huge figure of the crucified Christ, was awash with colour and to Avis, looked nothing less than exciting. As if something miraculous was going to happen. As if heaven itself was going to be present. It wasn't long before the music faded away to silence, all were seated, and the priest stepped out followed by a number of cherub-faced choirboys.

Unlike her visits to her own church, Avis became magnetically drawn into the centuries old service, and lost complete track of time, sang the hymns with passion, and tightly closed her eyes when asked to join in the prayers. The Catholic experience moved her beyond what she had expected. Which, at the time of her beginning to walk by the church, in the bitter cold, was very little, so deeply was she stuck in her malaise.

She pondered in the quiet moments of the service, if she had been drawn to the ensemble because Edith, in her death cell, had become the focus of attention by Canon Patrick Palmer whom Edith had grown to like very much. Indeed, so much that she preferred his company to the official Holloway chaplain whom disgracefully, had much to do with keeping the Canon away in the first instance. Edith had told Avis how very kind she believed him to be. Despite being an important ecclesiastical gentleman, he had spent a great deal of time comforting her during her long incarceration. His views on her death were not recorded.

After an hour and a half, Avis found herself back on the, by now, bitterly cold and dark streets of Forest Gate with a promise by the clergy himself that she would be welcomed to return, and perhaps take her First Communion Class. At that initial encounter, he, and the other people with whom she spoke, did not appear to recognise her, so she thought it wise not to mention who she was.

At the time, her awareness simply extended to the spiritual warmth and level of communication that had been offered...plus the slight and perhaps shy attention of the organist who had finished his repertoire, and had joined the mingling assemblage afterwards.

She had stayed for about twenty minutes chatting to various members of the congregation, being mindful of the time, and the fact that she had not told her parents she was going to be late. Reluctantly, she had said good-bye and left the gently buzzing crowd. She had turned briefly around to take one last look at the high altar, but instead had caught the eye of the organist who immediately looked away and down. It was obvious to Avis that he had seen someone with whom he found attractive.

Despite the freezing conditions outside, and the prospect of a difficult journey home, Avis was glowing. And she liked the feeling. The organist was tall, and people might say, skinny, but to Avis' eyes looked none the worse for that. He had been formally dressed in a blue suit and dark tie, and had the shiniest shoes she had seen on a man for a long time. They did not have an occasion to talk, but Avis knew she was being observed. And that made her feel warm in itself.

Unaccountably, the temperature outside had risen a little but the wind had increased. Then, astonishingly, Avis had taken no more than fifty steps towards the Romford Road, where she hoped to catch a tram, when the first pattering of snow appeared. Although Avis felt, as most people do, that snow after Christmas was hardly as exciting as snow beforehand, that night she quite relished it. So charged with positive emotion was she. Even though they were a little way into the year. By the time half a dozen snowflakes had landed on her eyelashes, and she had reached the main road, past endless empty and drab shops, her dark coat was covered as the flakes continued to swirl around her relentlessly until it all began to look rather pretty. Despite wearing her thickest gloves, she dug her hands deep in her pockets.

Romford Road, seven o'clock now being a memory, was essentially deserted. Almost certainly a consequence of the time and the conditions. Only the rumble of the occasional barrow on the stones and horse's hooves disturbed the growing peace. She stared left and right at the many industries and shops now barely visible through the increasing prettiness of the snow, before quickly turning left, and walking to the tram stop where she glanced at her watch.

Through the increasingly quiet gloom, across the road by the crossroads, the far older Church of Emmanuel stood like a stupendous fortress amongst its many trees, and did not give Avis the warm feeling by any means, she had experienced when standing outside St Thomas. Looking at her watch again, as she became colder, the warming effects of her spiritual experience beginning to fade, she looked west, in the direction of Stratford hoping a number eight might still arrive.

Within two minutes, an elderly gentleman leaning heavily on a cane, stepped forward from out of the gleaming whiteness of the growing blizzard, and slowing down just ever so slightly, tipped his hat with his free and gloved hand.

'No trams now Miss. Got far to go?'

'Manor Park.'

'Best get walking Miss. This place'll be covered soon. I wish you goodnight.'

Avis stared dismally at his round shouldered back, and pouted. However, resigned to her fate, she set off with snow blowing around her at an ever increasing rate. 231 was just over a mile away, but she found walking more difficult with every step. After a while leaving the crossroads, there was hardly any traffic, and those that were caught out in the storm, consisted of a few delivery vans being pulled by sweaty and driven horses, even their sounds muffled.

Minute by minute the Romford Road took on the appearance of a Christmas card, silent and attractive, but Avis as her mood changed was in the best state of mind to appreciate it. The only pedestrians braving the weather, except for several excited boys who were already becoming wild, gathering up the snow and screaming madly, were a few men hurrying along, most probably making their way to some public house. Or if their wives were lucky, to their homes and children. Nevertheless, despite being a lone female, she felt quite safe as she picked her way along the increasingly slippery pavement mostly by hanging onto fences and walls.

Eventually, her brown leather shoes soaked and much ruined, at Manor Park broadway, and under better lighting, she found the crossroads had been transformed into a tinge of blueness under what street lighting was provided. Turning left at the junction of Romford Road and High Street North, she crossed the wide empty street and carried on regardless, now with no more than ten minutes to go.

Avis would have normally taken a short cut through Salisbury Road, indeed would have taken that route had it been daylight, but decided not to risk it now it was under the cover of a threatening type of darkness. Even though she was a mature woman, it ought to be remembered how innocent she was in the ways of the world. Although, not apparently innocent enough not to have heard about the shenanigans that occasionally took place in that particular small part of Manor Park, respectful as it was.

At the telephone exchange, it was common knowledge that it had something to do with being so approximal to Manor Park Station. However, apart from that intelligence, and a certain notion that whatever happened to the unfortunate women who tended to accumulate there, she had no real idea what occurred except that it was probably not something a nice girl like herself ought to view.

Therefore, she had taken the ever so slightly longer route, and was forced to slow down even more as she mounted the slight rise, under which ran the railway, turned left into Church Road, and aimed herself at the bridge which would take her again back over the railway line. That took her another ten minutes though as the snow continued to pour out of the dark sky. Not a single train passed as she groped her way, holding onto gateposts and fences, now almost blind. Also, because the wind had risen even more, now Avis found she was in the middle of a veritable snowstorm. And she was bone cold throughout.

Finally, a little panic set in as now she was the only person seemingly left in the area. She was the only mad person out in the appalling weather, as charming and as silent as it appeared. Some measure of how fast the storm had come upon the county could be judged by the fact that some of the lower curb-stones had already disappeared. Unfortunately it was against one of those, just as she turned left into Essex Road, that her shoe slipped on the corner of one, and with a small cry, her body failed to right itself, and Avis fell backwards into the road, landing squarely on her back with a thump, her right elbow and head cracking against the cobbled stones. The snow not deep enough to spare her that mercy.

Her handbag flew open at the same time spilling a majority of its contents into the snow. Which ironically was deep enough to stop them from rolling far. Badly winded, her arm in a great deal of lancing pain, and a lump forming on the back of her skull, she lay in the road with a kind of certain knowledge that someone would assist her. That was her attitude, and that was what she expected. Dazed and frightened, she managed to look around, but saw only a cruel white wasteland, silent as a grave. It quickly became clear to her that no one was going to come to her aid, and even clearer, that it was unfeasible that she remain where she was. She called for help a few times as loud as she could, but as if to cement her feeling of isolation, no one came. And still the snow poured over her.

Therefore, rolling over onto her belly, and using her un-injured arm, she raised herself up, slightly cursing her de-cision to go for her walk. Gingerly, she gathered the con-tents of her bag and now, so bedraggled, so cold her fingers and toes were numb, and in considerable pain from both her injuries, she carefully limped the rest of the way home by continuing to hold onto fences and railings. Within an-other ten minutes, she found herself banging the knocker on 231.

When her mother opened it in surprise, for she and Wil-liam were not expecting a knock, but a key in the latch, she nearly collapsed in shock, looking at the condition of her daughter. However, her motherly instinct immediately took over, and she bundled Avis into the kitchen where she and William made a great deal of loving fuss over her at the same time as calling her, 'a very silly girl' for being caught out in such weather.

It was when the three of them discovered the extent of the injury to her elbow though that William took his coat and hat, and immediately set off to fetch Doctor Wallis. While they were waiting, Ethel helped her daughter change into her night-dress and dressing gown, bathed the back of her head which was sore and split, and sat her in her own chair next to the fire in the kitchen, and offered her a little of her father's whisky.

Naturally, Ethel wanted to know where she had been, and Avis was some way into relating her moving religious experience when the front door banged open and a snow-covered William and Doctor Wallis appeared. Who was kindness itself considering William had interrupted his supper. By this time, the bleeding of her elbow, which had been so evident before, had now been staunched, leaving only a dark red mass on the wet tea towel which Ethel had applied.

Whilst saying yes to a whisky himself as offered by William, Doctor Wallis cleaned both wounds, fishing out a small, but jagged piece of glass in the process from her elbow. He assured the parents that their daughter had not broken anything and dressed the injures. It was now Avis' job to keep her arm elevated as much as she could. Swigging the yellow contents of his tumbler back in one gulp, Doctor Wallis thanked them all, and said he would call back tomorrow. He gave strict instructions that under no circumstances was the patient to go out in the snow or go to work.

The whisky, plus a sleeping draft that Doctor Wallis had prescribed, soon began to numb any pain Avis felt. And soon, after a little soup, a slice of bread and two aspirin, she told her parents that it would be a good idea to have an early night. Therefore, by nine o'clock, she was helped into bed by her mother who sat on the side of it for a short time, while Avis continued telling her about her exciting evening.

Ethel smiled inwardly, as she had always had a notion that her second born had a nonconformist streak in her nature. One that was unexpressed of course. That had been Edith's position. In that moment as she smoothed Avis' short hair, she clearly saw her dead daughter within the eyes of her alive second one. Beautiful hazel eyes with long eyelashes. Just for a fraction, she quivered with the imagination that Edith was in front of her once more. The results of her lonely imagination vanished though as fast as it had arrived. To cover herself, she leaned forward and kissed Avis on her forehead.

'Will you go back there dear?'

'I think I will mother. The chuch had such a good feeling about it.'

'Reverend Vega might be disappointed.'

'Do you think so?'

'We're see my dear. You get in a good night's sleep. We'll be quiet downstairs. Thank goodness the boys aren't here until tomorrow!'

Ethel moved to the window and drew back part of the curtains.

'Goodness me! Look at it! Its not stopped. They'll be fun and games in the morning!'

'Night mum.'

'Night darling. You sleep well, and I'm glad you got back home. What a thing to happen! Quite put me out! What would I do if anything happened to you?'

'Oh mum, don't think like that. I'm here and it's all right.'

'Goodnight darling.'

As tired as she was, after Ethel had closed her door, the child within her could not help, out of sheer curiosity, from rising from her bed, and looking out of her window one last time at their snow-covered back garden, and all the other gardens. The trees, especially Edith, were laden with sharp and glistening sparkles, reflecting slivers of light, and the area had become an expanse of soft clean white. Even through the glass, she could distinguish the quietness that the snow had brought. The best kind of silence. The neighbourhood children would be having some fun tomorrow! Snow was still falling with increasing heaviness as she pulled the curtain back into place. Avis, in a way, wanted to sit by the window and watch. But she felt too tired. Beyond a certain natural excitement for the snow, as she snuggled into bed, her mind's eye only conjured up an image of an organist with yellow hair.

Eleven

Before Avis had knocked at the door of 231, William had been reading his paper and Ethel had continued her knitting, both of them rather full after one of Ethel's speciality; fresh herrings which she had brought fresh the day before, it being market day in East Ham. When the hurried knock sounded, both frowned as neither felt in the mood to entertain. They had that week, at last, received a number of letters from those to whom Ethel and her sisters had been writing, the stragglers, and all were either arrogantly dismissive and certainly unchristian in their humanity. Add to that, the story that Elizabeth had captured the hearts of the nation the moment she married The Duke of York, and Ethel and William were not pleased, if not downright angry. The royal family who let them down — betrayed is the word William used — they believed had no right to be so happy. Therefore the mood of the Graydon family was, and had been sombre for some while as they had begun to realise the power, the ignorance and the indifferent mercilessness of the Government and their King.

Reading the formal letters had been a bleak experience. Especially as they still, at that time, held positive hopes of recovering Edith's body. Within the words they received, which in themselves were not many, there was no optimism, no propitious happy road ahead. Ethel and William had not talked in depth about the rejections as their nerves were still too raw. Nevertheless, both knew without a doubt, that they ought to at some point. Both recognised that there was very little they could do, now that the king himself had been approached, and rejected each of their arguments. The royal dismissal had been particularly galling, especially for William when he thought back on all the achievements he had completed, and all the sacrifices he had made for his king and country.

Therefore, they wished to have a quiet evening, especially as all three of their boys would be staying the coming weekend. Avis, of course put paid to that. It truly was the sudden vision of witnessing Edith within her sister which allowed Ethel to imagine that somehow, somewhere, perhaps her daughter might...might be what? Not alive of course. But spiritually alive yes.

Ethel had heard of Spiritualism, but had never taken an interest. She had been taught that when a Christian dies, they go to Heaven to sit with God. A plain and simple doctrine. They don't hang around waiting to be summoned. Especially to talk about old Mrs Fielding's lumbago, or some other such trivial matter. Later, with the snow outside as deep as she could ever remember covering the land, Ethel, trying to sleep, listening to William's light snoring, smiled as she half remembered some argument she had once over-heard after a church meeting. Ethel was sure that, despite that legal label as a murderess, Edith had died a good and solid Christian so why shouldn't she be with her Maker?

However, like an injured moth to an eternal flame, the idea of further communication with her daughter would not let her go, and she tensed her toes with some small measure of delight in imagining Edith 'coming through' and talking to her again. Her heart even beat a little faster at the thought of the experience. And marched a little faster again when she imagined how wrong it was, and how, in order for it to happen, she might have to deceive her William, perhaps Avis and certainly, Reverend Vega. How much these thoughts troubled her can be recognised by how vividly she dreamed that night. A night of guilt. However, the box had been opened, and there was no one to advise her how to close it.

It was over a week until Ethel took positive action about her growing obsession. In that time, plenty of events happened in the Graydon household. Ethel took a hearty breakfast of egg and bacon up to the invalid's bedroom the following morning, and delighted her by swishing the curtains back to reveal...nothing! As Avis' vision corrected for the white overwhelming light, she realised that so much snow had fallen during the night, that it had obscured the world by covering the windows. Therefore Avis was suitably amazed. And excited.

However, a stern warning from her twinkling-eyed mother reminded her of Doctor Wallis' recommendation. Anyway, she continued, there is nowhere to go.

'How the boys are going to get here only heaven knows!'

But get there they did, each arriving far later than was agreed, and each bursting to tell how they managed it. The day was positively blue with not a cloud to mar the sky, and the brilliant low sun made the deep snow glow.

Avis' injuries were better, in that, at least, the lump on her head had diminished. Her arm ached though, and more aspirin was prescribed after she had risen. In her dressing gown, she was allowed to sit in her father's chair by the kitchen fire as the poor chap had donned as many clothes as he could, and was busy clearing snow from the porch, and the front garden down to the roadside whilst chatting to as many neighbours as possible.

A mass of people, principally boys, were having a grand snowball fight a little up the road, and William smiled gently as he clenched his pipe between this teeth and sucked on it. It had been a long time since he had become that enthusiastic about snow. Shifting it was good exercise, and he enjoyed the occasional greetings he had, especially when his friend and neighbour Mr Bristow arrived with the idea of mimicking his good work. William told him about Avis' accident, and Mr Bristow promised to pop in later about elevenses to wish her well.

The snow was indeed deep, and had compacted under its own weight. Where it had drifted, it came up to William's thighs, so, no doubt he thought, the storm throughout the night must indeed have been severe. Whilst attending to his manly duties, he saw no traffic, and therefore no deliveries. Not even the hardy paperboys. After clearing away the space in front of 231, with difficulty, he tramped up to the corner shop in High Street North, and spent a little time conversing with its owner and other customers. Eventually, he returned with milk but, to his annoyance, no daily paper as the truck hadn't managed to get through.

Perhaps it was the unusual weather, but any slight feelings of paranoia which usually accompanied him whilst in public dissipated that morning. Like sound, the snow seemed to sweep them away, as if people were more concerned about this current event than the big event that had been discussed with a frenzy by the nation. He recognised that most people come together in a crises, but he was pleasantly surprised when he failed to get a glimpse of those usual slight turn of the heads when he entered the shop. Those who recognised him, still did not know what to say or how to behave in his presence. After all, it had only been...forever? Therefore William arrived back at 231 in a happy, and because of the snow, quite a simulated mood. And was more than ready for his chair and the fire.

Over the weekend, the boys took as much advantage as they dared with the good temper of their mother, and disappeared occasionally as the whim took them. Nevertheless, despite their youthful foolishness, at each meal, Edith was remembered with a great deal of reverence as grace was said. On Saturday night, the six of them, joined by Mary to balance the sexes, played cards and backgammon until late, and it was good that the family had spent time with each other. Ethel was not the only one to notice, for the very first time, the embarrassing and clumsy emotional sparks that occurred between Newenham and Mary. William and Avis caught it too, although naturally neither man nor woman acknowledged it in the other. Amusingly, they acted like fifteen year olds.

This was indeed strange because they had known each other since they had been children, and before that night, had never shown any attraction for each other whatsoever. Nevertheless, while they were fumbling and exhibiting a combination of interest and contempt for each other, Avis was thinking about the music of Handle, and how well the yellow-haired organist had played.

Early on Sunday morning, as she felt better, the six of them went for a long walk over Wanstead Flats, and Avis was glad to finally get out. William and the boys threw snow at each other while Ethel and Avis stood stamping their feet. Harold threatened to put snow down Avis' back, but after a stern warning from Ethel, he thought better of it.

After an hour in the brilliant sunshine, they returned to enjoy a quick pot of tea before Matins at St Barnabas Church where Reverend Vega was welcoming his congregation by the front porch. As was usual, the Reverend asked people to pray for those who were not present, and the Graydon family, as one unit, felt a great deal of comfort in this, for it was clearly directed at them, and everyone knew it.

The boys disappeared late on Sunday night as they had work the following morning, and their leaving cast a soberness over the three remaining, which was accompanied by a little crying by Ethel and Avis. William shook the hand of each of the boys solidly, and wished them a safe journey home, and eventually they departed into the cold, crisp night surrounded by the sparkling stars in the heavens, and the blue shadows of the trampled snow.

As Avis had been told to take time off work, a note from Doctor Wallis was sent to the exchange, by way of Mary which was received by the staid spinster Miss Brown. By the end of the week, Avis received a clean bill of health, but information, delivered again by Mary, that the staid spinster Miss Brown, was not all that happy with her, having taken so much time off, saddened her, but that could not be helped, and Avis returned to her duties on the Monday the following week. By which time, the snow had mysteriously disappeared as in the manner of snow which settles sometime into the new year.

It was therefore, Avis' continued presence in the household which prevented Ethel from indulging in her forbidden idea of spiritualism although, since the boys left, she had thought of little else. On the same Monday as Avis returned to work, and having seen William off to his work after making his sandwiches, she took a walk, as part of a shopping outing, to her local library in the Romford Road where she nervously enquired about books on the afterlife.

The young woman assistant gave her request no more thought than she would any earthy subject, and showed her what few volumes the library stocked, which were few. Ethel tucked two under her arm so no one would be able to read their covers and walked into the book-lined and wood-panelled reference room where she settled down to ingest what she could. Here, amongst the readers of local and national newspapers, she imagined she was quite immune to the interrogations of strangers. However, this plan proved to be wrong. For after five minutes, a woman of about her own age, reached across and tapped her on her hand. Which, in the silence caused her to jump.

The woman, who had quite a pleasant face, and was well dressed with a fox fur flung around her shoulders and a colourful spray of feathers protruding from her hat, apologised softly immediately although there was no reason to do so as the severe-looking and ancient reference room lady assistant had left a moment before, no doubt on some errand. That was therefore why the woman introduced herself as, astonishingly, Mrs Thompson, and then pointed at the open book Ethel had been attempting to understand. It was called, *Spiritualism in the Twentieth Century.*

Announcing an interest in the subject, although modestly mentioning that she had no powers herself, she enquired gently if Ethel had lost someone dear. To which Ethel, immediately assessing the situation, rather coarsely answered.

'Why do you think I know nothing about the subject?'

To which the woman removed her hand completely from the space around Ethel's and deeply apologised. She then went on to explain that she was a widow, and not long

190

in the parish, her husband dying just some six months since they moved from Surrey, luckily so she could be near her sister. Immediately there it was, the unhappy expression which so accompanies the grieving process. Within a moment, Mrs Thompson was wiping her eyes and again apologising.

The appearance of tears certainly overruled her previous attempt at finding a new friend, and Ethel, sensing a common emotion, reached out and touched the woman's arm, apologising for her sharpness.

'My own grief has made me perhaps less friendly.'

Their conversation thus continued and Ethel, in turn, introduced herself and they quickly shook hands, with Ethel embarrassingly informing Mrs Thompson of her ignorance about that which she was reading. Mrs Thompson then told her that if she really hasn't much knowledge about the world in which they were interested, then she could do worse than to purchase a copy of *Two Worlds*, an established magazine on the subject. It was, she said, through that very publication that she had found a local church (relatively) which she visited as often as she could financially allow. This prompted the question of cost, but Mrs Thompson smiled, and told her it was donations only. It was the cost of the journey that took her money.

Affably, but excited, and continuing the conversation, Ethel asked if it would be possible to accompany her one day? To which, the talkative Mrs Thompson, replied she would be delighted if she would, and told her that the church was but a short distance away from Mile End Underground Station on the Bow Road, luckily only six stops away on the train. Ethel at the time wondered how little money the woman had been left by her husband that she thought a single journey on a train, all right, both ways, would hit her hard in her purse, but didn't give it any more thought.

Ethel soon put the book back as Mrs Thompson's almost encyclopaedic knowledge of the world beyond seemed overwhelming. Clearly she had been studying the subject for far longer than her husband's passing. This she confirmed as the two of them left the warmth of the library, and made their way over to a local tea-room near Manor Park.

There they chatted as easily as old friends about the mysteries of the unknown, many of which, made the hairs on the back of Ethel's neck rise. She was not used to having this sort of discussion. However the lure of even imagining getting some contact from her eldest daughter drove her, and she paid for another pot of tea.

She mentioned the loss of her own dear daughter, and the reason for her interest, but Mrs Thompson did not then make any connection. She only nodded gravely, and again, placed her gloved hand on Ethel's, and hoped that she would be lucky in her quest. She herself had had some wonderful messages from her Alan, and went on to describe some. One incident particularly moved her.

It was of such a personal nature though that the medium, a youngish and well-dressed man with swept-back hair styled with Brillantine, felt it best to relay it to her afterwards in private. It was therefore after most of the congregation had left that the chap had invited her to join him in one of the small back rooms and, with a face as red as a beetroot, had told Mrs Thompson that her husband had told her to go out and buy a new slip for the one she was wearing had a tear along the shoulders and he didn't want his wife wearing such an item.

Mrs Thompson's reaction was twofold. Naturally, she was highly embarrassed that an unknown male stranger had remarked on her undergarment, yet astonished that he had been exactly correct. The rip, some six inches in length had been caused by a clotheshorse two weeks previously, and she hadn't had time to make the necessary repairs. There wasn't the possibility in all the world that the medium could have known that. The incident had occurred just one month after Mrs Thompson had buried her husband.

This story impressed Ethel a great deal, and she felt her cheeks flush. A sense of hope. An end to the dreadfulness of the dark tunnel in which she and her family had been encased since January the ninth. She had the awareness that even if Edith contacted her from the beyond, it wouldn't be like a regular conversation, although of all the things she missed about her daughter, Ethel missed her intelligent opinion on so many matters.

She, as much as she loved her second daughter, had interests mostly apart from her mother, and discussions on many subjects went nowhere. Edith had been truly like her mother, a female chip off the old block. Ethel recognised so many of her qualities as being so similar to her own once. That was before she was married of course. Although it was not William's fault that those qualities of gregariousness and positivism left her. Marriage just did that around that period.

As this thinking occurred, a trace of anger swept through her veins as she fully realised that Edith had had it all, being raised in a new century with hope, freedom and with new and untold possibilities, and she had wasted it all on an illicit, stupid and foolhardy love affair behind the back of her perfectly respectable and likeable, if indifferent husband.

Mrs Thompson noticed the slight change in her, and asked if she were all right. She confirmed that she was. She was just about to tell her who she was, and with whom she hped to get in touch, when something told her to keep her mouth shut. Time enough for that.

After shopping, they walked back in the same direction along High Street North and parted company on the corner of Milton Avenue where they agreed they would meet in two days time at six in the evening so they could attend the Wednesday meeting. They shook hands again, and Ethel completed the rest of her shopping.

It was only now left for her to invent an excuse to be out on her own in the evening. Anytime she visited her sisters, William normally accompany her, and that would be a family visit as Avis often came too. Apart from the occasional visits to the church to speak with Reverend Vega, episodes which were becoming less frequent, she had no reason to be out after dark.

Therefore she decided that honesty was the best policy, and decided to tell William the truth. Or part of it. Over their evening meal she told him how she had met a new friend, and how keen she was at Contract Bridge. Ethel knew quite well that any mention of the game Bridge would send him into a deep state of boredom, and that is why she had never learned the card game. Nevertheless here was a woman who enjoyed teaching and playing it. She was to make up the forth player. Her problem was solved.

Or so she thought for Avis, now back at work, and her elbow healing well, expressed a sudden interest in learning. This put Ethel in a bit of a spot until she reminded her that the game was played by four people and, thinking quickly, an enterprise not in her character, told her that her new friend's two sisters were making up the numbers. However, she said guiltily, perhaps once I learn, I can teach you and Mary and then we will only need one other to put your father to sleep quickly! To which he replied that if anyone attempted to play that game in my house then I'll divorce you all!

The two days passed quickly and uneventfully, and at a quarter to six, Ethel, dressed in her best skirt, cream blouse and shoes, set out to meet Mrs Thompson. Who was on time, and within an hour, they had alighted at Bow Station. Mrs Thompson assured her that Bow Spiritualist Church was less than five minutes walk away, and soon they could look forward to an evening of clairvoyance.

The church was unlike any Ethel had visited before. The entire structure was made of wood and painted pure white.

It had a sloping roof and a small spire, also in white, built as if the architect was trying to imitate a traditional stone church. Attached to the framework at eye level was a huge wooden cross under which was printed in black majuscule letters, Bow Spiritualist Church. Four steps led up to the entrance, a plain white door.

However, the unpretentious exterior did not prepare Ethel for the beauty of the interior. What struck her most was the volume of garnishes, and flower arrangements scattered in vases throughout. There appeared to be hundreds, and their powerful combined scent was uplifting and vibrant. Carnations, chrysanthemums, daffodils, daisy, lilies, amaryllis and pansies, and a great deal more she could not readily identify were bound up with holly and other evergreen leaves.

Ethel was a little stunned, and a weary smile appeared. The church was small, of that there could be no doubt. But what it lacked in volume, it made up for in homeliness, for it was similar to a person's large front room. There was the obligatory altar, a slightly raised area covered in a royal blue cloth, upon which rested a wooden cross on its centre, center and a large open book, Ethel presumed was a bible. Three tall white candles glowed, but the main illumination came from gas jets of which there were six, and mounted equidistantly on the walls.

The quivering flames set the spiritual tone for the evening, and Ethel and Mrs Thompson took their seats amongst thirty others of varying ages and sexes. There were no pews as such, but surrounding the altar was a double semicircle of upright chairs, each provided thoughtfully with a plump red and gold-decorated cushion. At the back where they had entered, copies of Two Worlds were abundantly on display to buy, and the price of nine pence was quite reasonable.

As soon as they had sat, a cheerful tall woman recognised Mrs Thompson, and came over to greet her, and by introduction, Ethel, who had three leaflets immediately detailing the church's future activities dropped into her hand. They were told that tonight's clairvoyant was a gentlemen of much fame in the west of London and they were very proud for him to visit their humble little church.

She asked if it was her first time, and Ethel assented with a silent nod. The woman smelt brutally of lavender, a fragrance of which Ethel was fond, but not in the strength that accompanied that particular woman. It was almost enough to make her eyes water, and she blew her nose gently, as her tongue began to tingle with the olfactory disaster that had exploded around her. But soon she was on her way to other visitors, and Mrs Thompson elbowed Ethel gently with a smile.

'I ought to have warned you about Miss Bennet. It is a little overpowering isn't it?'

'Goodness me, Mrs Thompson, she must bathe in the stuff!'

Light hymn-type music came from a short elderly lady who gently played a mechanical harmonium, her legs pumping up and down on the wide black peddles as she had been doing since learning it aged ten. Obviously a pipe organ was either too large or too expensive to install Ethel noted. But the music, although a few of the notes were mis-played, was pleasant and certainly, when added to the mys-terious lighting, provided a suitably mysterious atmo-sphere. Ethel sat comfortably back on her cushion, and after scanning the leaflets and placing them in her handbag, watched the people around her take their seats.

Eventually silence came, and a short woman accompan-ied by a tall and an excessively plump yet distinguished middle-aged man stepped out from behind a side curtain onto the podium, and while he sat, she began the service which, to Ethel's surprise was surprisingly Anglican in its approach. They began with a hymn, and then prayers were said followed by another hymn. Then a different woman rose from the congregation, and read from the Bible before finishing with reading a collection of notices and requests for healing. During this time the harmonium was played again, and then it was time for another hymn.

Some twenty minutes of this passed before the short woman finally stepped forward, and introduced with a huge smile, their visitor for the evening. Although given a warm introduction, no one clapped, as an audience might as if a performer was about to entertain. Instead, a soft kind of silence overwhelmed the space, and all Ethel could hear was the light traffic outside, and the occasional barking of an irrelevant dog. The lights were turned down one by one by Miss Bennet who moved swiftly around the church.

The clairvoyant moved to the front of the tiny stage area, and did not welcome them at all, but stood quite still for a moment, eyes closed, his hands poised in a theatrical pose before speaking in a deep and clear voice which Ethel found extremely appealing. At the same time, he thrust out one arm and pointed to a man sitting in the first row. Just three chairs away from Ethel. He opened his eyes.

'A man here. An old gentleman. Name of Samuel. Can you go with that madam?'

'My father was so named.'

'Ha! He says you ought to take more care of your money.'

'Thank you.'

'Coming to this lady with the feathered hat in the second row.'

'Yes sir?'

'Yes, I have the letter P here. I see it hovering over you. Has anybody passed on recently owning a name beginning with P?'

'Yes sir, my father. Name of Percy. Just a short while ago.'

Her voice was cracking a little, and as everyone was staring at her, she felt her friend tighten the grip she had on her arm.

'Yes, he wants you to know that it was not your fault. That is to do with...Simon? Can you take that?'

The woman obviously did because she dissolved into tears, and her companion offered her a hanky. She did not have any time to question the great clairvoyant though as he had turned, and was already addressing another, his finger relentlessly pointing accusingly, the information, it seemed to Ethel, coming quicker than he could deliver. She hoped the spirits were impatient.

'Coming to this lady at the front.' Mrs Thompson jumped a little and held on to her handbag tighter. Her lips tightened.

'I see a tall man. It is not clear. I cannot see his face. But he limps.'

'My son limped.'

At this revelation, Ethel held her breath for a moment. Mrs Thompson had said nothing about a dead son. And she had talked plenty about her family as she was one of those women who did, freely and effortlessly. However, Ethel had offered nothing about Edith either so perhaps she had no right to be surprised.

'He refuses to offer his name, but says that you ought to be more understanding. Does that mean anything?'

'Not really sir. I had a son...'

'He fades now from my reality. Bless you and remember. Perhaps it will mean something later.'

'Thank you.'

Both she and Ethel looked at each other as the great clairvoyant moved on to another, this time to one of the organisers who sat at the far back. He continued in this manner for some forty minutes, occasionally returning to those with whom he had already spoken, but not once did he direct his steely finger at Ethel although several times, he looked at her directly, and appeared as if he wanted to repeat something which he possibly had psychically seen or heard, but found the courage not to.

Close to the end of his performance, he drew out a large handkerchief and wiped his face and neck. After, he only delivered one more message and once finished, the short lady rose again, and interrupted him by clapping which of course was taken up by the congregation. Obviously pleased with his performance, he bowed, stepped back and sat.

Only to stand again for the collection plate to go around, the last prayer and a final hymn, Awake, My Soul, And With The Sun, one Ethel didn't recognise. She was naturally extremely disappointed not to have been given a message, but as Mrs Thompson pointed out, it was only her first time.

To the side, there was tea and biscuits prettily laid out on a wooden fold-out table covered with a light blue cloth while steam vapoured out of a large silver urn. Cups and saucers, stood in line like soldiers with milk and sugar available. While there was a general excited hubbub as people grouped, and collected their refreshments, few noticed the great clairvoyant speaking to Miss Bennet discretely on the platform.

Ethel began chatting generally to those who smiled at her, whilst endlessly repeated the same thing; that it was her first time at any spiritual church, and how she had found it most interesting and how disappointing she must feel at not getting a message, and how she hoped to come again... Mrs Thompson had drifted somewhat away from her side, and was mingling socially in her own way, excitingly chatting about all they had heard, when Ethel felt a slight tug on her sleeve to find that Miss Bennet was quietly asking her to come into the back of the church.

Taking her two tea biscuits, and not being able to signal to Mrs Thompson, she followed the lady who was dressed in a wonderful purple skirt and top, up onto the low podium and passing it, moved beyond the curtain. There was just a single room back there, and one lavatory further back. The room was obviously used for many purposes as she could tell by the clutter, and Ethel noticed the remains of cut flowers everywhere. It was positive cornucopia of boxes of candles, vases, paintings of Red Indians, broken chairs, mirrors, lamps and a mishmash of too many things for Ethel to fully take in.

However, there she was personally introduced to the great clairvoyant who rose to greet her before offering her a seat opposite his own. Miss Bennet, her duty done, retired. But not before Ethel asked her to tell Mrs Thompson where she was. Under the intense gaze of the great clairvoyant, she began to feel a little nervous.

'Please excuse the dramatics, but I thought perhaps a one-to-one session, however brief, would be favourable. The church is useful and necessary, but one cannot function properly, spiritually I mean, when so many eyes are on one, and expectations are high.'

'I see.'

There was a hint of weariness in Ethel's voice because he corrected her immediately.

'Please, have no fear. Yes, I do charge for private sittings, but not with you madam. Not with you.'

Ethel swallowed rather hard, and waited for him to speak again. Which he did not, so she broke the silence.

'I didn't get a message tonight. Was I just unlucky or was there perhaps a reason?'

'Madam, I received several, but imagined, considering whom they were from, you would have wished me to offer them to you in private.'

'That was very considerate sir.'

'You are most welcome...now...I have a young lady here...Adel. Can you take that?'

'No...no, that name means nothing.'

'She is telling me that she is your daughter. I am afraid to say you do have a daughter in spirit don't you?'

'Yes.'

'Then, yes, she is here.'

'But that's the wrong name.'

The great clairvoyant twisted his head sideways with a strong grimace, as if by performing that action, more information might be gained.

'She is weak. Things are indistinct.'

'If you are aware of who I am, then you probably know her name...which is not at all fair.'

'Madam, I am aware of your family's sad recent history. I do recognise you I am afraid to say.'

'Sir? I came here for proof. An ailing mother wants to speak to, or hear her from her child again. I'm begging you not to let me down, but firstly, to be honest. You seem genuine and I want to believe...'

Ethel's anxious words floated away to nothing as the great clairvoyant's eyes and mind reached into the hereafter.

'Yes, I know her name was Edith. I know it but the child that stands here...oh! I see. Yes, it is your daughter.'

The great clairvoyant's gaze returned to Ethel and he reached forward, as if he was going to touch her knee but stopped himself.

'Madam, you came for proof, but how can I not be aware of your very particular circumstances? If I say your daughter is with me now in spirit, what must I do for you to believe me?'

'I don't know sir.'

'She is saying that you must stop writing letters. That they serve no purpose.'

'Well, in that she is right.'

'She says, she cannot stay long with us. She is recovering.'

'Could you tell her I miss her please?'

'She has heard you madam. She wants...she wants...'

'Want's what?'

The great clairvoyant smiled a little and nodded.

'She thanks you for the tree.'

Ethel's hand shot up to her mouth and tears instantly formed.

'She says you must forgive those who wronged me.'

'Forgive them!'

'Forgive them madam.'

But how can I forgive those who took away my daughter?'

'She is gone madam. I'm sorry, but she was weak. But she will become stronger.'

Ethel was left a little breathless as the great clairvoyant stood, hopefully indicating that he now wished to be left alone. Ethel took the hint, and after shaking his huge sweaty hand, left and met Mrs Thompson who was waiting for her by the tea urn. Who, of course wanted to know why she had been chosen to personally meet the great clairvoyant in private, and instantly and rather innocently fired question after question.

It was only when she managed to see past her own selfish personality that she realised Ethel was entirely upset, and as the two of them said good-bye to the few remaining, and after unfortunately smelling Miss Bennet once more, they passed out into the cold night air and walked back to Bow station.

The decision to let Mrs Thompson in on her private family business was not an easy one. Yet considering her emotions, and what she had undergone, Ethel felt an urgent need to tell someone.

The news about the tree had stunned her. Although it had not been planted all that long ago, Ethel occasionally walked around it, in the weak winter sunlight, and imagined that Edith was under it, one day to nourish it. It was macabre thinking yes, but better that her loving daughter might one day become part of a beautiful tree rather than uselessly rotting in an unknown hole in the ground. A place where no person visited except to add another poor soul's body to the unnamed and unspoken for collection.

Ethel, despite her initial excitement for the evening, did have an amount of reservation, and even scepticism about the process, but considering her position, was prepared to be a little open-minded. On the whole, she had been impressed by the level of accuracy during the evening, and she assumed innocently that no one had been a 'plant'. Of course she had a feeling that the great clairvoyant had recognised her, as did a few others in that evening's congregation, and therefore what chance had he to offer her anything when the whole of the woman's world had been dissected, and offered up for worldwide discussion? But when he had mentioned that tree...

It took seconds for Ethel to tell Mrs Thompson who she was, but rather longer to tell her what the judiciary had done to her innocent daughter. All through the train journey back to Manor Park, the normally talkative Mrs Thompson, who naturally felt a need to discuss her own small good news that evening, listened with an attentive ear that did her proud.

In her defence, she had just about heard of the Thompson and Bywater's case, mostly by heresy for she was not a person who interested themselves in politics or current affairs. Mostly because she believed she did not have the brain to understand such matters. The loss of her disabled son, her only issue, seven years previously had cut her down to a bare human being, and she had never fully recovered. She had lost interest in everything, had spent time in a sanatorium, and even attempted suicide whilst there for which she was jailed for a year, suspended for two years on account of her circumstances, and placed on probation.

The two women were therefore subdued to the point of almost saying nothing as they walked up the metal steps at East Ham station and prepared to say goodnight. Although Ethel was not a woman who found socialising easy, she invited Mrs Thompson around for coffee the next morning, and offered her her address. An offer that was gratefully accepted.

William was reading the newspaper and smoking his pipe when Ethel entered, but apart from uttering a brief 'hello', he did not look up. Avis was at her knitting at the kitchen table, and thought her mother's entrance a good time to take a break and make a pot of tea. As Ethel lied continuously about what an interesting evening she had had, all the time feeling her ears burn, she saw William's paper getting closer to his face as he was distancing himself from all that which he despised. Ethel even began to simmer down and grinned at his foolishness.

She took off her coat, laid it briefly over her chair and, leaving her handbag on the kitchen table, stepped into the dark night to visit the lavatory which was outside next to the garden. When she re-entered the kitchen, she saw Avis, a pot of tea on the table, looking down at it. Or so she thought until she realised that she was not staring at the pot, but at the contents of her open handbag.

'What's this mum?'

Ethel rose defensively immediately, and went to snap it shut but did not reach it until Avis had read part of one of the leaflets which Ethel had just placed on top of everything else.

'A Spiritualist church? And it said tonight! Is that where you've been mum?'

Ethel was now like a rabbit caught in headlights, and she angrily snatched her bag away thereby telling Avis exactly what she wanted to know.

'Don't be stupid, and that's none of your business young woman.'

It was a known fact that in the Graydon's family, whenever Ethel or William called their children young something or other, then they meant business. Nevertheless, although Avis was flushed, and embarrassed that she had discovered her mother's guilty secret, a better part of her would not let the matter drop.

'What is Reverend Vega going to say mum? That is not Christian mum. That's partying with the Devil mum. What were you doing there?'

'None of your business.'

'You lied to us mum. For that?'

At this, William pulled down his paper, unconvinced he could not remain anonymous any longer.

'Where have you been Ethel?'

'I've been to Mrs Thompson's. I told you. For Bridge.'

'What did Avis read in the bag then?'

'Just...just some silly things that were being given away at the station that's all. There's no need to make a song and dance about it.'

'Well, that's all right then. As long as you didn't lie. I mean, if you wanted to go to one of those places that'll be all right wouldn't it? I mean, it's your life Ethel. You ought not to let Avis' persecution mania get to you.'

'I resent that dad.'

'Pipe down Avis. Ever since you found that Catholic church, you've been nothing but a bore. Your mother and I don't want to go and that's that. Our families have been with the C of E for donkey's years, and we won't change now. And wherever your mother's gone tonight, the last thing she wants is you breathing down her neck, and telling her she's going to Hell because she believes in something different.'

'I didn't say anything like that.'

'Yes, but you would of done. You're like an open book my girl. Transparent as glass.'

Avis now sat in a huff and played about with the cups, suitably subdued. But William hadn't finished.

'So...Ethel?'

It was a damning moment, broken only by the sound of Avis pouring tea, splashing milk and the 'plink, plink' of falling sugar lumps, and Ethel clutched her bag against her chest as if it were a favourite and much cherished doll. She shook her head as she realised that once again, it was impossible to keep anything from William if he really had a mind to uncover information.

'All right...I went there.'

'Told you so!'

'Avis? Shut up and pour the tea for your mother and father, and I'll have a slice of cheese on toast while you're at it. So you visited this church? And what happened there?'

It took her almost as long to relate the contents of the evening to William as it did the content's of the trial to Mrs Thompson earlier on the train, but when she had finished, William had eaten his cheesy supper, and was on his second cup of tea. Avis sat at the table, now absent-mindedly picking at the knitting, and quite horrified at what she had heard, but too much in awe of her father to say anything. So she sulked.

'I'm going to bed. And I'll pray for you mother.' But her Christian words did not extend to closing the door quietly.

Ethel was about to give her another piece of her mind when William cut her short.

'Let her go Eth. She's got a bee in her bonnet, and it's not worth arguing about. Let her calm down. Bloody religion! This is what happens when you take it too far.'

'I expect she only finds the same comfort that I did to-night Will.'

'You women stick together don't you? Half an hour ago, she was at your throat.'

'It's still only a couple of months Will. We all need to find a way to help us come to terms with what's happened.'

'And yours is to believe she's some spirit or something? God, that's a lot of nonsense Eth. Are you that desperate?'

'Yes, I am! And I'm surprised you're not too.'

'You think I don't have feelings woman? You don't think...'

They sputtered to an angry silence, both too afraid of what they might say in the heat of it all. William re-stuffed his pipe from his brown pouch, and lit it until fumes clouded over him.

'I don't think it's stupid William. To want to believe that my child is still around somewhere, even if it is in spirit. Whose to tell? Whose to know?'

'I can't argue Ethel. It doesn't make any sense to me. It just seems like you're holding on to the past, and that isn't right. Edith's with God and that's it. And we've got our lives to live and others to look after. That's the way I see it.'

'So how did the man know about our tree then?'

'I don't know! He guessed! Lots of people plant trees in honour of their loved ones. It was probably a lucky guess. Anything else he read about you in the damn papers.'

Ethel stood.

'I'm going up Will. Remember to put Joey out. He messed the scullery last night.'

William barely nodded, and picked up his paper again. Now he was in a mood she thought and would be tossing and turning all night. He was like that. Avis was really very thoughtless. She knew her mother and father were not pleased at all for converting to Catholicism. Especially without their knowledge. She was aware that her daughter did not need their permission, but a simple admission would have been welcome. Just to arrive home one evening and bring that down on the family...

Naturally extremely awkward questions were asked by friends and neighbours such as, where she was, and why didn't Avis attend church anymore? Reverend Vega more than most was not so much displeased as perplexed. One Sunday afternoon he had spent over twenty minutes with her in their front room, and ventured out none the wiser. Or at least, as much as he was going to pass along to Ethel.

As she passed Avis' room, the light was out, but she knocked gently anyway. There was no answer, and as it was impossible for her to have fallen asleep so quickly, she presumed quite correctly that Avis was being stroppy. So Ethel pursed her lips, and continued along the short cold corridor. It was going to be a cold night all round.

Twelve

A few bitter months passed, and the Graydon family, fractured emotionally as well as geographically, arrived in the middle of spring, each member unconsciously beginning to devote himself or herself to what they did best. William felt the magnetic pull of the garden, and as each week passed, found himself increasingly pottering and mowing, clipping and watering, raking and sewing. William was never happier than when he had honest soil between his fingernails, and it was one of his hobbies where Edith had liked to help, whereas Avis enjoyed the sitting and the scent of the flowers, but did not have much of a green thumb.

Ethel's home interest turned to baking. That is when she was not spring cleaning or mending curtains, quilts, clothes and bed-sheets. Each year, the entire house would be examined from the cellar to the rafters, and each room would be given a thorough going-over with assistance from Avis after she had put in a day's work. At the weekend, they would shop for replacements that had worn out or were unserviceable. What was worse about this year was, they were on their own, as Edith always used to arrive to help with what everyone came to know as TGC or 'The Graydon

Challenge'. It didn't matter that Edith had had her own house to clean, it was traditional.

Both felt Edith's absence acutely being that it was an all-girl activity. Her singing while washing the clothes, just ever so slightly off tune, her prattling on about the shows she had seen, or was intending to see, the latest fashions '*to die for*', or her silly imitation of her father doing the Tango. She used to do it with a broom, and have them in stitches. Not something she did in front of him of course. Her smoking only the most expensive cigarettes, her pernickety, bordering on snobbish behaviour she had become about wine, her fantastic wardrobe...

The boy's only escape from this once a year ritual was to leave home, which the three of them did just as quickly as they were able. Their actions were not as a result of wanting to remove themselves from the family so much as a desperate need to improve their lives. Positions in different parts of London and the country, plus the joys of bachelor life urged the three of them to set up for themselves. Although each were mindful of their family's past, they had the opposite of a cavalier attitude when it came to identifying themselves to new people.

They would each visit the family home at 231 frequently right up to when the house was sold. In later years, when wives and babies accompanied them, it became crowded, especially on the anniversary of Edith's death when as many of the family got together as possible. That too, eventually became a family tradition like TGC.

The two women of the household eventually put away their religious differences, although it was a subject never again discussed. Like an ache which would not dissipate, the furious and unprecedented row seemed to drive a wedge between them for the very first time since Avis had been born. However, it was only a very small wedge. Any stranger appearing at their table, or meeting them in the street would not have noticed anything other than a contented mother and daughter.

However, when the subject of religion was voiced, or a question asked about where they went on a Sunday, or what they would do after, each would automatically look busy, and subtly change the subject. Reverend Vega only made extremely rare visits to the household after the spring, and although the family did not openly pray for her, Ethel did in her heart. Not for Avis' soul to be saved from oblivion, but for her daughter to re-enter the family fold again. However, despite her praying, it was never to happen, and Avis died a resolute and faithful Catholic.

This then became the second family secret, the first not even being mentioned to any of the Graydon descendants, the eventual children of Newenham, William and Harold.

219

For many years, they would be told that they had ever only possessed one aunt. They would eventually discover the truth in their own painful and humiliating way. In a damning but almost necessary social decision, Edith was wiped from the family's name. Only those who where there, who had undergone the pain, or who were old enough to remember, knew the truth.

Only when the children became too old, did they stop the family anniversary on the 9 January and took it subtly, but completely into their hearts in the evening when they were alone. Therefore, William and Ethel's grandchildren grew up, never once realising that they ought to have had another aunt.

The second family secret, Avis' religious change, ought to have lasted for only a few days, perhaps a week or so, but because it was an event, which occurred so early in the year of Edith's death, it reconstituted all the emotion and despair of the terrible events of January. And Avis was, by a significant degree, the cause of it. Adding to her dismissal of the Anglican religion, both William and Ethel felt betrayed beyond all measure. Even though Ethel had instigated the original argument, Avis' part in the affair was made to seem worse.

This was brought to William's attention one Tuesday morning when a work colleague playfully tossed a newspaper across a table to him during their morning tea-break. On page two, with the most terrible misgivings, he saw a picture of his wife, Avis and an unknown woman leaving what looked very much like a tea shop. All three appeared to be on the verge of panicking as they realised their photograph had been taken, and he furrowed his brow as he tried to comprehend what this new mystery was about. To his credit, the work colleague did not add anything playful. But the story itself, William found difficult to understand.

The World Tea Rooms in Holloway Road, he read, had become the centre of an increasingly bitter row about prison security concentrating on a suspended woman prison officer called Miss Amy Baker. Miss Baker had been arrested by undercover police attempting to smuggle confidential papers out from the muniments room, and was being held at Highbury police station charged with offences against the Official Secret's Act. At her home in nearby East Finchley, which was searched immediately to the distress of her mother and father, a number of items were discovered, including the name and address of a certain mother whose daughter had recently been executed...

Once this was public knowledge, the news-hounds of the day, who naturally wanted a photograph of the doomed prison officer, searched their records, and very quickly found the shot of her and the account of her assignation with two unknown women taken back in January. Who did not remain unknown for long as they were immediately identified. The infamy of the older woman's executed daughter, rocketed the story from being a fairly interesting one to one that the editor was sure to sell many tens of thousands of copies, the Thompson and Bywater's case still relatively fresh in the public's perception.

That afternoon, on William's arrival home from work, the small area outside his house was cluttered with three police cars, and a smattering of neighbours and interested bystanders. Two men in long brown coats took pictures of him as he opened his wooden front gate. Once inside, he had the dubious pleasure of a tall policeman opening his own door for him from the inside. Ethel rushed into his arms crying and sobbing such as he had not seen for months, clearly extremely distraught.

He immediately demanded to know who was in charge, and by what right they had to be in his house. Whereby a heavily moustached, middle-aged gentleman stepped out of the kitchen into the hall and introduced himself as Chief Inspector Anderson. William's response was stoic, and he quietly waved his hand in the direction of his front room where he, Ethel, the Chief Inspector and two plainclothes detectives sat after William and Ethel took their place on the sofa. Joey jumped into Ethel's arms, and she stroked him unconsciously.

While one of the plainclothes detectives flipped open a note pad, Chief Inspector Anderson cleared his throat gently, and firstly apologised for the intrusion. It was not his intention, he said, to open up wounds, but he was charged with investigating a serious breech of national security, and it was necessary for him to speak to all concerned. He then turned to Ethel and asked her exactly what had been said on the day of the meeting between Miss Baker and herself and her daughter. To which, Ethel, as much as she could remember, gave an account of that afternoon's informal chat, and what was more important, from the Chief Inspector's point of view, Miss Baker's reason for it.

This took Ethel over half an hour and during it, a commotion outside alerted them to the sound of Avis arriving home from work. They saw flashes of light through the curtains, along with the characteristic whooshing sound which could only mean one thing, that she too was being photographed. She too was let in by the tall policeman, and directed immediately into the front room where she was comforted by her mother as she continued her story. William though, sat, stone-faced throughout, and Avis found that far more upsetting.

Up to four o'clock that day, Avis had been entirely un-aware of the story until Mary had shown her the photo whilst they were enjoying their last tea and cigarette break of the day, the accusing picture being in a late edition brought in by one of the evening shift girls. Avis had stared at it with increasing horror, and thought immediately of her mother and father, and if her other little secret escapade might also be discovered. The small matter of visiting Ruth Brown, of which she had just completed her eighth visit.

Between that new relationship, and now the newspaper picture plus her earlier rejection of the Anglican Church, and conversion to Catholicism, Avis felt that nothing was going right between herself and her parents, and that her personal life was in danger of collapsing around her. Once finished for the day, she apologised to Mary, and rushed home as fast as she could only to find outside her house, in the dusk, a road full of objectionable sightseers who did their best to mock and jeer as she struggled to get past the reporters.

Satisfied that his detective had written down what was said, the Chief Inspector, surprisingly, did not question Eth-el, but turned to Avis who swallowed hard.

'If you would be so kind Miss Graydon? To speak your side of the story.'

'We didn't do no harm. She came to us you understand.'

'If you wouldn't mind Miss? If you please?'

Therefore Avis related intermittently, complete with a great sense of embarrassment and wringing hands, her mother's plan to place the flowers outside Holloway, and how it went wrong, and what happened after. She took about the same time to relate the rest of the story and, to William's ear, it sounded the same. When she had finished, he spoke for the first time since sitting.

'So, inspector...'

'Chief Inspector.'

'I do beg your pardon. Chief Inspector. I don't hear anything said here tonight which warrants any further investigations do you? No crime has been committed by either my wife or my daughter, foolish as their actions may have been at the time.'

'Mr Graydon. We are speaking here of extremely sensitive information leaked by an employee of His Majesty's Prison Service, and my superiors have deemed it important enough to send me to the other side of London to collect what information may be had in order to fully prosecute the range of offences that this woman has committed.'

'But she only told us what happened to our Edie.'

'Miss Graydon, she has committed several offences, each of which could land her a substantial jail sentence. Mr Graydon, I hope I have made myself clear. I personally don't believe there is any reason to believe your wife or daughter colluded with Baker in instigating her to get the information, and therefore, for that reason, I am not tonight arresting them. However, they are required to give written statements, and that is best done tonight. I suggest we drive now to your local station, which is East Ham believe?'

'Tonight? I haven't had my supper yet!'

'Mr Graydon, the sooner this is over, the best it will be for all concerned.'

'Will the young lady lose her job?'

'Mrs Graydon, perhaps you underestimate the seriousness of the situation? She is in custody, ironically, Holloway, awaiting a hearing. The evidence collected tonight will form part of the prosecution. This is an extremely serious matter. When she joined the prison service she signed the Oath Of Allegiance to His Sovereign Majesty, and promised to adhere to The Prison Code of Discipline. This is a serious breech, and she will certainly be dismissed from the service if found guilty, with probably a jail term following. Her actions have brought the service into disrepute'.

William stood. 'Well, if we have to go, we have to go. But can your men clear those sightseers away?' He seemed not to care about the speech.

'I'm afraid not sir. It's a Public Rights of Way, and as long as they do not cause any interference with my duty, there is little I can do about them. They can take as many photo-graphs, and shout as many questions as they like. Of course, it's entirely up to you if you answer them back, but I would not recommend it.'

'They are a damned infringement Chief Inspector. I don't know what the country is coming to when the police cannot protect honest people from men like that.'

'That may be true sir, but honest people do not receive clandestine information from rogue prison officers do they sir?'

A harsh statement and delivered with a flat voice which made it sound truer than it was. The press took another four photographs, and an overwhelming barrage of ques-tions filled the street as Ethel, William and Avis climbed into one of the large black police cars. After they moved off to the Barking Road, Ethel had a momentary flash of panic as she remembered how the police took her Edith away that day from her house in Ilford. That was the last time her daughter ever saw her beautiful home, her final four months being spent in Holloway.

With that knowledge therefore, it crossed her mind whether the same was going to happen to her, and if she might wake up in that dreadful prison in North London. With those thoughts, she clung on to William's arm but he, at the time was indifferent. He had the sense not to resist the police, and knew that they were only discharging their duty. But inside, he was fuming. For so many reasons. Not the least being with the one who was clinging onto his arm at that moment, and his daughter who sat opposite, staring forlornly at the darkened streets. With no sense of hopeful expression on her face whatsoever.

Avis was alarmed for more than one reason. Although her fear did not run as deeply, and as imaginatively as her mother, she was extremely concerned that the investigation might uncover the fact of her visits to Holloway. It was therefore out of concern for Ruth Brown that she did not want their meetings discovered. Any problem with her current situation had a possibility of leading straight back to Ruth, and that gave her possible complications the nature of which she had no wish to think about.

In her visits that she had made so far, Avis believed that she had made a reasonable amount of progress with Ruth. The prisoner no longer saw Avis as a threat, and she had begun to chat about her considerably arduous and hard life. But not in any great detail, and not in any sense of complaining or bitterness, so it did not appear to be like counselling. Nevertheless, at the end of each brief twelve minutes, Ruth felt a little lighter, and even after the third visit, even remarkably stopped getting herself into trouble with the guards.

Who in turn quickly noticed her improvement in character, and soon associated Avis with her progression from delinquent to very nearly, an upstanding detainee. By the eighth visit, for now Ruth was allowed more frequent visits, the guards actually smiled at Avis on her arrival, although they still remained as silent as ever. Avis fervently hoped that they might have recognised by that time that she was only there to do some good. Not that anybody knew, at that time, her real emotional reason for continuing to visit. On each appointment she would take hundreds of cigarettes which were inexpensive to purchase, and later on, she gave Ruth some scented soap, and a small bottle of lavender hair wash, both of which she was expressively grateful the next time Avis visited.

There came a time though, when a splinter of suspicion crept in, and Ruth asked her one day, with only some two minutes to go, why she was doing all this for a perfect stranger. The only thing Avis could imagine at the time was the reason she had offered on her first visit. Which was to thank her for showing such compassion to her family on the day Edith was executed. Ruth accepted this, but only begrudgingly. But then the time was up.

'Next time Avis. We'll talk again,' she had said, and winked.

Avis adjusted her coat, left the police car and followed her mother and father into East Ham police station as she remembered that last interview in Holloway. Her problems now were, should she visit Ruth again? And should she tell her parents? There was no question of admitting and writing down what she knew about Miss Amy Baker to the Chief Inspector. Of this she was certain, but her mind was consumed with the thought of complications all the same. Interview rooms were quickly prepared, and while William kicked his heels near the front desk next to an uncommunicative sergeant, Ethel and Avis disappeared into the depths of the warm police station. He was to follow shortly and, not surprisingly, was the first to finish.

Mother and daughter reappeared an hour and a quarter later. The Chief Inspector led them both back to William, signed them out and signalled for a car. He seemed satisfied about William's statement, but warned them all that should the case go to court, and there was a possibility that it would, then they would certainly be required as witness'. With that final depressing piece of news, they were driven home in complete silence, and were more than relieved when they saw their road was empty of all newspaper men.

The two women pottered about in the kitchen, and while Avis made tea, Ethel boiled some potatoes, and put out some ham. As soon as they had made themselves comfortable and tea was brewed, both women prepared themselves for the expected angry onslaught from William. Who, all this time, after he had slipped off his shoes, and lit his pipe, had stoked up the dying fire, and sat in his chair, just silently watching the flames. Avis placed a cup of tea next to him on the occasional table that William had brought with him on the occasion of his marriage. A table made by his father.

'Aren't you going to talk to us dad?'

'What is there to say Avis? What can I say to a twenty-seven year old woman who ought to have known better? How can I let you how disappointed I am?' William nodded glumly. 'Perhaps I blame myself. Look at what this family has turned into. One has been executed for murder. My wife and daughter taken from the house they live in and dragged publicly down the police station. My daughter doesn't attend church anymore, I've been humiliated at work, my previously strong faith in the church, the government and our royalty has been dashed to smithereens, and my wife is hunting for ghosts like a mad woman. I've been thinking that the best thing we can do now is move. Move far away, perhaps to another city.'

'I can't move Will. I have to be near my sisters.'

'Well, if we stay here, we'll be the bloody laughing stock of the entire area. Is that what you want? Can anything more happen to this family?'

What made Avis open her mouth and say what she did, she never quite figured out, but she imagined it had something to do with how much she loved her dad.

'There is something else dad. I'm sorry but there is.'

'Avis? What more can you do to us? You've made a public display of yourself as regards the church, you're unsettled, you ought to be married off by now, and giving me grandchildren not still living here. What else can you do to me? Tell me you are joking. What have you done? Do you know about this Ethel?'

'Avis? What have you done my girl?' Obviously her mother didn't know.

Avis sat and looked at her shoes briefly before she made an effort and spoke clearly and directly at her father.

'I've been back to Holloway dad. I've been visiting a prisoner.'

William glanced at Ethel, satisfied that his wife was as ignorant as he was at this latest piece of news, and by the knitting of her brow, of the reason too. But William remained exasperatingly, to Avis, calm.

'What? Is that all? No bank robbery? No grand larceny? No exposé of any kind? You're slipping Avis!'

'I'm serious dad. It's a woman, and she showed such kindness to us as a family when we was last there. When we viewed...Edith.'

'Avis, we didn't meet any prisoners on that day. We went to the mortuary.'

'No dad, you're wrong. Don't you remember the woman who was chained and shovelling coal?'

Both parents took a drink of their tea before shaking their heads.

'There was no woman, and they don't chain people there. We're not in the nineteenth-century Avis.'

'Dad, I've been back heaps of times. Her name is Ruth Brown, and she lives in C Wing. That's the long-term wing. She has about two and a half years of her sentence left to do, but she stopped working that day when we walked past, and she figured who we were, and bowed her head. That moved me dad. She was the only one who showed some emotion over our grief and loss. I wanted to do something for her, and no one visits her at all.'

'So where is her family?'

'Up north mum. She's from Newcastle. They can't get down.'

'What did she do?'

'She was a look-out girl for a robbery in the West End.'

'Heavens! She knows all the lingo Will.'

'It's just what she told me mum. There's no harm in it.'

'So what do you do for this girl then?'

'Nothing much dad. We talk. I take her a few ciggies. I think I'm having a good influence on her.'

'Yeah, and when she gets out, she'll rob you blind and take everything you've got.'

'I thought you'd be more angry dad.'

'Avis? What you've just told me is like...a pea put on top of a football. Ethel? How's dinner. I could eat a horse.'

'I'm going to keep seeing her dad. I have to.'

'You do what you have to Avis. It's your life.'

They were the words which upset Avis more than any other that had been directed at her in living memory. Those were the words which separated father from daughter. That was the intention, which told her that he didn't care about her welfare anymore. Truly, her life was falling apart, and she was shocked into silence.

While Ethel mashed the potatoes, and her father sullenly returned to the fire, for the only time in her life, Avis felt like an outsider in her own family. Anger she was used to, on the occasions she had played up as a child, and the occasional smack across her legs only proved in a back-handed way, that her mum and dad loved her, and wanted more than anything else to protect her from the wickedness of the world. Annoyance was routine of course. The petty occurrences to which all families were prone. Beyond the negative though, there was always love. Overwhelming love both demonstrable and imaginable, and which welled upwards, and cascaded away from each member like an invisible yet golden stream of light, touching all, and setting their hearts to beat as one unit. The Graydon family.

When Edith was taken from them that dark morning, that heart had suffered greatly, as if a great hole had appeared. In those early months of 1923, that gap was in no danger of being healed with any speediness, the outcome being that the family's life-force was spent unwisely. At a time when they most needed each other, there was the constant danger that the opposite might occur. When so injured, it was easy to look the other way, and to indulge in self-absorption, introspection and aloneness. The most tragic thing about being part of a family in those days, was that, for people in their class, there was no one to guide them except their own sense of morality.

There had never been any great tragedies attached to the Graydon family. No miscarriages, no broken marriages, no life-changing accidents of any kind, no terrible birth deficiencies or defects, no life-threatening illness either, and no overwhelming tragic love stories. That was what made them remarkable. They were so ordinary. Grandparents died of course, in the natural way of things, and grief expressed. Both Edith and Avis were rightly mortified when their mother's mother died, and they grieved for months, but at least continued to operate in the world, and go about their business.

But losing Edith was of a different division altogether. Each of their imaginations conjured up the very worse scenarios, as sick and upset minds tended to do, about how she suffered, and what she had to endure, with the result that when it finally happened, the anonymous tragedy had uncountable effects. Like many families, they were so close that what happened to Edith, happened in a subtle way to each of them. The sins of one were visited on the many.

The collective feelings of the Graydon family when Edith was put to death were too shocking to be acknowledged. They were even too shocking to be authenticated. Apart from tears, these feelings remained fixed like hard rock, imperious to human efforts to change. But life would alter them slowly, and eventually, would move them back on course. Not entirely the course they had before, but fairly close.

The overwhelming influence Edith had had on her family could not be estimated, but it could be occasionally measured. As Ethel served up ham and mash potatoes, Avis felt an overwhelming need to not be in the kitchen. As if she was suddenly with strangers who cared little or nothing about her welfare. She rose and excused herself.

'But I've just served. Aren't you hungry?'

'No mum, I've got a few sweets in my room, and a bit of cake from work...a friend's birthday. I'll say goodnight.'

Her father did not take his eyes away from the flickering red flames. Not even when his dinner was placed in front of him on a tray. Avis stared only briefly at the back of his bald head and quickly left.

Thirteen

Avis was true to her word and herself, and continued to visit Ruth Brown. By June, everyone was taking advantage of the summer, and it appeared that Ruth's days of causing trouble for herself were a thing of the past, although Avis was concerned about the amount of cigarettes she was smoking, which was almost forty full strength Capstans a day.

Her bad habit became obvious when one day, Ruth arrived at her seat, her eyes streaming, and hacking away like an old sea captain. Surprisingly, one of the guards, normally unemotional, brought her a cup of water. After taking a few sips, it took her a few moments to recover her voice.

The first thing she did when she regained her composure was to apologise. But as she explained, while waiting, she had begun a coughing fit from which she found it difficult to recover. The guard, overhearing this, suggested to Avis that she cut back on the amount of cigarettes she brought, which was two hundred each time. Although that worked out to just less than thirty a day, not all that much she thought for someone in prison with nothing to occupy themselves in the evening, later she was told by that same

guard that any cash Ruth earned as part of their rehabilita-
tion program was also spent on cigarettes, and that she was
probably smoking between sixty and eighty a day which
was both shocking and damaging for such a young woman.
Even the prison doctor thought her consumption excessive.
The guard told Avis with the best of intentions, and Avis
certainly believed her. Avis herself smoked about ten a day,
which she considered low compared to many of the girls at
work. It was, after all, a tedious job.

Avis asked her if that was the first time she had coughed
so badly, and she imagined Ruth answered truthfully, but
could not be sure as Ruth's foxy eyes had a lifelong habit of
swivelling side to side as if forever on the move. As if she
had gained a habit, the action of which would keep her
alive. Forever alert to danger, and open to the possibility of
attack. Avis recognised that that part of her defence was
continued lying and deceit and, although no expert, saw it
as a part of her inbred nature, which might take a lifetime
to dissipate.

Ruth mostly began by relating to her how welcome her
twice-weekly letters were. It was not always possible for a
guard or the chaplain to read them for her, but she had
found another woman, some ten cells along, one a little
older who would. And for her trouble, Ruth cut a deal, and
gave her one cigarette per page read. It became a satisfying

arrangement, and she hoped that she didn't mind another inmate reading about her. To which Avis had no objection at all. After all, it was just trivial things; work and play.

One thing Avis did not mention was her growing association with the organist with the yellow hair. Him she kept to herself, even when Ruth particularly asked if there was a special man in her life. To that question, of course, Avis blushed spectacularly, and looked away while Ruth smiled knowingly. At twenty-five, she had known a few lovers back in Newcastle before she had arrived south especially to help out with that robbery. And all for her brother. She would never trust him again. She then told her it was not her business anyway, but she liked the way Avis' ears had blushed!

The twelve minutes was often up so quickly, and with protocol broken now that the system knew who Avis was, and was deemed not to be a threat, they were allowed, for the first time, to shake hands. Ruth's skin was unnaturally tough, and as Avis withdrew, she looked down at her own hands in surprise. Ruth gave her her usual look of apology, and rubbed her palms together, explaining that it was the rug-making and the sewing. Avis made a mental note then to bring in some hand cream, and asked her if that would be all right, and that nobody would ridicule her.

In the remaining seconds, Ruth answered that that would be fine, and that it would be a brave woman who ridiculed her! She winked at the same time, and Avis smiled ruefully as the prisoners were led away. Ruth smiled again over her shoulder just before she disappeared through the doorway.

The fine weather was turning to rain as Avis waited for the tram to take her back to Holloway station. She was already making a list of subjects about which she would mention in her next letter. However, the organist, her mother's and father's feelings, and the general atmosphere of indifference in her home, were matters of discussion that were not placed on her mental list. As fond of Ruth as she had become, because she was a secure prisoner with a long-term sentence to work through, even the slightly naive and certainly innocent Avis thought it best not to reveal too much of her personal self.

And the organist was one such part. Whether it was the Catholic church calling her, or the thought of meeting and spending time with him, Avis was not aware. She believed it was the church, and that satisfied her for the moment. Since that first and almost accidental time just before what became generally known in the newspapers as *The Great Snowfall*, Avis had become a regular visitor. The church was more than ten times the distance than St Barnabas' in

Browning Road, but it made no difference to its newest and most enthusiastic member. She was treated like the prodigal daughter (except she never left in the first place) and quite soon, after a meeting with Father Clifford, a large man whose face was wreathed in grey whiskers, she began attending meetings once a week in preparation for becoming a Catholic.

This was a lengthy process, and she was told it would probably be completed by Easter of 1924, but the time alone did not concern Avis as she was allowed to attend all the services and meetings. Moreover she was glad to report back to Mary (the only person to whom she was able to talk to about her experiences) that the grand and warm feeling she had had on her first visit was not diminished by any degree on her subsequent ones. She even told her it was as if she had a second home.

There was a bible study class on a Saturday in which Avis was particularly interested. Mainly for the reason that it was for adults, but also that she had seen the organist write his name down for it on the Sunday evening it was announced. Swiftly, she had scuttled over to the desk at the back of the church, and next to several leaflets, a pile of bibles and the poor box, was a sheet of ruled paper. She wrote her name under his; Simon Derry.

This was only some two weeks after *The Great Snowfall*, and Simon had also been quick to notice the return of the brown-eyed young woman with the curvy figure, and the sweet singing voice. Although naturally shy himself, after he had made discrete inquiries from one of the women elders, he had smiled upon noticing her name under his. At that first meeting, he made sure that, after the tea break, he sat as close to her as he dare, noticing not for the first time that she wore no wedding band. Avis herself had arrived some five minutes late though which had caused him a little distress. Initially due to some upheaval and disturbance on the Tottenham & Forest Gate Railway line, she, that day, had travelled from Holloway. When she had not appeared at the required time, Simon had spent a few anxious moments fidgeting and glancing at his watch, for he did not possess the most moderate of temperaments.

He was known by the congregation as a decent, and solid bachelor of thirty-three whose main unfortunate problem was that he had contracted diphtheria as an infant. Bright and naturally eager, after he had recovered from the occasionally fatal illness, due to a complication with maintaining a sufficient supply of oxygen, a matter over which his father, a local doctor, suffered greatly from guilt, and which was to end his life by way of suicide, there was a small amount of brain damage which affected his level of intelligence more than anything else.

Therefore, although he seemed perfectly normal in all respects, Simon had difficulty in concentrating, though not in an excessive way. This fundamental ability had hindered him throughout his schooling, and he left showing no aptitude for almost anything except drawing, painting and music of which he eventually became quite accomplished in all three due to the continued and patient efforts of his devoted mother. Due to the newness of the term, he was not diagnosed as suffering from it, but dyslexia was the result of his neurological problem.

His involvement with the church had been from an early age as his mother made sure he had attended as soon as he was able to walk. When she died eventually of a broken heart, some ten years previously, the friends of the church were all he had. As he lived in his parent's huge house just around the corner in Windsor Road, he was involved in many of the activities of the church who employed him as a handyman/cleaner as well as their resident organist. His ability on the keyboard again could be traced back to his mother. Occasionally, he would sell his pictures, especially the Christmas ones, which a local printer made up yearly as greeting cards.

One thing Simon could never be described as, was a ladies man. His shyness made this impossible. However, as he grew older and reached his thirties, an inherent natural type of confidence began to emerge, which overran his unfortunate medical condition, and for the first time began to look at women as, unfortunately, objects of sexual desire. This was an embarrassing issue that he kept strictly to himself, and as many of the females who came and went concerning their business with St Thomas', were either married, too young or too old, the sudden arrival of a woman of appropriate age, not to mention her beauty, quite literally stung him, and he was mesmerised.

Simon was a fairly plain chap physically, and could best be described as lanky and docile. His mass of yellow hair was a talking point, and with no one to monitor him, it often grew too long, and it was Father Clifford who had the job of reminding him to visit the barbers. In general then, he had no faults, was completely dedicated to the Catholic church, and for all practicable purposes, was a good catch for marriage being that he had a viable property and a separate, if small, private income due to the perspicacity of his mother.

This positive diagnosis about the man was what Avis was told when she enquired, in the most general tone possible, about him to the lady who made the tea and supplied the biscuits, although she was not given as many details. Just enough to let her know that he was unmarried, an orphan, and once was the son of a local doctor, and a once respectable family who had supported the church a great deal. Avis at the time, did not question her about using the word 'once' twice. And the woman did not expound on her explanation, as suicide was unlawful by the teaching of Holy Scripture and of the Church, which condemned the act as a most atrocious crime.

This then was the burden Simon carried, and his remaining without a wife was judged by those less charitable, to be his atonement for his wicked father's action. All this Simon knew, but it did not trouble him. Some original part of his thinking simply overruled gossip. It was his manner of surviving.

When therefore he managed to sit next to Avis having returned with his tea, he offered her a Jammy Dodger which she politely refused as she had two already. She could see that he was somewhat nervous, but as she had taken a deep fancy to him already, she helped him along by chatting about herself until it was time for the circle to resume.

They hung about after, almost as a couple, much to the amusement of a few of the regulars who knew Simon of old. An elderly man had winked at him as he left. Simon eventually, as the church was emptying, retrieved Avis' coat from the row of hooks in the vestry, and she allowed him to help her on with it. For the first time, as he stood behind her, he momentarily smelt her hair. Lemony.

After he had escorted her outside, there was a certain amount of awkwardness as they both fumbled for appropriate words in the foyer. Behind them, the gently smiling, and plump Father Clifford closed, and locked the double doors, and there they stood in the unsettled weather until it occurred to Simon that he might walk her safely to her door. As this was what Avis was hoping he would ask, she accepted willingly, but warned him of the distance.

His willingness to continue, cheerfully disregarding the milage, found her approval, and she linked her arm through his and they set off for the tram stop, talking nonstop about what they had learned that evening. They did not have long to wait, which was just as well as, as they reached the stop, it began to rain and Avis discovered that her new umbrella was faulty, and wouldn't open properly. Therefore, for those few minutes, they huddled by a shop window until Avis' spectacles became quite steamed up.

The rain did not stop when they alighted at Manor Park Broadway either, and after assuring her that it was not a problem, Simon continued to escort her to her front door where there was more bashfulness from both parties until, with a daring that surprised herself, Avis moved forward, and planted a kiss on his cheek, ever conscious of her painful shyness, especially around men.

'Night Simon.'

'Night Avis.'

'Hope you don't get too wet going back.'

'I doubt if I will.'

'It was very sweet of you.'

'I couldn't see you go home on your own...in the dark.'

'Well...no, but thanks.'

'Perhaps I can see you again Avis? We seemed to have such good chats.'

'I'd like that Simon. Of course I work during the week.'

'But in the evenings?'

'Oh, evenings I am free of course.'

'Perhaps the flicks?'

'Yes, that'll be nice.'

'Douglas Fairbanks as Robin Hood is on at the Electric Empire.'

'Oh...I like him. On what day?'

'Would Tuesday be all right? Say at seven? Meet inside?'

'That'll be fine. Well, goodnight again.'

And after that lengthy conversation, what more could she do but offer him another kiss. This time she was not so coy, and noticed how she had to stand on tiptoe to reach his face despite him leaning down. She also noticed his five o'clock shadow which was rough yet exciting. The second kiss took slight longer than the first, and his dark coat smelt of freshly cut wood. That was because he had been sawing logs during the afternoon.

Then it really was time to go indoors. If she stayed any longer she was afraid where her actions might lead. She did find him attractive. He was thoughtful, quiet and not without a certain sense of dry humour. So clutching her bag to her bosom, she opened the front door with her key, and regretfully smiled one last time. Which was his signal to leave. But he did not.

This sent her into a singular apoplexy. How could she be rude enough to close the door when he was still standing there? So she smiled again.

'Aren't you going?'

'I don't really want to.'

'You'll get wet!'

'I've my coat.'

'You'll catch your death!'

'Sorry. I've just enjoyed walking you home.'

'You're very sweet, but I have to go in now.'

'All right then. I'll have to go I suppose!'

'You're crazy!'

Simon smiled. 'See you Tuesday Avis. Bye.'

'Bye.'

Then he was gone, leaving her to safely close the door without hurting his feelings.

Truthfully, Simon did not feel the rain as he walked back to Forest Gate. He did not wait for a tram. He just wanted to walk and walk and walk. He had been kissed twice by the woman of his dreams, with a certainty of a second date. He found himself smiling for no reason. The traffic sung. The increased rain stung. His clothes became soaked. There was even a hint of a whistle on his lips. The sky was the darkest black, the opposite of his heart. A favourite piece of Mozart, Symphony No. 40 in G minor echoed in his mind, round and around. He had not felt like this before. A thought. How would he be able to concentrate on the film on Tuesday with her sitting so close? He smelt lemon again in his mind. Fresh and tangy. No, the rain never bothered him at all.

Fourteen

The family atmosphere at 231 improved over the following months. Nevertheless, for a time, but not more than a week, William had been preoccupied with private thoughts, not even allowing Ethel to know what they were, much to her annoyance. He was restrained and depressive. He particularly avoided speaking to Avis. But as she had somebody new in her life, and most definitely on her mind, she didn't really notice, or, at that time, care.

The three of them went about their daily lives as if no family breech had occurred. If it had been a matter of lesser importance, the problem may have been forgotten quicker. But the possibility of giving evidence in court again, any court, so close in time to Edith's own appearance at the Old Bailey was not easy to ignore. Each day, William would scan his paper for some news on the story, but noticed nothing.

Eventually, just over a month later, he wrote a letter to the Chief Inspector asking about the case, and was told in a swift reply that Miss Baker had pleaded guilty to all charges, and that she received five years imprisonment. He was happy to add that no action was to be taken against

Mrs Graydon or their daughter. William was therefore extremely angry that he had not been informed at the time of the hearing, and complained in another letter about the shabby way his family had been treated, causing them unnecessary hardship. He ended his diatribe by informing the Chief Inspector that he would be drafting a letter of complaint to his superintendent.

Which was never written. William was the type of man with high morals, and during his life, had very rarely breached the law. He was always on time, raised his children to know right from wrong, often spoke of dignity, the necessity of courage and honour, rarely blasphemed, and always told the truth. If he said he was going to do a thing, then it would be done. He was a proper Victorian East-Ender. So when, after three days of being shown the letter, Ethel knew that the letter to the superintendent hadn't been written, she knew that William, although appearing to be the same man, wasn't.

At fifty-six years of age, he was not so young anymore, and suffered with several age-related complaints such as a stiff back in the mornings, a little deafness in one ear, spots before his vision, a runny nose upon rising, a troublesome knee and a smoker's cough. His knee caused him to limp a little, but only when the weather was cold. He had been limping since Edith's trouble began last September.

However now, Ethel noticed he was eating a little less, his feet were more pungent at night, almost becoming an olfactory nightmare, and his skin and grey hair was dry. To her, it was obvious that the strain of the last six months had begun to tell. She herself was undergoing symptoms of a similar nature, although she had no cough, and her feet didn't smell. Nevertheless most days she was tired long before a woman of her stamina and age ought to be.

Doctor Wallis understood what was happening to them, and on the occasion of them both visiting his surgery, just coincidentally to renew prescriptions, and for William to have a painful boil lanced, he took the opportunity to suggest that as the warmer weather was right around the corner, they might consider some sort of holiday — and for God's sake, he had said, you both need it.

In the midst of their unhappiness, a holiday seemed the most unlikely event. Nevertheless it took the combined efforts of their four children to convince them it was not such a bad suggestion. There was no effort involve in William getting time off work. Indeed his manager welcomed the suggestion, and immediately offered him two weeks.

Ethel fussed about leaving Avis alone, but secretly prayed they could get away. A close neighbour, Liz, the wife of Mr Bristow at 229 had said that getting away from the associations of the last six months would do her a world of good, and she would only be too pleased to keep an eye on the place when Avis was at work.

Therefore with the endorsement of his employer, and over a fish and chip supper one Friday, William addressed the subject again, and asked if Ethel wanted a few days away. Her answer did not surprise him as he had seen how eager and willing she had been when the doctor had first suggested it. And after all, it had been some years since they had been away. Perhaps three she recollected.

Therefore, travel arrangements were made, and ten days bed, breakfast and an evening meal for two was booked at Palm Garden House in Barnstaple. William's only stipulation was they book in under an assumed name which they did, choosing the name Larkin, William's manager's name. Ethel didn't particularly enjoy being called Ethel Larkin as, to her, it sounded as if she was slightly simple, but the bookings were made under that name nonetheless. Although slightly against his principles, William was content to allow the change of name to avoid being recognised.

On the day of leaving, just after an unearthly early breakfast at five in the morning, while William was polishing his walking shoes by the sink, Ethel gave a stern warning to Avis not to overfeed Joey, and to behave themselves, as by this time, both William and herself knew about her friendship with the 'Catholic organist' as he was known.

And she stared hard at her daughter as if to press home the point that she did not want to return home to find her in any different condition. All that was conveyed with one glare, and Avis, reddened, and told her mother not to be so silly. She was, after all, nearly thirty.

'People do such stupid things nowadays.' Ethel reminded her.

'Just get on that train mum, and don't concern yourself about me. I'm a sensible girl.'

'Better be. Please don't give your father anymore trouble. We're going away to forget them, and we don't want to come home to have another face to feed.'

'Mother!' Stop it. Just have a good time, and everything will be all right here.'

Within another thirty minutes, there was a kind of tearful good-bye on the doorstep, and in the dark, the cab driver assisted William in loading the suitcases. Ethel kissed Avis one last time, and promised she would send a postcard first thing. William, quiet as usual, and with not a trace of a smile, give Avis a peck on her cheek, and reminded her to look after the house. She was sure he had wanted to say more, perhaps something personal, but a kind of family propriety stopped him. Perhaps it was because they were outside. But this she doubted.

Ethel waved furiously through the back of the cab's window, but William only waved once. And then without turning around. Avis had Joey in her arms, and raised one of the cat's paws, and waved it up and down absurdly. Within a few seconds, they had vanished around the bend and that was that.

Avis returned to the kitchen, poured some milk for Joey, washed up the breakfast things, noticed the silence, and prepared herself for work. As she washed and dressed, her mind aimlessly drifted over to her date which was to take place that evening. At first she had wanted him to enjoy a meal at her house, but thought it best not to ask Simon there for the first time without her parent's permission, or indeed, them not being present at all.

Since her father's general disappointment with her, Avis had walked on eggshells around him, and did her best not to make the situation worse. Although she had told her mother about Simon, they had yet to meet him. Her mother had suggested after their holiday, which seemed like a fine idea as her father was almost certain to be in a better mood. It therefore would not do at all if Simon had wandered in, and it had come to light he had been in her father's house already.

Therefore they had arranged to meet at the junction of Romford Road and High Street North under the gas fitting of the Earl of Essex where they would take a drink before going on. He was waiting for her when she arrived, and as they had reached the stage of exclusivity, they slowly kissed each other on the cheek romantically.

For both of them this was an exciting time, and Avis certainly thoroughly enjoyed getting to know all about Simon. She had admitted that she played a little piano, but was nowhere near his standard. She would have kept up her childhood lessons, she told him, but her father and her uncle broke up the old upright one day, although why she still had no idea. She assumed it had been taking up too much room as the family grew. She and her sister and her brothers were told strictly to stay indoors on the day they did it.

While he had his usual half a pint of bitter, she supped her bitter shandy, exceedingly grateful that Simon was not a man desperately fond of alcohol. After an hour of fond and deeper inquisitiveness about each other's lives, which Avis would have wished to go on all evening, they took a tram to the The Grove Picture Palace where they enjoyed a recital of Chopin.

After, both of them humming concerto number 2 in F minor, occasionally in harmony, they drank a cup of coffee at a roadside cafe by the side of St John's church before Simon showed her where he lived. He, naturally, did not dare to ask her in, not at the stage they were, but was attempting in a fairly crude way to show her how independent and autonomous he was. This she understood, but nevertheless, a small part of her wished that propriety did not play so important a part in their lives.

By this time, after some ten dates, Avis had begun to understand the reality of Simon's condition. It would be true to say that another woman, given an uncharitable nature, would have looked about for a more deserving catch. However, Avis was not an uncompassionate woman, and besides his occasional bouts of simplicity, she had the ability to see beyond his individual nature.

She had never been a woman who naturally commanded a great deal of attention from men, despite being physically attractive and naturally kind. The reason for this was never entirely clear, but she had her suspicions. Possibly a combination of a vivacious and slightly older sister, plus a natural shyness, had combined to make her somewhat invisible when out socially.

It said much of the period in which she was born, that a great many of the very few gentleman she did meet were only interested in the commonplace and the trite, whereas she and her sister had most probably taken after their father in their appreciation of culture. However, having such an effervescent older sister so close in years, the shy Avis had tended to occupy a place in Edith's shadow.

The three men with whom she had become familiar since her parents had allowed them to escort her out had all tried to become a little more familiar than she had expected, and therefore none of the situations went further than one date. Avis had not exactly resigned herself to spinsterhood, especially at her age, but it was true, she admitted to herself, she was getting older...

Consequently, and she could be forgiven for believing she settled for second best, the appearance of a cultured, if not exactly highly intelligent man of the right age and background, at her time of life, was nothing less than a stroke of good fortune.

Not that she allowed him to guess her poor grasp on relationships. For she was coy when the situation warranted it, captivating when she wanted something, and occasionally deliberately infuriating. All techniques she had learned by observation from her older sister. Simon though, given his only slightly more extensive dating experience, recognised such primitive attempts of play, and counteracted with the only precedent an honest man had...love.

'It's a huge house Simon!'

'Yes,' he answered with his usual bonhomie, 'sometimes I think of getting something smaller, but I've so many memories of my parents. I'm sure they wouldn't have wanted me to move.'

'And you were an only child?'

'I remember mother getting a little plump when I was about five, and I imagined I was getting a little brother, but maybe she just enjoyed food as she got older!'

'You joke about that?'

'Yes, Avis. I can. Mother had a great sense of humour.'

She took his arm, and leaned against him a little, already imagining herself running the household, perhaps even with a couple of rosy-cheeks children playing in the extensive front gardens. If nothing else, Avis had a vivid imagination, and often indulged in a great deal of progressive thinking.

'Is that a lime?'

'Yes, I was told father planted it.'

Avis remembered their own tree, the earth not yet settled around it.

'For any particular reason?'

'I cannot say. I remember playing around it as child. There is an extensive back garden you ought to see sometime. And the conservatory.'

'I'd like that Simon. Better in daylight though.'

'Of course. Come round for tea soon?'

'Might I bring Mary? I think my mother might feel better about that.'

'Yes, of course she can come with you. I don't want the neighbours to talk.'

'I ought to get back.'

'Of course. Shall we walk or get the tram? How are your shoes?'

Avis had been having a little trouble that evening as a result of a new pair of shoes being too tight.

'Hurting actually. I'd prefer it if we waited for the tram.'

The evening was cool and breezy, but wasn't too uncomfortable as they stood at the stop watching the light traffic trundle past. Avis still clung onto Simon's arm.

'I hope mum and dad arrived safely. Devon is a long way away.'

'I expect they are. Going anywhere is very safe nowadays. You'll get a postcard in a few days telling you there're having a spiffy time. I can't wait to meet them Avis.'

It was then that Avis' eyes froze and stared once again at the big old church so black and gloomy on the opposite corner. And that seemed to reflect within her the dark knowledge her family held. Like a half-forgotten memory interrupting the pleasure she had with this man, like an aching tooth that she was trying not to acknowledge, her sister's face arose sharply in her memory, and she knew that very soon, she would have to tell Simon the family secret. By the fact that he had not mentioned it, it was almost a certainly that he had not guessed who her sister had once been.

Fifteen

Ethel and William allowed their moods to change for the better once they left 231. As they bounced their way along to Paddington Station, a journey which took them two hours due to road-works in the City, what began, on William's part as frosty, seemed to thaw the further away from his home he became. By Holborn, amidst the early morning rush of other taxis, trams and the mass of people streaming into the capital, coughing and sniffling because of a heavy fog which had descended overnight, he took a deep sigh, folded up his newspaper where he had been reading a round-up of that year's news thus far, which included the great battle of Dublin, and the wonderful news of the official ending of the Great War, and reached across almost coyly, and took Ethel's hand.

She, still sleepy, her eyes opening and closing, fighting back the effects of waking so early, was pleasantly surprised, and silently squeezed his hand back. A smile was exchanged, and she moved closer and laid her head on his shoulder. By eight o'clock, they were settled in a smart railway carriage waiting by platform number one along with three other holidaymakers; a plump man, his very plain wife and their young son who looked a little white and ill. On the hour, a shrill whistle blew, William glanced at his fob watch approvingly, and the train gave a little jolt as it began its long journey across England.

Pleasantries were exchanged, William using their fake name, but the four adults, finding they had nothing in common, eventually quietened and settled down to the five hour journey to Exeter St Davids where the Graydons would change to a branch line which would take them to Barnstaple, a total travelling time of seven hours. Apart from a sideways glance from the man after the families had run out of conversation, William believed they had not been recognised which cheered him considerably.

The question of whether he or Ethel would be able to spend their holiday without any sort of intrusion from the press, or from individual persons, had weighed heavily on William. It was not at all as it was when he was a child. Local news then meant issues stayed local, and disappearing to another part of the world meant that for most purposes, a person could remain anonymous. Not so now though. Express trains, long distant letters arriving within days, hours even, wireless communication and the growth of news agencies put a stop to that. William had a perfectly good reason to hate them all, and hoped the people of the West Country had short memories.

One meal, a selection of sandwiches and two pots of tea later, at exactly three o'clock in the afternoon, and with Ethel and William feeling more tired than they could remember, with a hazy yellow sun trying so hard to break through the clouds, the branch-line's equivalent of an express eased gently into Barnstaple's terminus known as Barnstaple Junction. There was a queue of holidaymakers on one of the other platforms awaiting the Ilfracombe 'puffer', and most of them looked carefree, dressed lightly and were slightly tanned, three conditions in which Ethel hoped to be before many days had passed. A considerable amount of bunting was still flapping in the wind as the line had just celebrated joining the Southern Railway.

A friendly and talkative cabby with a strong and unmistakable West Country accent drove them away immediately as not too many people had alighted at Barnstaple with them, and within a few minutes they drew up outside the spacious and well decorated Palm Garden House which was to the north of the town. After signing the register with his new fake surname, William allowed a smart-looking boy to heave their luggage up to room number seven, after which he tipped him sixpence. Then, left alone, they both laid on the deep and comfortable double bed in their overcoats, and remained there exhausted with the raucous screaming of gulls outside the only reminder that they were on holiday. Both fell asleep for over an hour.

Late in the afternoon, somewhat refreshed, while William went downstairs to get a timetable of meals, and to collect pamphlets and leaflets and buy a few postcards, Ethel, romantically pleased with their view of the River Taw, its tide advancing at the moment, unpacked and then, finding the tap water extremely hot, decided to take a bath. By the time she had finished, changed and re-entered their main room, William was laying back on the bed reading.

Ethel was pleased to note that his demeanour had changed a great deal since leaving East Ham that morning, and he even made a joke about Bombo, one of the musical events that happened to be showing at the Theatre Royal that evening, to which she enquired if he wished to go.

'Not tonight my dear, too tired.' He rose and strolled to the wide window. 'But we can get some tickets tomorrow if you like? It says here that it's a runaway success! Didn't you read the book sometime?'

'I did and it was funny. It'll be interesting to see what they've done with it. Edith prob...sorry Will.'

'Don't apologise Eth. That's stupid. She's bound to come up in conversations occasionally and yes, she loved the theatre and yes, she probably saw it in London. She seems to have caught most popular performances.'

'Don't be angry Will.'

'Do I sound it? Sorry. Don't want to spoil our time away.'

'It's going to take time isn't it?'

'She's not been long in her grave, and it feels like years.'

'I know it does Will. We have to give ourselves time.'

'If only I'd have known. I would have clouted that Freddy so hard he wouldn't have got up for a week.'

'Well, you were not to know was you? No more than me. She was a grown woman Will. She knew what she was getting herself into.'

'We ought to have brought her up better. More stricter.'

'Will, don't even think of such things. We brought them all up the same way, and the others have turned out all right.'

William gave an uncharacteristic sniff of disdain, and silently brought his eyes away from the ever changing cloudy scenery back to Ethel who continued.

'All right, Avis' is going through some changes at the moment, and we did something silly, but you can't blame her for that. That was my fault. She only carried the flowers.'

'I just can't see...it all feels broken somehow Eth.'

'Will? I'm in no situation to offer you advice, but we have to manage somehow. I know we've lost her, and under the worst possible circumstances. We can't grieve at her burial site. We don't even know where she is. But we have a duty to our other children. Will? Getting angry with Avis won't help either you or her, and you ought to say something when we get back.'

'Such as?'

'Make peace with her. Show her that you are still her father.'

'Well, what else am I?'

'Oh, you know what I mean. You've been so distant, and she's very upset, but she doesn't show it. She's hasn't done anything wrong. Isn't it possible that you're taking it out on her? It was Edith that did wrong.'

William returned to the sky, and leaned his forehead against the pane of glass. It was very cold.

'We shouldn't have started this. I feel rotten now. A fine way to start a holiday.'

Ethel walked across, and put her arm through his, her eyes staring at the same scenery.

'Will? We have to approach this now from a different angle otherwise we're going to get lost. Can't you see that? You're head of this family, and you have to show our children that we can get on without Edith. Somehow.'

'How?'

'By being strong and praying to God for help. Reverend Vega helped didn't he? Let's ask him again if he can spare us some more time. I can't believe Will that we can carry on without any hope at all. There has to be something other than time which will help us as a family.'

'The boys won't go along to see him again. I know them. They seem to have recovered quickly.'

'Is that what you think? Have you spoken to Harold recently about his sister? He's still very upset, and goodness only knows what Newnie and Billy think. They won't even talk to me about her.'

'Well, you said it then. You're their mother, the softest option. What chance have I got?'

'I'm talking about Avis Will, and she knows how angry you are with her. Look, the church thing doesn't really matter does it? So she goes to a different building. She still has prayer and God in her heart.'

William sighed, and shook his head sadly.

'And anyway,' she continued, 'if she hadn't stumbled in there, she wouldn't have met this organist feller. She seems very keen on him. Perhaps this is the one she's been waiting for. Son of a doctor...big house!'

She nudged him with a sparkle in her eyes trying to wrestle him away from his thoughts. 'Maybe grandchildren...'

As if the very mention of that word animated him, he turned swiftly and grabbed her waist.

'What about a sixth for you and me?'

'William Graydon! Get away with you! At my age...oh, you ought not to joke like that...!'

William snatched a kiss to stop her talking, but she eventually pulled away and, quite flustered yet smiling, smoothed down her dress, and ran a hand across her hair.

'What time's the evening meal?'

'Six thirty. Can you hold out until then or do you want a snack?'

'What I want is for you to talk pleasantly to your daughter when we get back. Invite her young man to tea or something. Show her that you are her father Will. Be kind.'

'All right woman. And all right, we'll see Reverend Vega again. He must be fed up with us by now.'

'He understands Will. Let's face it, We've had an experience, a loss, that not many people have undergone.'

'Mrs Bywaters has. I wonder how she's coping?'

Ethel had no answer to that stinging question. Freddy Bywater's mother had often passed through her mind, and wanted to speak to her about the whole thing, but her intuition told her it was not the right thing to do or the right time to do it. Yet. Nor could she see how to go about resolving the differences of the families, even if differences existed. Yes, she knew where she lived, but she had no idea how she might have been received had she even attempted a visit. Perhaps the woman may even attack her. Ethel had no idea, and there was no friendly third party with whom she might contact.

On the one hand, as far as Ethel was concerned, Freddy's despicable and insane actions had inadvertently brought disgrace and shame to three families. However, Mrs Bywaters may well argue that it was Edith who perhaps mesmerised him into murder. At the trial, Freddy's mother, like her, was inconsolable, and wailed continuously when sentence was given. Even beyond her own shock, Ethel would never forget those closing scenes. And after, that was the last time she saw her although, like her own, pictures of her and her family continued in the daily papers for weeks.

'How about a short walk before our meal?'

*

Their ten days passed so rapidly that it seemed time passed at a different rate in the wild and windy peninsular of North Devon. Apart from two days of tragedy, three days of rain, one of which was spent in Palm Garden House itself playing drafts, chess and backgammon with other residents, and the other two in various museums, galleries and places of historic interest, they spent their time walking, sight-seeing and occasionally taking a charabanc to various towns along the North Devon coast.

It was on the fifth day that tragedy struck in its worst form. With flasks and sandwiches generously supplied by the owner of Palm Garden House, a woman called Mrs Chambers, they had booked a ride on one of those chara-bancs to explore the North Devon coast. And so it was with ten other couples, mostly middle-aged, that soon after breakfast, William and Ethel set off eastwards to follow, as close as the driver dare, the often used route to Minehead some forty miles distant.

This afforded, on a clear day, which it was, two perfectly spectacular and opposing views. On their left was the Western English channel and Celtic Sea, a blue flat surf of breathtaking sparkling reflections, above which they rode high on their journey on top of the cliffs. And to their right, the almost everlasting heather; the bleak, ancient brown and green moorland tracks of Doone Country as their driver called it in his flowery baroque.

Or as Londoners like William and Ethel recognised it, the vast and unknowable Exmoor forest, a place of ambi-ence, magic and dark colour with its hilltops and ridges, en-igmatic stone settings and circles, medieval settlements, prehistoric enclosures and forts on hilltops. A world several steps away from all with which they were familiar.

Pools of huge areas of swiftly moving sunlight spotted both land and sea as the sun played hide and seek with the mighty white clouds. Overall it was clean and fresh, and about as far away from the experience of dirty old London Town as anyone could hope for. Women covered their heads with scarfs as protection from the wind, and the men generally sucked on pipes and occasionally peered at distant objects through their binoculars.

Having made a stop in the quaint village of Berrynarbor for morning coffee, the party motored on, and eventually settled for lunch at what Ethel was to recall later as a beautiful and charming inn, delightfully and enigmatically called the Haunted White Lady, a little way north of Martinhoe where the driver found a delightful shady spot outside, under the dappled light of the now warming sun. Everyone agreed that the views were breathtaking, and the service of the inn extemporary.

William consumed a large fish pie while Ethel contented herself with the small. Chips and peas accompanied the main dish, while strong dark beer washed it down. Ethel left her half a pint deciding that it was not to her taste, but it was all she could do to prevent her husband from downing it after he had finished his. They *were* drinking in public after all.

The driver of the charabanc decided that the engine needed some water, and to cool so he invited the crowd to take a wander around, but advised them to return in about an hour. The sea is in that direction, he guided them. However, maybe it was because the service was so sterling or the beer that strong, it turned out that only Ethel wanted to stretch her legs. Therefore with the greatest reluctance, William lifted himself to his feet, rolled his eyes in submission, and allowed his wife to take his arm where they proceeded to stroll along a slightly downward-sloping path, covered with a soft layer of sand to the sea.

At this meeting of sea and land in Devon, Woody Bay, it was only possible to approach it by walking the well-trodden paths. For to walk directly, as a crow might fly, a visitor would have to clamber over nearly a thousand yards of low-growing bushes and stumpy trees. Therefore, mindful of the time, and with a great wish to stand next to the water, they hurried along as fast as they dare, given the slippery nature of the sand underfoot.

The bay itself, from the air, looked like a crater, half of which was covered by water, and there was not much sand as the tide was in. In many parts, the water, unusually calm that day, was lapping gently (for Devon anyway) at the ring of rocks. What was unusual too was, despite the beauty and calmness of the scenery, there was not a single soul to be seen.

William and Ethel reached the top of the very low cliffs, and decided that they were not going to be able get to stand next to the sea without walking down the last part of a steep path, which they decided was a little too dangerous. So they did the next best thing. They sat and stared at the panorama which stretched before them. Seagulls of course filled the air with their noise, but they didn't concern the visitors who enjoyed the peace, the gentle breeze, the strong sun and the smell of the salt and the seaweed.

Here they sat in complete silence for some five minutes until William, who had better hearing, nudged Ethel and mutely pointed downwards. Following his finger, Ethel abruptly stood, and squinted as a high-pitched scream of a woman reached them. For towards the sea, in a break in the rocks, where they had long ago parted and left a tiny triangle of sand, was the figure of a woman who seemed to be flinging herself back and forth, kneeling over something whilst a smaller figure stood still by her side.

William's binoculars came into play immediately, but reporting back to Ethel, said he could not make out at all what was happening. But as it was clear that the woman was in a great deal of distress, both of them were therefore motivated to take that last spit of a path, and were soon approaching the scene. The woman, who only wore a dark blue bathing suit, was still kneeling, but it was the other person, now recognised as a child, who saw the Graydons coming, and she alerted the woman.

Who looked around immediately and cried out for help. It was not until William and Ethel had entirely arrived next to the figures that they saw that what had happened was a tragedy. And even then, the awfulness of what they saw seemed to scramble their minds, as if their brains could not fully recognise or understand what they were seeing. For at first, William thought it was a large fish over which the woman was wailing.

But it was not. It was a child. A very dead child. As white as a sheet because she had bled out due to a gaping tear in her thigh. Straight away, William and Ethel knew there was nothing they could do despite the woman's urgent pleas to help bring her around.

William made an immediate decision, and told the women he was going for help. Within a moment therefore he had disappeared over the extensive greenery leaving Ethel to find two towels, one of which she put around the woman's shoulders, and the other around the standing child's who appeared to be in an equal condition of shock. Ethel ordered the girl to sit, which she did with no hesitation. She quickly discovered their names, but could not get any more information out of the adult. The distressed woman only continued to hold and rock her dead child whilst sobbing in the most intense way Ethel had been witness to for a long time.

Being somewhat isolated, it was a while before William returned with a small body of men, one of whom was the driver who knew a little about first aid as it had been taught to him during the Great War. However, when that particular chap saw the body, he bulked a little, and shook his head stubbornly before informing the two women that a message had been sent by car to Lynton, but that it would be some time before a doctor arrived. His suggestion was that the girl be taken back to his vehicle.

By this time, Ethel was making some headway in talking to the woman whose name she discovered was Mrs Groves, and by degrees, told her that it was too late and even, eventually eased her away saying that the men would take her back up to the inn. A fresh group of men now hurriedly arrived carrying a stretcher, and they gently placed the girl's body onto it.

Therefore it was a slow and silent procession of figures, except for Mrs Groves who could not stop weeping, which edged their way back to the inn up and along the sandy path. William could not help noticing that the other child, perhaps slightly older, although seemingly content to hold Ethel's hand and be led along, really looked quite frightened.

They did not have very long to wait for the authorities to arrive, which they did in a large white Ford. Courtesy of the owner of a local golf club who had happened to be talking to Lynton's only policeman at the time the message came through. Therefore from it, stepped a uniformed officer, who immediately put on his helmet, and a middle-aged man with a dark leather bag whom William assumed correctly was a doctor. He was shown the body immediately which had been set down on a makeshift table in one of the stables. Someone had had the decently to close the girl's eyes. Mrs Groves was standing alongside her, holding the dead girl's pale hand, as well as Ethel's with her other when he walked in, and introduced himself. The policeman and William followed him whilst Mrs Grove's other child was left with the wife of the landlord.

Introductions established, the doctor quickly performed the most elementary of inspections before drawing himself up and declared the time of death to be one thirty-eight in the afternoon. He turned to the weeping mother, and asked her gently what happened, and from her came a story which chilled Ethel's heart.

The two sisters had been playing in the sea. Only a shallow pool she was quick to assure them. She imagined they were safe as the tide was retreating, and the weather and the conditions were fine. She was reading her book when some part of her noticed that the children were not screaming in their usual playful way. The way children do on a beach. A chilling silence took hold of her. Therefore she had ran down to the water's edge only to discover her youngest laying in a huge rocky pool which was entirely coloured red. She had tried to wake her she said, but she could not stop the bleeding. After that she said she could not remember anything until a woman helped her to her feet.

'That was me', offered Ethel.

'Bring in the other child,' ordered the policeman.

'No John, best not in here. Let's go outside.'

As the landlord offered one of his back rooms, a dark and foreboding place which smelt of stale beer, that is where the group retired where the older girl was questioned gently by the doctor. Her responses to his gentle probing explained everything. They had been playing, she told them. Just playing and Mary had slipped on the rocks, some seaweed she thought, and fell. The amount of her sister's blood had frightened her, and she didn't know what to do. She still seemed stunned. Her mother, at last, put her arm around her and held her close. They shivered together.

'Why didn't the deceased call out?' asked the doctor.

'She was mute,' replied the mother simply.

'And why were you alone Mrs Grove?'

'We are here alone. My husband perished in the war. He was a Major.'

'Do you own the Morris outside?'

'Yes, we drove here this morning from Weston-Super-Mare.'

'I see. The deceased will have to be taken back to Lynton Madam. Are you up to driving yourself and your daughter?'

'Yes, what about Hanna?'

'An ambulance will be sent for. Please don't trouble yourself. It would be best if constable Harris accompanied, and booked you in somewhere. I'm afraid there will have to be an inquest of course, and a further examination of the body.'

'Constable? Do you need any form of statement before we leave? My wife and I were first to get there and raised the alarm.'

'In which case...'

'Mr...Graydon. This is my wife.'

'In which case, Mr Graydon, your presence and your wife's will certainly be required at the inquest. May I ask where you are currently staying? I assume you are holiday-ing?'

Excusing themselves for one moment, there followed an intense discussion between William and Ethel on whether they ought to accompany the mother and daughter back to Lynton, or leave with the charabanc which had decided, out of respect, to return to Barnstaple. Many of the holidaymakers felt the same way after witnessing the poor child's body being brought up from the coast.

Ethel certainly thought that as the mother had no other relative present except her shocked little girl, she implored William to allow her to travel with her. Whereas he, as sympathetic as he was, looked on the practical side, putting the case to her that perhaps the woman might wish to be alone. A single question to the mother quickly answered that dilemma, and William and Ethel were bundled into the back of the Morris with an assurance that a police vehicle would escort them back to Barnstaple after they had given statements. Although they would certainly be required to attend the inquest and give evidence.

Those last words stung both of them, but while Ethel continued to offer comfort to the mother and her remaining child, William sank morosely back into the deep brown leather seats, the policeman now driving. Mrs Grove had attempted to drive away from the inn, but had not been able to locate first gear because her hands were still shaking violently. At which point, the policeman gently took hold of her, and guided her to the back seat where Ethel had welcomed her, and wrapped a blanket around her and her daughter, a sweet, fair-headed child of twelve who still remained uncannily silent.

True to the policemen's word, a car was made available after William and Ethel had given statements, each in a different room of the tiny police station which also doubled up as the constable's home. More police had been drafted in from Exeter, including a sergeant to assist with the paperwork and organisation. It wasn't long before the press arrived as well. William and Ethel were not pleased about that development, but luckily they managed to evade them by moments as a car took them back to Barnstaple under cover of darkness.

Mrs Grove had been given a sedative by the doctor, and her remaining child sent to bed by the time the Graydon's left. They were thankful that they had not seen any reporters, especially as they had heard they were arriving soon. But were utterly dismayed to hear that they would be required to give evidence at the inquest on the day after the next. The same car would pick them up again. The police were extremely grateful for their assistance, and while they were there, offered them every comfort.

These tragic events had a detrimental effect on William, and that night, after their evening meal, he told Ethel he was going to take a walk along the river, and moreover, he desired to be on his own. Ethel could only surmise what was going on in his mind. He returned over two hours later, by which time, the landlady had to open the front door for him, and Ethel, after finishing her book, was almost asleep on their little sofa.

He climbed into his own bed as silently as he left, and wasn't talkative the next morning over breakfast either, offering little more than grunts, and was certainly not friendly at all. Quite upset by his mood, soon as she had finished eating, Ethel silently rose and disappeared upstairs. By the time, William entered their rooms, she had vanished for the day. And moreover, she did not return until it was time for their evening meal.

It took her less than fifteen minutes to wash and change, and William, by the way he was staring at her, wanted an explanation as to where she had been all day. Their short spat of heated words was not resolved by any means by the time the gong rang for the evening meal, and so they both put on their bland English faces, and walked downstairs and entered the dining room which was packed. There was not a spare room to be had in the building.

Whatever the essences of their individual disappearances, both understood that their behaviour really had very little to do with each other's conduct, and everything to do with situations over which neither had any control. Perhaps six months previously, such a confrontation of words might have lasted for days, each blaming the other. However, now their perception had matured.

Each had experienced the very worst emotions a human being could undergo, and in the process, cried more tears than each of them had previously unleashed before. Almost all in private. It almost seemed a sin to be annoyed with each other. And they both knew it. Whatever closeness they had forged throughout the terrible dark ordeal they had undergone, could not now be marked or undone in any way. They were twinned for life with a higher perception, about which ordinary mortals could only dream.

Therefore, by the time the pudding arrived, their hands had reached and found each other's, while a few inquisitive residents who had noticed this profoundly affectionate act, found it cute and had smiled. Not one of them knowing just what the couple had had to undergo to have reached that stage of forgiveness. There was peace between them. Even as they discussed the distressing events of the last thirty-six hours, and the looming inquest to which they had to attend the following morning at ten sharp.

Naturally, they had no appropriate clothes for the formal event, so they wore the clothes in which they had arrived, and waited rather nervously for the police car to pick them up. It was a different policeman that morning, and their embarrassment was complete when he asked in reception for the Graydons. A name the owner of course was unaware. However, it did not take long for the confusion to be resolved, and with a curious look from the landlady as they walked to the car, William prayed for the day to go quickly.

The journey both there and back in suitably overcast weather did not inspire in them the beauty they had felt when on the charabanc two days previously. Now the same views, both sides, appeared threatening and dangerous, the seaward side especially so. Apart from a couple of hair-raising traffic events caused by a constable whose speciality was not driving, they reached the wooden village hall of Lynton with ten minutes to spare. Apart from Ethel wishing to use a lavatory, they were pressed inside immediately and told to sit on the right. The hall had been arranged to resemble a small courtroom.

The inquest itself, once the small public gallery (basically a double handful of chairs) had been filled and a jury sworn in, did not take long. Only Mrs Grove, her eyes darkened for lack of sleep spoke, and the doctor gave details of her daughter's single injury to her right leg. William and Ethel were not asked to speak, but their statements were read out. To William's surprise, no one appeared to recognise them, and realising this, palpably relaxed.

Mrs Grove broke down several times as she described what had happened. The jury was informed of the pool of red-stained sea-water in which Hanna had been found, and the doctor assured them that death would have been swift as her blood-loss would have been great. Too great, he empathised, for anyone in that lonely stretch of land for any lay person to have staunched it. The long jagged wound being caused by a fall onto sharp rocks.

To which the jury, consisting mostly of elderly farmers and shopkeepers, swiftly brought in a verdict of accidental death. After the proceedings had been dismissed, Ethel had a mind to spend a little more time with Mrs Grove after she had enquired as to her own health, and what her plans were, but it was clear to her that the distraught woman was in no mood for chatting with a virtual stranger. Ethel therefore wrote her home address on a slip of paper and wished her well, never expecting her to write. Mrs Grove thanked them both personally, but made the excuse that she had to see the funeral director with the aim of transporting her daughter's body back to Western Super Mare.

There was after, no point at all in remaining, but even so, they found a small pub at the top of the town where they took lunch and had a beer. Both had the feeling that they were being watched, but as the expected hoard of reporters had not arrived, they dismissed their feelings. Only later, in London upon their return, would they realise how naive they had been. Only one hurdle needed to be faced and overcome. And that was an explanation to the landlady as to why they had booked their holiday under a false name.

Upon their return to the Palm Garden House, Mrs Chambers was ready to ask them to leave, being that she naturally suspected the worse, and that she was harbouring an illicit love affair under her roof. However, when in the privacy of her private back parlour, William reluctantly explained who they were, and why he had misled her, she, with good grace, accepted the explanation perfectly before her face turned into a sorrowful map of condolences. Something neither William or Ethel wanted to experience.

Yes, she had followed the case in the paper and thought it was such a shame that that lovely girl had been put to death. And wasn't she innocent? She believed so, and always had from the start. Yes, it was a shame. Not a tragedy or a catastrophe. Not a cataclysm or an annihilation. Just a shame. What William and Ethel hoped most of all, happened after though. The landlady never mentioned the subject again.

Woolacombe eventually proved to be their favourite retreat, and they visited it twice, both times spending the entire day sunning themselves on the wide, clean expanse of golden sand. Deck-chairs hired, a packed lunch, and a few bottles of beer convinced William that given the circumstances, it was a place where a man could forget almost anything. Except when he saw middle-aged men walking about with their daughters. At least, he thought, he hoped they were the men's daughters.

Society had changed so much for William over the last thirty years since he was a young man, that he believed anything was now possible. Even lecherous old men walking about in public with their concubines. It seemed to him that socially, the world had turned upside down since the old Queen died. As he lay in the warm sun on his deckchair, he half remembered how devoted his own father was to Queen Victoria, and even claimed to have seen her once at some parade or other in London in far more innocent times. William never doubted for a moment where his enthusiasm for the Royal family originated.

But with the appearance of the telegraph and its descendent, the telephone, about which he had heard and read a great deal, the rise in feminism, radio transmissions, the scandalous chicanery of modern politicians, the fast motor car and swift and cheap travel to name only a few items about which he had concerns, William felt as if he were being left behind. Memories of the Great War became petrified in his mind, and very few seemed to care, except on one day of the year in November. Concerns about the rise in youth crime, and the decline of the British Empire also occupied his free time.

These troublesome thoughts whistled through William's mind each day as he sat baking in the sun, whilst alternatively reading his paper, and placing it across his face so he could doze, while Ethel's head resounded with little more than knitting patterns, and what she intended to do to the house, and what was more important, what she wanted William to do in the garden when they arrived back home. For there was vegetables to seed, transplant and collect, paths to maintain, their little greenhouse to be cleaned and weeding to do. Because as sure as God made little apples, Ethel imagined, the boys will not have bothered to pop around, and do any of those chores as they said they promised they would. And Avis was not a gardener.

William and Ethel's evenings were mostly spent in a pub, and they discovered, on a recommendation from another couple, a local one called The Bull and Gate, constructed in the eighteenth century that still retained all its original fixtures and fittings. Ethel thought it was like going back in time, and upon their first visit, as it was early in the evening, she fully expected a corseted woman in a wide fancy frock to walk down the stairs.

They always sat next to the fire in the huge grate which seemed to burn continuously day after day, and the landlord was as friendly a man as ever William had known a publican to be. He also thought the local beer was very good. Strong and 'woody'. After her tongue told her what the alcohol content was likely to be, Ethel became his personal conscience, and told him that if he made a fool of himself, then he would be walking back to the Palm Garden House by himself. Thus so warned, each night, he never had more than two pints while Ethel contented herself with a couple of weak shandies made from the same ale. At about nine in the evening they always ordered the same food; a plate of crab and tomato sandwiches for supper which they ate whilst writing postcards.

On both of the Sundays that they spent in Devon, they attended morning service and evensong at a local church along with a couple their own age who had a room directly under them. This couple were slightly more puritanical than the Graydons, or the Larkin's as they were still known, and spent much of their time drinking tea and reading in one of the exquisitely fashioned lounges. This was designated as the quiet one, the other had a radio which was seldom used because there was very few broadcasts, but it was a talking point nonetheless, and certainly a reason to make their neighbours jealous as very few houses owned one.

After ten days, they very reluctantly packed up their clothes, and said their good-byes. The house dog, an old yellow Labrador with a remarkably sweet disposition, and a calm gentle manner, which Ethel was very sad to leave because, in the times she had used the lounges, he used to lay at her feet with his head affectionally laying on her foot, appeared as if from nowhere and rubbed his soft fur against her legs, something he had not done before. She imagined of course that he knew he would not be seeing her again which she thought was sweet. She also imagined that in his own doggy way, he was offering comfort to her, he with superior intuition, somehow aware of her hidden grief.

Of course, they promised to return soon, which they did year after year, and just before they entered the waiting cab, Mrs Chambers, pushed a paper bag into Ethel's hands, and wished them good luck. In it lay buttered bread, cold roast chicken and a salad for the long journey which she knew they were to undergo. Later, after a day or two, having become accustomed back into her old life, Ethel wrote and thanked her for her courtesy and her confidentiality. It was the start of a sure friendship, which lasted until the woman, Sarah, upon the death of her husband thirteen years later, emigrated to Canada to live with her brother. Letters still flew back and forth across the Atlantic of course, but with ever diminishing frequency until one of them died.

However, despite Mrs Chamber's friendship, and how close they became, she never once revealed the Graydon's business, and never once communicated with any third party about the true identity of her friend, and of the unhappiness which once affected them so tragically. As the years went by, all the Graydon children knew about this perfect woman, and even teased their mother about it. Amusingly, Mrs Chamber always wrote to the Larkin family. She often received a few queer glances from her postman though who was desperate to know who this Larkin family was, but as he had no cause to ask them, he remained perpetually in ignorance. A an aside, Ethel and William never heard from Mrs Groves again.

They reached home at eight o'clock in the evening, and Avis had a beef stew waiting for them with dumplings, potatoes and bread. The couple were so exhausted, it was all they could do to eat a plateful, and take themselves off to bed leaving their daughter to clear up. But she didn't mind at all for her father seemed to be back to his normal self, and her previous transgressions appeared to be forgiven. And as the days passed, her assumption was correct.

Sixteen

The date for the *Great Meeting*, as Ethel had embarrassingly named it, was set for the middle of June. It was a sweet and warm evening, and Simon was due at seven. William, although certainly interested in the man who was pursuing his, now only daughter, did not wish to get involved in any of the preparations. Which consisted of a thorough clean of the front room, the kitchen and the outside lavatory along with any of the interconnecting corridors. All this Ethel managed while her daughter and husband was at work. When Avis arrived home, the hallway smelt of strong polish and every surface gleamed.

'Goodness me mother! He's not a prince!'

'Doesn't hurt to give a good impression young lady. Dinner is on so go and wash that old office smell out of you!'

'Mum! I do not smell.'

'Hurry up, your father will be home soon and he'll want to use the basin too.'

'I bet he won't. He never does normally.'

'Less lip, more washing! You have an hour. Off you go.'

Avis trudged upstairs to change, reservations already forming. William certainly normally did not wash himself upon his return from work. His usual routine was to kick off his boots, drink the tea which awaited him, while he spent fifteen minutes finishing off the day's crossword until his evening meal. However, like Avis, when he arrived, he was pressed into washing and changing and then obliged to sit in the normally chilly front room, but which for that evening, had been transformed into a warm paradise given the amount of coal that Ethel had heaped on the fire blazing in the grate.

Dinner he knew was still at least an hour away, so Ethel brought him some biscuits when she gave him his tea once he had washed and changed. He looked a little odd, him wearing a suit and tie in the evening, as if he were a stranger in his own house, but as Ethel had chosen from her favourite wardrobe as well, they both caught each other's eye and hoped the effort was worth it.

Avis joined him, after redoing her makeup twice, and they both sat quite still, nervously awaiting the dreaded knock on the front door. Which seemed ridiculous to her as she was now meeting him at least five evenings out of seven. However, inviting him to meet her parents was a big step, and all four knew it.

For Avis was just not getting any younger, and from what she had told her parents, they imagined that there was a distinct possibility that this man could actually become their son-in-law. They had seen a photograph of him, taken over Wanstead Park with what used to be his father's camera, and had had certainly approved of him. Moreover, he appeared to possess a sense of humour by the way he had stood and larked about whilst pointing at the camera in a manner not at all formal. Therefore, by what little Avis had let slip about her darling man, they expected the evening to be harmonious.

The *great meeting* was marked on their calendar in the kitchen, and Ethel spent a great deal of enjoyable time deciding on what she was going to feed her daughter's beau. The eventually decided upon fare was simple. Tomato soup as an appetiser, followed by roast pork and a sweet pudding. Avis had already informed her that Simon had a decent appetite, so Ethel's modern gas cooker was full. William found his mouth filling up with saliva as he and Avis waited patiently for seven o'clock. He finishing off his crossword whilst she read and reread lines from a cheap novel as she mentally sweated over the family secret.

Avis was not clear about this part of their relationship. They had known each other several months by this time, and not once had Simon approached her, or mentioned, even in passing, anything about her executed sister. Naturally Edith had a different surname, but the newspapers had been full of the family Graydon, and it didn't take a genius to put two and two together. But of course, Simon was not a genius.

She was completely sure that quite a few of the members of the church knew, and she had told Father Clifford some months previously. In the strictest confidence naturally. As she had decided that her move to Catholicism was going to be permanent, she wanted no secrets.

Yet Simon still had not mentioned it. She was aware that he did not take an interest in current affairs, but found it difficult to believe that something, anything had not been mentioned slyly to him. After all, she had reasoned, if someone had, wasn't it the sort of thing a lover, for that's what she now thought of him despite not having indulged in carnal relations, would wish to know about? An executed sister?

As their relationship deepened though, an additional problem occurred to Avis. Which was, the longer she maintained her silence, and the longer he did not mention it, or give any sign that he even knew about it, the harder it became to approach him. What could she say? How could she begin? 'Oh hello darling. Simon, we've been walking out now for some months, and I have to tell you that, by the way, my sister was hung for murder.' Under what possible circumstances could she even make that sound acceptable?

The longer the issue continued, the more agitated Avis became. She found she was spending an increased amount of time cogitating about the problem, running through various scenarios to wonder which one might soften the blow the most. A walk across Wanstead Flats or a day trip to Epping Forest? Over a cosy drink in a pub? After enjoying fish and chips? A favourite habit which they partook on a Friday evening after a visit to the cinema. Or sitting in his garden (she had got that far) on a Sunday afternoon?

Yet all of these seemed perfectly unacceptable when it came to delivering a speech involving an executed sister. She had imagined that while her parents were away on holiday, she might have found the courage to just blurt it out, but as each situation arose, it did not seem at all appropriate. Then her parents had arrived home with that awful story of how the child died. She could see how much it had affected them that she too, had become numb once again to even thinking about the secret, let alone mentioning it finally to her sweetheart.

Then mother had placed pressure on her to arrange a meeting, as she thought it was about time they met him, and as the days slid by without anymore suitable circumstances arising, they had now come to this evening, and he still had not been told just with what family he was about to enjoy a meal. Avis jumped when she heard the characteristic squeak of the garden gate's hinge, and her mouth became instantly dry. Her father, not having heard the rusty noise, remained unflustered, but looked up with a smile as the front door was gently hammered.

Avis jumped to her feet, obviously in distress.

'Calm down Avis. It's only a fellow for dinner.'

'Someone open the door?' That was Ethel calling from the kitchen.

'Thanks dad, I'll open it. Oh...by the way, I haven't mentioned about Edith. You'll say something won't you?'

In a flash, she was out of the hot room, and into the hall. Smoothing herself down, she opened the door.

As the Graydon family had, Simon had dressed for the occasion for he was wearing a new suit which Avis knew he had only brought within the last month. His shoes shone like a pair of polished buttons, and his unblemished white shirt appeared almost professionally laundered. Completing this ensemble was a sky blue tie and a grey trilby, which was instantly removed once he had been welcomed in. He immediately thrust a posy of freshly cut flowers into Avis' arms with a smile. These she took and breathed in their scent before looking up at him. He looked slightly different thought Avis, peering at him with a slightly turned head and expression.

It took her a few moments to work out that he was growing a moustache, and as introductions were made and hands shaken, Ethel hurrying along the corridor drying her hands on a teacloth, and William appearing in the doorway, she decided that she liked it. It could be a little darker she criticised in her mind because he was so fair, but perhaps it would darken later? Although he did not voice it, William thought it looked as if the chap had eaten a jam doughnut, and fallen over onto the carpet. A witticism he was reminded of from an incident that had recently happened to an apprentice at work.

Simon was immediately offered a choice of tea, coffee, beer or something stronger if he wanted, and immediately received a mental 'thumbs up' from Ethel when he chose tea, which she scampered off back into the kitchen to brew. Meanwhile, even in the short period in which Avis had taken his coat and hung it in the hall, the men had already found some common ground, Simon remarking on the small photograph of Vic Watson which William kept on one end of the wooden mantelpiece.

Therefore, while the men began a passionate discussion on the outcome of the 1923 FA Cup Final in which West Ham lost against Bolton Wanderers, Avis stole out of the room, and attempted to help her mother. Who shooed her out of her hot and steamy kitchen. But not before she had gained a first impression of what her mother thought of him.

'Nice...well dressed...hair's a bit long. He'll do', she said with a smile.

'They're talking about football already mum.'

'Better than silence love!'

'I suppose so. I hope dad gets around to mentioning what I asked him to mention.'

'What's that?'

'Oh, nothing, shall I take the tea in? When will the soup be ready?'

'Avis Graydon! What?'

'Simon doesn't know about Edith yet.'

'I beg your pardon?'

'I didn't get around to mentioning it.'

'But you've been walking out for months! Didn't it ever come up in conversation?'

'Not really mum. I don't think he reads the papers either. I mean, how can I...I mean how was I...I've just not told him.'

'Well, don't you think he has a right to know? He's here to dinner. He must be fond of you. As much as I don't want it mentioned, he ought to know what sort of family he's getting involved with.'

'I know, I know. That's why I asked dad to say something.'

'What! Oh goodness me! Dad'll make a right mess of it. As subtle as a bull in a china shop is your dad. Here, take the tea, and make sure they keep on talking about football. Dinner will be in ten minutes. I'll just check on the table.'

Dinner was to be taken formally in the back room, the only room in the house that was hardly ever used. However, that day, all of its surfaces had been polished, and a fire burnt in its grate to take off the chill. The table had been extended thanks to some clever woodworking design, and had been set for four as the boys were not expected.

When Avis, baring a tray of tea, clattered back into the front room, clearly the conversation was no longer about football. Horrifyingly, the men were not speaking at all, and William looked guilty. So with that expression, he embarrassingly lifted himself up and made a space on the table so Avis could put the tray down. Which she did and looked at them gravely.

'What's happened? Dad?'

'It's nothing Avis. Nothing.'

'Dad? Simon? What's my dad been saying?'

But Avis was too disappointed for words, or relieved, she didn't know which, when her boy-friend reluctantly revealed that her father had made a discouraging remark about the goal-keeping prowess of Ted Hufton. She paused for a second, her eyes flashing from one to the other.

'Who?'

'Ted Hufton, goalkeeper for West-Ham,' answered Simon, 'he let in two goals in the final.'

'Oh dad! Can't you talk about anything but football?'

'What else is there to talk about? I like this chap. Any man who is game for The Cockney Boys is all right in my book...even though he thinks their goalie is good.'

'Goodness me, you men! Simon might be an armed bank robber for all you know, but as long as he likes the football, he's all right with you!'

'Quite right. Are you an armed bank robber Simon?'

'Not any more sir.'

'There you are! I'll take the chap's word for it.'

Avis turned away to the door. 'Mum said dinner will be ready in about ten minutes. I'm going to help her. Dad? Football isn't very subtle is it dad? *And* I'm sure there are other things to talk about.'

Avis' eyes were almost wide open as she left the room. Despite her mother's fear at her father lack of subtly, she, by that time, much preferred to have him say almost anything to Simon rather than for the stupid charade to continue. Unfortunately, by the slight shaking of William's head in the direction of Avis when she came to escort them into the back room, it was clear that he still had not broached the forbidden subject, and therefore the tricky subject about the death of William and Ethel's first daughter remained unspoken.

William invited Simon, as guest, to say Grace which he gratefully did in a suitably low, yet clear manner, and his words about salvation and forgiveness particularly moved the rest of his dinner companions. Then Ethel served the soup, and for a while, silence reigned as bread was passed around, and they ate. This silence was only broken by Simon, perhaps not exhibiting the best of manners, who pointed at a photograph on the mantelpiece with a piece of bread, just before he dunked it, and asked who the other woman was.

The photograph in the slightly green and handsome onyx frame obviously contained Avis, but the others knew immediately that he meant the other woman. Both wore summer white dresses, and were obviously extremely happy by the way they appeared so relaxed and smiling. The other woman wore a flower in her hat, and amusingly held another in-between her clenched teeth.

'That's obviously you Avis. Whose the other woman? Best friend?'

'That was taken on holiday a few years ago Simon.'

'Oh, well you look happy.'

'Simon can you pass the salt please?' interrupted Ethel.

'She was my sister Simon. She's...not with us anymore.'

'I'm extremely sorry Avis. I didn't wish to pry.'

Avis quickly glanced at her mum and dad, but they gave no indication of what they were thinking. She was most defiantly flying solo now.

'There is something I wanted to tell you for some time now Simon.'

Ethel finally made a scraping noise with her spoon.

'Avis, is this really the time?'

'Mum? Is there ever going to be a time? Simon, my sister was called Edith Thompson. Ring any bells?'

He shook his head, his hair rolling softly. 'fraid not Avis.'

'Really? It was back in January. She died.'

'I'm so sorry.'

'Simon, she was executed. For murder. Except that she didn't do it.' Avis added quickly.

Simon's spoon almost by itself, gently lowered, and finally disappeared under the red, thick soup. There was a short silence broken only by the clock ticking the seconds.

'I don't understand. I didn't know. I take very little interest in things of that nature. I'm so sorry. I cannot imagine...'

'Avis has had a problem mentioning it Simon because of what you may think of us.'

'Mr Graydon, this makes no difference at all. Jesus told us to forgive all sins, and that's the way I try to live. Oh my word! How horrible for you. I suppose...well, I don't know what to suppose. I can't imagine.'

'Perhaps Avis can tell you now. We, as a family are still trying to face down the notoriety that the case has brought us.'

'Avis? I'm so sorry. You know that I know what it's like to lose someone?'

'Mum and dad know Simon. I told them about your father.'

A silence descended over the four of them, with only the grustling of the fire and the clock sounding the half hour as they finished their soup. Soon after, Ethel rose and gathered their plates asking if Avis would help serve the main course. That gave William a little time to extrapolate the details of their tragedy to their ever-more astonished guest.

Seventeen

The Graydon family story did not instil in Simon the disgust Avis had feared it would. Later that night, when she was in bed, reviewing the evening before she slept, she reprimanding herself for imagining and conjuring up such fears. Why ought he to have minded she asked herself? He was a committed Christian, a peaceful soul who believed in the power of forgiveness. She had tut-tutted to herself at her own folly.

There was not the slightest danger that he would sever their growing relationship because of an occasion which happened before he had known her. These were Simon's own thoughts as he walked home, his belly full of meat and vegetables. He could tell that Mr Graydon had been painfully embarrassed as he told him, in the lowest tone possible, what had happened, and he remembered thinking at the time, at least the sister never actually did anything. It did seem like a travesty of justice to him. The story interested him enough to think that perhaps he might find a book or a magazine, and read up on it a little more.

However, in the warm night-time air, walking back to Forest Gate, he quickly forgot about the Graydon situation, and concentrated on Avis herself as he hummed a little Fugue composed by Bach. Now that he had been introduced to her mother and father, and seen for himself that they were people of good, if not rather poor standing, a vision of joining came into his mind. His own mother, had she still been alive, would not have approved of the Graydons, he was almost sure of that. Too poor, not Catholic, and now, worst of all, a socially mortifying story of murder and execution. No, Simon could almost hear his mother's high-pitched shrilly voice forbidding him ever to see Avis again.

Her tone echoed though to a much younger man. Now, that evening, he shook her memory off, and was glad to do so. For the truth was, he was very fond of Avis. There was something, possibly a weakness, about her which brought out what protective nature he had, and this was a charming and powerful feeling. He wondered if it was love, but could not collaborate that question. It was a warm and comfortable feeling though, and that in itself was new.

He had spoken to Father Clifford about their situation, and received nothing but encouragement and smiles. The middle-aged priest though, his belly now enormous with the goodness of life, had been careful to remind him of the sacredness of remaining pure, and had lectured him on fornication, mortal sin, and the value of the confessional.

However, considering himself to be a modern man, he advocated holding hands, cuddling and perhaps kissing.

This advice Simon found amusing as he had already spent a number of times with his lips pressed firmly up against Avis'. Mostly as they were going to say goodnight, but he had managed to snatch a few kisses occasionally during the daytime, when out and about. Some of those had made Avis' ears red, but she loved the feeling and the naughtiness of it. They were undoubtedly committed to each other, he had told Father Clifford.

When Simon reached home, as it was only eleven o'clock, and still with the essence and image of Avis fresh in his mind, he walked to the conservatory where he uncovered a watercolour painting of Avis on which he had been working for the past month. To most eyes, had anyone been around to view it, it appeared finished, but not to the artist. There he spent another two hours working under the dim gaslight until his eyes tired. Soon, he would present his not completely unexpected gift to her.

He had captured Avis in the late spring, and had initially sketched her on one of their walks in West Ham Park. There, quite often on a Sunday, they would enjoy the usual brass band, which began playing once the weather warmed, and would sit with, mostly, fifty or so people in the warming sunlight holding hands whilst they enjoyed lemonade or ginger beer along with a packet of Jammy Dodgers which had become part of their thing.

That particular afternoon, after a light shower, there had been a quality of light which had excited him a great deal, and he had tried to convey his painterly enthusiasm to Avis. However, she, not having an artist's eye, was content to simply smile at his eagerness as she struck a comically dramatic pose while sitting on his coat on the wet grass. An action which was immediately pounced upon, and her willingness to be his subject turned to his advantage.

So with a little patience, he manoeuvred her so she faced the sun, arranged her dress and her hair and then took out the small sketchbook which he always carried from his inside pocket, licked the tip of a soft pencil, and began to stare intensely at her wide eyes. A soft breeze moved her hair, but that did not distract him. Within five minutes, he had captured her basic form and then, despite her increasing fidgetiness, finished the sketch within ten.

Avis was extremely flattered when she was shown the sketch. No one had ever drawn her before, and the effect on her emotions was nothing short of extraordinary. For some while, she had stared at the remarkable resemblance, at the correct nuances of the eyes and skin, the roundness of her cheeks and lip before looking again at her boyfriend in an entirely new light. Not having seen any of his work first hand, only his collection of work on cards, to actually witness his skill first hand was, to her, nothing short of a miracle.

Therefore, it was that well-executed depiction which turned her attraction of him from a boyfriend to potential lover and husband. Any person, in her opinion who could make her look so wistful and charming had to be in love with her. It was an impossibility that he was not.

She had demanded it of course, but it was lovingly withheld with a smile. Perhaps when he had turned it into a painting. Wide-eyed, she had mouthed, 'a painting? You're make a painting from this? Of me?'

'Yes, Avis, If have your permission.'

Her silence and a shy smile told him precisely what he wanted to hear, and he had begun his new project that very night. Now though, he re-covered the canvas, turned off the gas, and made a hot chocolate which he drank before prayers and bed.

That night he dreamed of Avis for the first time, which he thought was strange as by now, she certainly consumed his waking hours, and had done so for some time. Normally, he did not remember his dreams, and had even convinced himself that he never dreamed. But that night, sometime around three o'clock in the morning, he awoke in a sweat which drenched the sheets, and saw him running for the nearest lavatory which, in his house, was on the first floor.

After, he drank some water in his cool kitchen, too scared to return to bed. He imagined, because of the nature of the nightmare, that it was greatly to do with the conversation that had occupied the rest of the evening over the main course but he could not be sure. Over and over, the strong images surfaced, and he was not able to easily dismiss them until he had returned to his bedroom, and settled himself by sketching in the most abstract way possible, a facsimile of what he could remember. After an hour, his sheets changed, he slipped into sleep again, this time into his usual, as he mistakenly thought, dreamless sleep.

Eighteen

September came late that year, and the vast amount of trees which grew in the streets and surrounding fields took ages to lose their green cover. Avis, who had by then, almost made the Windsor Road house her second home, had got into the habit of spending her free time there, in one of the large downstairs living rooms which tended to make William and Ethel's front room, look miniscule. Simon only used that room plus the kitchen, bathroom and one other as the entire property consisting of thirteen rooms in total was too expensive to heat. Simon may have owned an elegant and desirable property, but his income certainly did not warrant it. Therefore he was glad he did not have any brothers or sisters, as almost without doubt, the property would have been sold off, and divided long ago.

Avis' best friend Mary had certainly accompanied her on her first visit as was agreed, for that was deemed appropriate, and the two women had been overawed by its size, the fact that only one person was in occupation, and its condition. Which was not at all dirty as Simon employed a local woman, Margaret to dust and perform other menial but necessary tasks. This she did for twelve hours a week.

Mary in particular thought Simon living there by himself a 'great waste and an injustice', especially as she and her two bothers and other sister plus her mother had to live in a house just a little larger than 231. To Mary's growing socialistic mind, a burgeoning condition, which would test her future husband's patience, it was nothing short of a crime, and during that initial walk home, that time not accompanied by Simon, she made her views known.

Her personality suited her changing appearance, which was growing more boy-like and severe by the month. Whatever she wore became looser and more shapeless. Her bust was suppressed, her waist disappeared, her shoulders became broader, and her hair shorter and shorter becoming more garçonne. Her flattened chest and womanly curves may have appealed to Mary's modern attitude, but it didn't work well for Avis. Or Simon either.

But nothing that day could dampen Avis' thoughts for she had seen the future, and it lay in becoming the mistress of the Windsor Road house. Even the name naturally sounded posh, and in her mind and her secret diary, she often referred to it for her own amusement's sake as the House of Windsor. There her boyfriend and she would play music, read books aloud and chat endlessly.

Avis was quite surprised when she first viewed Simon's living room. It reminding her so much of her grandmother's home, but was about ten times the size. For it was clear that he had not changed or replaced one thing since his mother had passed, or even, since his father had done the deed of which the Catholic church so disapproved.

The double room was a positive Victorian time machine. Apart from the abundant amount of plants which grew in the oversized white enamelled pots, of which there were many, Simon had been proud to announce that it was just as his mother had left it. There was a generous amount of heavy furniture, and long dark decorative curtains, which were either half pulled open or half pulled closed, Avis could never make up her mind.

A plethora of heavy-framed portraits of serious men and women covered the walls almost obscuring the detailed, but now faded green wallpaper of leaves. To one side close to the French Windows was a piano with sheet music laid out as if an artist had just left to make a pot of tea. Ample plump red velvety chairs were arranged around the fireplace, accompanied by fireguards, and there was a large round, finely made table near the front bay windows so arranged as to enable the sitters to take tea while spying on the neighbours and those walking by in the road.

Curiosities abounded. From the stuffed fox under a canopy of glass, endless ornately carved wooden boxes filled with knickknacks and conversational pieces, to the abundant clocks which ticked continuously, the living room reeked of the past. A Persian carpet covered the entire room, but it was now faded and extremely worn, even becoming tattered in places, while the original candle chandelier hung down prettily from the ornate ceiling rose.

But what astonished her most of all, positioned as if the owner had just left the room, was Simon's father's pipe and tobacco pouch, and his mother's now dated magazines. Their shoes too were near the fire as if they had just slipped them off. Avis, secretly found that a little spooky.

She certainly did not approve of the Victorian clutter as she was a thoroughly modern woman, but the sheer amount of it took her by surprise. Her condition of silent exclamation continued when Simon had presented to her his kitchen. It was like going back in time, and she imagined her making small changes day by day until she had introduced this man she was hopelessly in love with into the twentieth century.

Occasionally Simon would paint, and she would knit, now that it was summer, sitting in the conservatory together. She had long ago been allowed to view her completed portrait, and it now hung, with a definite sense of pride and accomplishment, in the room they most used, cradled in a magnificent gold-painted oak frame purloined from an old Victorian print, of which his father had once thought a great deal, for it reminded him of his young wife, and which Simon had rediscovered in the loft.

The picture was hung there as it was thought by Avis to be extremely inappropriate to have hung it in her own bedroom much as she would have liked, for she thought it the most wonderful gift she had ever received. The little original sketch though, true to Simon's word, had been given to her, and now was a keepsake in her jewellery box at 231.

Much as she now loved Simon, she thought it was a shame and a pity that Mary never returned to Windsor Road with her. But Avis knew that she was busy making a life for herself outside of their friendship. As that consisted of, as the summer ended, becoming the fiancée of her brother, Newenham, it was undoubtably a shame that the two couples did not share enough common interests to walk out together. However, Newenham was utterly unlike Simon, and Mary's continued disgust at the size of his house, continued to irk her.

Avis used to joke that when she became Mrs Derry, and they filled the place with children, then the problem would certainly disappear. But this demonstration of equality was not pleasing to Mary's ears as Newenham's navel wage only allow them to get a small mortgage. It has to be admitted, it was the only issue that divided them. However, when they were not fawning over their boyfriends, they still spent time with each other, mostly shopping with the occasional visit to see a show.

It was in the autumn that Newenham and Mary announced their marriage, and the two families could not have been more pleased as they were considered a good match. Among the heady and general festivities that occurred between the two families, were two parties, one taking place at the Graydon's and one at the Page's, the blushing bride and Avis, who had been delighted to accept the position of bridesmaid, found time to celebrate on their own.

Which they did with a meal and a show in the West End one Saturday evening. As they travelled to Leicester Square on the Central Line, both of them outfitted in their finest lace-toned flapper frocks and fox furs, adorned with exotic magnificent orchids, a journey neither of them had undertaken for some years, it crossed Avis' mind that although a special once a year treat for her, such a night would have been bread and butter to her older sister. However, that brief maudlin thought did not interrupt her happiness, and soon they were sitting down at their reserved table at the Kingston Dinning Rooms in Shaftsbury Avenue.

They ordered the pork in a curry sauce, after the Waldorf salad on the recommendation of their waiter, and were not disappointed. All through the meal, a young fellow circled the tables playing wistful laments on a violin through which both women had a fit of the giggles, but would have been entirely lovely had they been with their men. Both of them, separately, made mental notes to make a follow-up visit with them.

Over a sweet of moulded jelly pears, and the help of a bottle of house red, they discussed the finer points of Mary's special day which she had not been able to discuss with anyone else. Not even her mother, or her doctor. This was a subject about which Avis could not help her, as her own level of information about such physical matrimonial matters was almost zero, but nevertheless, listen intently, and nodded as Mary talked and threw out question after question.

She understood about seeds and eggs, having read about them in a library book but, like her contemporaries, had, because she had always been a good girl, little idea how those things worked in practice. She knew that a gentleman had urges over which he had little control, and that it was important not to over-stimulate him. She understood well enough that that part of marriage, the nightly transactions of the flesh, was a necessary evil. Or at least that was what she had been led to believe. However, the married women at the exchange seemed to cope with the nightly invasion, and one or two even seemed to enjoy it.

Therefore, at her present age of twenty-seven, Avis could quite reasonably admit to being confused about sex. However she was sophisticated enough to know that she could not become pregnant by sitting on a chair warmed by a man, and that she would not be in danger of going to hell if she kissed a man outside of marriage. After all, her new priest had practically told her it was all right. She knew also that the man, in order for her to carry his child, had to penetrate her, and this concerned her a great deal for she was not overly fond of injections, and even Avis knew that that part of a man wasn't as thin as a needle. She had seen the occasional male dog, and worked out on her own the possible dimensions of the offending part given that the ratio between it and the size of the dog ought to be approximately the same as a man. She hoped. She saw no reason why it should be any different. She had a slight knowledge of evolution, and fifteen inches in length, although a little long, she supposed was average.

Thus she became rather silent as Mary chatted on about her fears which oddly, she found to be virtually identical to her own. She had seen animals couple, and found it intriguing when she allowed herself to think about it. But she could no more shed light on Mary's questions than she could sprout wings and fly back to East Ham. In the back, and the front of her mind as well, she blamed her mother of course, for conversations like this made Avis uncertain in social circumstances.

However, on her third glass, Mary demanded some answers, possibly in too aggressive a tone, and which drew glances from those tables closest. Therefore it was all Avis could do at the time, to advise her in a low voice that she was to calm down which thankfully, and being the lady she was, took her advice, and the incident was soon forgotten especially as they left, and reached the cold night air of bustling Shaftsbury Ave. The lights and the sounds almost overwhelming them after the quiet ambience of the restaurant.

The musical comedy they had booked, the rags to riches story, Sally, at the Winter Garden Theatre, they enjoyed tremendously, and they clapped until their hands stung. By the time they had left, both felt exhilarated and far from tired. A coffee bar and more music was therefore needed, and as they had at least another hour and a half before the last train, a helpful burly policemen, more attuned to dealing with drunks, drug addicts and women of the night rather than innocent visitors to the West End on a night out, pointed the way to Arnold's, off Wardour Street, one that he himself recommended for 'nice young ladies such as yourself'.

It was almost that remark which put Mary off, but at the insistence of Avis, after descending into the cellars of the building, they found themselves seated, amongst huge ferns which graced unexpected corners, in a semi-darkened coffee and wine house while a seven-piece band amused the mostly young audience with fast jazz. Which was played quiet enough for them to continue talking, but not too quiet so as for them to lose their heady excitement. There were some twenty or so tables, each occupied with a mixture of both sexes, and the air was thick with tobacco, pipe and cigar smoke, chinking glasses and high speed chattering.

Many of the men, accompanying the women were formally dressed in tuxedos with both black and white ties, while the women wore the latest fashions. There was a great deal of laughing, smoking, drinking and tomfoolery, and it was clear that these young people were liberating and distancing themselves from the extremely wearisomeness period of the Great War. Even though that monstrosity had ended over five years previously. Obviously, Avis whispered to Mary, these were the bright young things about which she had read. Although Mary nodded, she was more concerned about where Newenham was going to get a tuxedo.

Both wished, their shoes tapping wildly, after only one cup of coffee that they did not have to leave. Nevertheless, making their way home if they missed their train would not prove to be impossible. However, they agreed that the cab fare would have been impracticable. Even split between them. And that is even if they managed to find one willing to drive all the way out to the suburbs, for East Ham was considered a long way out.

The pace of the music fell away, and a young crooner stepped up, and invited couples to dance which several did. Again, silently to themselves, Avis and Mary thought that this would be a wonderful night out with their men. Avis called one of the cigarette girls over, and brought a packet of Chesterfield. She tipped the girl well for two reasons; the first being that she thought she looked bored, and the second being that, from across the dance floor, amongst the shadow, she imagined her to be a good likeness for her sister.

Again the tempo changed, and more coffee was ordered. At the request of the crooner, a chirpy little dance number began, and soon the floor space around the band was packed with mad and energetic young things dancing in a way that almost certainly their mothers and fathers would not have approved. To Avis, the place was beginning to resemble a packed asylum full of very happy drunks. But a very excited and desirable one. Noticing that some women had paired up, Avis and Mary thought they would give their legs a stretch, and wandered onto the dance floor where they, thanks to the magazines which showed the steps of the latest dances, and which they brought each week and practised with, the two women did not embarrass themselves up as they danced the Black Bottom.

Laughing gaily, and a little out of breath, the two almost skipped back to their table where a waiter was finishing replenishing their glasses. When questioned, he offered Mary a note, which she silently read before passing it to Avis.

'Is there any reply madam?'

Their looks of astonishment and quickly shaken heads gave him his answer, and he pointed to a table of eight men and women, whereupon a tall and strikingly handsome man stood and half bowed as he lifted his glass. Avis was embarrassed, but Mary was not so coy. She lifted her own glass, shook off Avis' gently restraining hand, and raised it to her lips as she smiled.

'Mary? How could you? You don't know who he is!'

'Oh, he's nobody! He just noticed us dancing that's all, and wants to reward us.'

'I don't think it's wise to accept a drink from a strange man.'

'Look, have we had a good time tonight or what?'

'Yes.'

'Then let's enjoy ourselves Avis. I want to stay actually. Did you see the notice in the foyer when we came in? It doesn't close until five! In the morning!'

'Oh, I don't know Mary. My parents will wonder where I am.'

'How old are you Avis? You're not fifteen. You're twenty-seven, and you ought to be able to stay out if you want. We aren't children!'

'But if only we could tell them where we are. Mum will be worried sick if I'm not home by twelve. She'll have the police out looking for me. You know what's she's like now.'

'Well, do you want to go and I'll stay?'

'I can't abandon you Mary! Here? And you're marrying my brother in a week, and that man's just sent over this wine.'

'Then you'd best stay with me little sister! I'm going to have to stay Avis. I'm not going to be able to do this very much again am I when I'm all bunged up with his children am I? This could be my last chance at having some real fun, and it's been a wonderful evening hasn't it? Please don't spoil it for me. Although I will stay here if you go.'

Avis took a sip of the wine, and although it tasted cheap and slightly vinegary, it was just what she needed at that moment. In a second, she weighed up the possible consequences of leaving her best friend to the mercy of the ever-increasingly manic crowd with the possibility of her being abused and ill-treated by the tall, handsome cad, against the possible hostile reception she almost certainly would get if she arrived home on a Sunday after the sun had risen.

She lit another Chesterfield, and blew smoke at her waiting friend, and at the time, the music hotted up again, the frenetic dancing, the movement and swaying of the crowd and the general excitement was compared to going home on the underground to a cup of Horlicks...and the club won out instantly.

'Shall we buy a bottle of better wine than this then?' she smiled.

'Oh, honey, I could hug you!'

'Well, you only get married once you know, and I have to look after you otherwise my brother would kill me!'

'You are a smashing person Avis and a good friend. We're be all right you and I. Come on, I want to dance again and then you can buy the wine!'

'Hey!' Avis smiled. But she was already being tugged towards the dance floor again. It was time to show people how well they had practised the Shag, a dance both particularly enjoyed. Learning the difficult steps had been a nightmare.

Nineteen

A daylight nightmare awaited Avis when she arrived home at a quarter to eight the following morning. Both of them having to walk from the station for there were no taxis, and both were looking, as it was teaming with rain, and neither had thought to take an umbrella, as if they had been dancing in dirty water all night. With their mascara smeared, not a trace of lipstick left, and their hair damp, and so far from their original style, they appeared virtually comedic. Their shoes were scuffed, and discoloured with the damp, the lower part of their stockings soaked, and Mary had a red wine stain on the front her dress, which began at her waist, and ended at the hem, an accident that occurred at three in the morning near the ladies toilets.

Avis' dress fared no better as there were flesh-coloured powder stains over her right shoulder, a misfortune when she happened to collide with a woman who was in the drunken process of reapplying her makeup by the side of the dance floor. Having consumed two bottles of wine, plus the one that was originally sent to their table by the tall gentlemen, both of them had never been so tipsy and friendly, and when they left the club and tumbled out into the dark warm streets of Solo, nether cared one bit how dangerous their situation possibly was.

However, a middle-aged man, with whom Avis had danced, and who was as smashed as they, spoke to them outside, and laughingly insisted that he looked after them. He therefore took them to a café in Old Brompton Street where he introduced them to the large swarthy man behind the counter as his old friends. The Greek owner, well known locally for his generosity, had insisted that coffee was to be given all round, and after being introduced to his new shocked cliental, that's where the two women stayed, learning about the facts of life, laughing eventually to the most filthy and crudest of jokes, and hearing about the lives of West End villains in general. All of which shocked the closeted women to their very core. Yet they never did feel afraid, not even once.

The collection of men and women drinking coffee, and eating odd meals throughout the night could easily be described as motley. They consisted of prostitutes, and their procurers, down and outs, night workers on a break, delivery men, the odd drunken passer-by and men from the nearby street market. All seemed to know each other, but as rough as they were, the two unknown women were treated with respect.

The café consisted of eleven plain brown wooden tables, each deeply scored with writing and marks. The counter was covered with off-white and well-used mugs. A whistling machine, from which a continuous stream of steam appeared, dominated the counter. The plain green walls were streaked with ancient fat, filth and dust. It looked as if no one had cleaned the place for many years. There were no seats as such, just long planks of wood which stretched between the tables.

There was one prostitute that drew Avis' eye, one that seemed slightly more withdrawn than the others. She was not so pretty. Rather big-boned and wide-shouldered...and rather tall. This she noticed when the woman took herself off to powder her nose. One of the men, a factory worker, around whom a smell of strong cheese hung about him like an aura, sitting next to Avis, noticed her little brief stare, and nudged her, saying that they didn't make too many women like her, as he gave a happy little smile. She didn't answer. However, she stared again as the woman returned, realising something that filled her with thoughts so shocking that she could not bring herself to mention them to Mary. She, herself hadn't noticed her.

At some point in the conversation, it became clear that neither of them understood a particular joke. This led to a bit of jovial, but penetrating questioning, and when it was uncovered that the women's education in the sexual arena was far from comprehensive, despite their sophisticated appearance, the oldest of the five prostitutes, a hard-boned fat woman took it unto herself to publicly amuse her friends while offering a full on explanation of the adult version of the birds and the bees.

Mary never once mentioned her forthcoming marriage which she thought was a wise move as she didn't know how much ridicule she could take that time of the morning from well-intentioned but perfectly horrid strangers. Eventually, they said their good-byes, Avis glaring incomprehensibly at the oddly large woman who was allowing a man to touch her in places that seemed positively scurrilous given the time and place, and walked out to a now chilly and wet morning. But one where, at least, the underground was running.

Avis had kissed Mary lightly on the cheek at the corner of her road, refused her offer of coming in to explain where they were, and turned her key in the front door expecting a torrent of abuse. Which did not arrive. For the good reason that there was no one at home.

As her mother's green day coat was not on its hook, and her father's fedora and grey macintosh was missing, Avis presumed the worse and sighed deeply. To add to her misery, she was slightly hung over, but not too much, wet through, extremely tired (she and Mary had dozed on the train to the amusement of other travellers, but not the elderly ones) and was hungry, their last refreshment being a cup of strong tea and two biscuits in Leicester Square at a vendor's stall.

She knew sleep would be impossible until she had spoken to her parents so she changed, washed her face and hair, and decided that bacon and eggs would go down a treat. Unfortunately, just as she had poured herself a cup of tea, buttered a slice of bread and lifted the eggs out of the frying pan to join the bacon which was already on a plate, a click from the front door alerted her, and she moved around so she could see the door.

When her mother saw her, she rushed into the kitchen with a crying sort of a sob, and threw her arms around her neck while William simply glared ferociously. But that welcome only lasted less than five seconds before Ethel shoved her rudely away, spitting at her in anger.

'Do you know where we've been for the last three hours? Down the bloody police station that's where. Signing bits of paper and trying to report you missing which they wouldn't accept because you haven't been missing for twenty-four hours, and you're an adult.'

'Just what the hell do you think you've been playing at young lady?' spluttered William. 'Have you any idea what you have put us through? Where is Mary?'

'She's gone home...I couldn't get in touch with you and ...'

'So you thought you'd stay out all night galavanting about up the West End? Do you know how dangerous it is up there for a young woman?'

'We missed the last train.'

'What about getting a cab?'

'The expense mum!'

'Damn the fucking expense! What about thinking of us for once in a while? We didn't know what had happened to you. You could have been dead, laying dead somewhere. How are we to know?'

It was the use of that word which stung Avis into sub-mission, and with a deep humility, looked down at her slip-pers as she placed her hot breakfast on the table. In all her life, she had never thought to hear it, or any words similar, cross her parent's lips, particularly her mother. Occasion-ally, one or two of the more cruder women at work would use that particular word, but then only in a low whisper, and about somebody whom they really didn't like. Was that how her mother felt about her?

She had heard her father swear, and utter the word 'bloody' and 'damn' and even once, 'piss', but it was always directed at an object or a situation, and anyway, she understood those words to be fairly harmless. However, that word was loaded with meaning, and it was a word not used often, and never at 231 to her knowledge.

Her mother continued venting her anger and helplessness at Avis until her breakfast was cold, greasy and unpalatable, and her tea had developed a thin scum. Almost all of it was fear about what could have happened. Her father had let his wife continue until she had run out of words, and then, after she had told her to get out of her sight, had advised Avis to get some sleep.

Despite the verbal roasting, she had fallen asleep immediately in defiance of the neighbour's dog which went on a barking spree. When she awoke at two in the afternoon, it was her father knocking on her bedroom door and telling her that Simon was downstairs enquiring why she had not been to church. William told her in the most unfeeling tone possible, that he had told him that she had a headache, but would be down shortly.

Therefore, with an actual real headache, wrapped up tightly in her dressing gown, she met him in their front room where a little electric heater had been placed to take the chill off the room. Pleasantries and kisses on each other's cheeks were exchanged before Avis invited him to sit. She was fine, she informed him, all better now. He enquired how hers and Mary's female night out had been and she, with a margin of guilt, but truthfulness, answered in the most honest way given the circumstances.

'We saw a great show. It was so funny, we laughed all the time, and the meal was spiffy too, and there was loads of people around us all the time so you need not have worried.'

'I wasn't Avis. I know you can take care of yourself because you're a sensible girl. What time did you both get home?'

'Oh, it was fairly late, last train and all that. What did you do? How was double choir practice?'

'You know me, I enjoy it. What gave you the headache?'

'Oh, too much wine I guess! No...only had a glass with the meal. I think it was a bit off though. You know...red?'

'Red can do that so I've been told. I'm glad I don't drink. Well, look, hope you feel better soon. You still look a bit peaky if I may say so, so maybe you need a strong cup of tea. I wanted to ask you if you wanted to go to a subscription dance? I take it you won't be along this evening? It's just that I can buy two tickets from Joan today if you want to go? It's for next Friday.'

'Well, next weekend will be busy then seeing as the wedding is on Saturday.'

'Yes, I realise that, but this is for the children's home, and I thought it would be in a good cause.'

'Then count me in darling. I'll take some extra vitamins during the week!'

'That's lovely then dear. Okay, better rush back. Just a few jobs to do before this evening. Coming over after work on Tuesday?'

'Wouldn't miss it darling. As usual. Bye for now then.'

As they stood, they automatically moved towards each other, and their lips met. And as passionate a kiss as ever they had experienced passed between them. Which, when they had finished, leaving Avis highly flushed, she felt even more guilty for not telling him the truth.

As much as she was fond of her best friend, that next weekend, she hated Mary for forcing her to wear the hideous dress a bridesmaid had to traditionally wear. This particular one was in a glaring shade of lemon, and the only satisfaction she gained from the experience was knowing that Mary's slightly younger sister was wearing an identical one. Together, they agreed they looked like a couple of newly baked French cakes. The wedding, at St Barnabas, brought a mixture of joy and sentiment to the

Graydon family as that was, of course, where Edith had married Percy over seven years previously.

Somewhat soberly, as Avis stood behind Mary and Newenham while Reverend Vega took the service, it was all she could do, to imagine that somehow, in the wildest flight of her imagination, she had travelled back in time, and was once again attending the wedding of her dear sister. From the back, at least, they might be similar. Except for the hair. And the size and shape of Mary's body.

Similar thoughts were overcoming Ethel, and William knew it by the way his wife tightly clutched his arm. When a tear fell down her rosy soft cheek, he was damn sure it was not for Mary, and he chewed the side of his tongue in agony to stop his own tears from appearing. Secretly, he was appalled at discovering how much emotion he still had over the matter.

The wedding march, which ought to have had the Graydon family smiling with pleasure along with the rest of the hundred or so people, felt like the worst day of the month, and after the heads had turned, Ethel and William were the only ones still facing front. Staring at the empty altar with its two pure white candles. Avis, unlike her parents, at least wore a resemblance of a frozen grimace as she followed the bride and groom out into the glorious sunshine.

When they had woken that morning and prepared themselves, although they had known they might feel unhappy, they had no idea how strongly and significantly the smell, the words, the music, the bygone happiness, the sense of God, the peace, and the solitude of St Barnabas was going to affect them.

Ethel's sisters, to an extent, guessed what was happening as they stood behind her with their husbands. As they were the last to leave the pews, Lily took Ethel's arm, and gave her the most comforting and knowing smile she could. It was all very difficult. Massing for the taking of the photographs, the entire family, against the backdrop of Browning Road, and the few passers-by who had stopped to watch the blushing bride, hid their emotions as best as they could although they were glad when the cars returned to take them to Mrs Page's house.

Newenham, who before the service, had looked positively anxious, forever glancing back at the double doors from where his beloved was to appear, once he had drank his first pint back at his new mother-in-law's house, had relaxed, and for the first time since he had awoken that day, finally appeared to be enjoying himself.

But he was the only Graydon.

Twenty

The first Saturday in October became something of a milestone for Avis. For she took Simon to visit Ruth. He had known about her visits to Holloway prison, since he had innocently overheard Mary asking how Ruth was, and if she was now eating properly. Naturally, he made enquiries, and when the two women became suspiciously quiet, he asked again.

Simon certainly wasn't annoyed at Avis for caring about someone, even if she were a prisoner, as he was quick to mention. It was the sure fact that she didn't trust him to know what she was doing, and about all the times she had lied to him. All the times she said she was shopping with a woman friend on a Saturday afternoon when she was not. Back in Late August, that clash of words had taken days for them to recover. A truce was finally agreed upon over a long walk over Wanstead Park in the late evening sunshine, and they had finished it holding hands, and promising never to lie or withhold from each other again.

After, they had continued the walk, and finished next to the fairground which had pitched itself ready for the bank holiday event. However, although he uncovered her secret, he was not invited to accompany her at the time. Mostly because Avis knew that Ruth would probably not welcome him. Which, on her next visit, and after she told her the story, she found her intuition had been true. Ruth had no desire to meet her boyfriend.

It was only in October that Ruth became more aware of just what Simon meant to her visitor, and she became intrigued as she noticed how dewy-eyed she would become when mentioning him. Intrigued enough to finally do a U-turn about her former decision. It was therefore on a sunny and bright and, for the time of year, warm day that they both sat against that long table and awaited Ruth to be brought to them.

The meeting went as well as Avis believed it would. Mainly because Ruth, by this time, had changed from being a *'persecuted little cow'* as she had renamed herself, to a mature woman, comfortable to be with even though her accent and use of words were occasionally difficult for Avis to understand. But it is not to be doubted. The continued presence of her visitor had made a great deal of difference to Ruth, and she now took reading and writing lessons as well as holding down a privileged position in one of the prison's three vegetable patches.

She was not angry anymore either, was respectful to the wardress', and helped the first-timers find their feet. Almost becoming a kind of mother figure to the younger hot-heads. The staff had not only recognised the immense change in her personality but, gratefully, had mentioned it to Avis on more than one occasion. Part of the privileges that she earned weekly was an extension to her visiting time. Not the frequency as that would involve a Home Office ruling, but the length of time her visitors could stay.

Therefore, on that occasion in October, Avis and Simon were allowed to chat for a full twenty minutes. At the end of which, Avis handed a wardress Ruth's usual two hundred cigarettes. Not that she hardly used them anymore, having cut down considerably. But they were still useful as prison currency. Ruth told her it was because she was allowed outside now in the gardens that her need to smoke had almost disappeared. Avis was pleased for her, and mentioned that if only she could kick her own habit so easily.

The ragged scar on Ruth's arm was still red when she showed it to them, but it was healing as well as could be expected given the prison's poor diet. The three of them chatted about nothing in particular, but towards the end, because she kept looking at the large clock on the wall, Ruth told Avis that, in her opinion, she had a *'good'un there'*, which made Simon smile.

Just before they left, before the cigarettes were handed over and signed for, Simon gave a small marble-covered ring box to the guard, and asked her if it could be delivered to Ruth. Naturally, she opened it and, to her surprise, as well as Avis', a metal cross laying on a bed of cotton wool glinted in the little anti-room. The guard smiled, and considered that Ruth would probably like that very much. Then she signed for it as well as for some soaps that Avis had also brought along.

As they left the huge dominant prison, in the yard Avis looked hesitantly around. Something she had become accustomed to doing. In the faint hope that she would see something of her sister. She knew this was an impossibility, but she was drawn to do it nevertheless. It was something about which she had become obsessive, or even compulsive. But she knew that if she did not look in a particular direction, the feeling of dread would not leave her. She knew that her beloved sister was there somewhere. Impossible to meet. Impossible to say with any certainty where.

Being that this time, Avis did not have to rush back to the East End, normally to meet Simon, and because it was such a beautiful autumn afternoon, they decided to walk along Holloway Road, and do a little window shopping. Eventually, after walking the length of it up to Junction Road and back, they decided to take tea in Jones Brothers' department store, where they found themselves a table for two overlooking the high street on the first floor. An attractive young waitress took their order, and they settled back, Avis' feet particularly tired for it had been a long day. A gentleman played a soft tune on a piano in one corner, and the afternoon light streamed in, causing the fine combination of Edwardian craftsmanship and Art Deco decorations to look sparklingly splendid.

Tea came, Avis poured, and they quietly and happily munched on the biscuits that were provided as part of the service. They were both sitting parallel to the window, by each other's side, she next to the aisle. Just by a turn of the head, they could see out of the wide window to the road below. It was while Avis was doing just that, looking past Simon, her china cup raised to her lips, her brown and cream cloche hat just about shading her eyes, when Simon caught a sudden unusual movement out of the corner of his eye to his right on Avis' side, not all in keeping with the calm and smoky interior of the tea room. What happened next was so shocking, and so unexpected that he had no time at all to prevent it. When it happened, all he recognised was a blur of an unknown woman walking past.

It was not the most fortuitous time to meet Mrs Bywaters. Or the best way. For three weeks earlier, on the Thursday at work, it had been brought to William's attention, by a local newspaper, that an auction was to take place on the last week of September, and it was pointedly asked of him, 'Wasn't that your lass' place Will?'

William had stared at the advertisement, a single column and perhaps six inches in length describing the sale of goods and chattels of 41 Kensington Gardens, Ilford. The address carried its own infamy, and the professional advert carried no mention of the person who once owned it although he knew to whom the house had been eventually bequeathed. Edith's murdered husband's brother. A man who positively had no time for the Graydons, and had done much damage against them in the press.

The advert simply stated that the auction catalogue was one shilling. When his daughter had been taken to Holloway, the beautiful house, along with a majority of Edith's personal things had been sealed by the police after the upstairs lodgers had been evicted, and after her death, the wheels of probate turned as slowly as they ever did, requiring six months for insurance claims to be settled. Then it passed to the brother as the ninety-nine year lease was in Edith's husband's name.

This final indignation William had kept from Ethel as he assumed, quite correctly, that she would go to pieces if she knew. Yet he himself was intrigued enough to purchase a catalogue which he eventually kept as one of his most personal and treasured possessions. Unknown to Ethel, he took a day off work, and accompanied by Harold, father and son secretly attended the auction which took place at the company's premises off Little Ilford Lane.

They immediately recognised so many of Edith's beautiful possessions that, William in particular, was overcome while Harold felt an intense rage burn within him, because neither of them could afford a single item. The bidding was fast and high for every piece, demonstrating that the public had not forgotten the tragedy, and the infamy that was Edith Thompson's life.

All of Edith's clothes had been removed long ago, and given to the family, but that did not quell his mind at all as he saw the greediness with which the mob tore apart Edith's home. In a surreal moment, he was glad she was not there to witness what he and his son were seeing. But continued thoughts of her body laying unmarked, and so alone and deep in the cold and hard ground within Holloway became overpowering and he eventually had to leave.

Harold brought him a whisky in a small pub in the Cranbrook Road, but it was a quiet drink for neither had anything to say. Both knew that the sale of the house, and its contents was yet another event which let them know how completely dead Edith was, and how uncomfortable that fact was to assimilate. Apart from when the glass touched his lips, William's face assumed a mask of grief, his dark grey eyes simply staring at the bare wooden floor. He had imagined the worse was over that day when he last saw her body laying so still in that mortuary, but amongst the clamour of the pub, he had never felt so distant from the world, or from other human beings.

Eventually, Harold pulled him to his feet, and the two of them walked back to East Ham, by which time, Harold managed to jar his father into talking, simply with the aim of not letting his mother know where they had been. Thus it was, for Ethel's sake, that William pulled himself together, and when she asked them how the game went, he answered as cheerfully as he was able, that West Ham had won, one-nil.

Nevertheless, supper that evening was a muted affair, and it was on such occasions, when the parents were on their own, for Harold had returned to his digs, that Ethel knew it was best to give William some room. It was with her own thoughts then that she decided to have an early night, and kissing him on his forehead, left him alone in the kitchen next to the gently dying embers of their fire.

It was therefore Avis who discovered him when she arrived home, and immediately became confused as to what was happening. Had he now fallen again into one of his depressive periods? Which did not last long, perhaps normally just a few days, but nevertheless, was difficult to witness.

William had endured a difficult relationship with his one remaining daughter since the incident of her overnight disappearance. The two of them never quite catching up to each other in the same manner they had been before. She, in his opinion, bringing disgrace to the family. For her part, she became only too aware that if Edith had remained alive, her indiscretion would have been forgotten within a week. But not having her there, and Avis now being, not only the eldest of their children and the only female, made everything very different.

There was a dark space, a void as vast as it were possible to imagine, between father and daughter. In the everyday world in which they lived, very little appeared to be different. Ethel though, knew the family, knew her child and husband, and there existed a chasm now where none existed before. Subtle as an unanswered question, a look away, a raising of the newspaper or sometimes, as hard as ignoring her altogether, it existed.

Therefore when she entered the kitchen to find her father staring blankly at the red embers, she could not immediately figure out whether it was him reacting poorly to her, or if he had descended into one of his moods.

'Dad? Mum gone up?'

'Your mother was tired.'

'You okay dad?' After she hung up her coat on the small row of wooden hooks on the back of the kitchen door, she sank down to her knees before him and touched his hand. There were occasions where Avis could be overly tender, and as she had spent a romantic evening dancing, her happy and kindly nature continued to flow from her. She curled her hand around two of his fingers and gave them a squeeze.

'Anything I can do dad? I know there's nothing I can say but...'

William dragged his eyes away from the heat.

'You had a good evening? How's Simon?'

'As good as gold dad. I think he may pop the question soon.'

'What makes you imagine that?'

'Don't know. He's been acting all fidgety lately, like, as if he's got something to say, but never comes out with it.'

'Probably got fleas.'

'Dad! You okay?'

'Not really my child.' Avis definitely knew something was not terribly right as it had been years since he had called her that. Before she could express surprise, he continued.

'What makes people want to own a piece of other people's possessions?'

He asked the question as if he were speaking to thin air.

'Dad? What's brought this on?'

'Do you know where your brother and I have been today?'

'No dad.'

'We've been to see...as if it's not enough that she's dead and buried in an unknown place...all her things have been sold off.'

'Have the police released 41 then?'

'Released it and sold off. Sold everything. Snatched away by ghouls.'

'What's happened dad?'

'There was an auction today. Of your sister's house and everything was snatched up. We couldn't afford anything. All her furniture...all her treasured things...everything...gone. Disappeared into thin air. Broken up. Scattered.'

'Oh dad!'

'I'm telling you now Avis, your mother must never know. I've told her Harold and me went to footy, understand?'

'Of course I won't say anything. Oh dad!'

His hand eventually curled around hers as well, and silently they looked again into the fire, no words necessary or possible. But Avis did feel a slight cracking of the icy conditions, a thawing of emotions. William though felt an additional sadness that it took such an awful event for him to feel close again to his one remaining daughter.

After a while, she rose, and made them both a cup of hot chocolate, and they went upstairs, he to slip silently into bed to warm his freezing feet on Ethel's warm legs, and Avis to continue her adventure into *Bleak House*. Although the emotions connected to what her father had told her dissipated somewhat overnight, at breakfast, both were still subdued. Ethel imagined William's nature to be a continuation of his condition, while she imagined her daughter's was from tiredness.

Avis had worked that day as usual, and she and Simon had their fish and chips as normal as they had discussed the following day's visit to the prison, and what he ought to expect. Therefore, the visit to Holloway slightly exacerbating her state of mind already, and combined with what her father had told her two days previously, she was not entirely clear of unhappy memories, and which even perhaps contributed to a slight day-dreamy sort of reality for her.

Later on, when discussing the situation with the police, she therefore doubted very much if she would have seen or noticed the woman, or had any idea what was going to happen to her in the Jones Brothers' department store tearooms. For one moment she was gazing past Simon to the sunshine outside, her tea cup almost touching her lips while her other hand rested on his arm, when an unexpected whoosh of scalding tea was sloshed into her face accompanied by the most fearful stream of offensive and noxious screaming words.

'You fucking cow! How dare you show your face in this part of London! Why don't you leave me and my family alone you fucking bitch?'

Avis' cry was the only other sound as the woman stood less than three feet away, and screamed obscenity after obscenity.

'You and your family haven't any right to be over here. Not with what she done.'

She then turned, and faced the twenty shocked and repulsed diners, all resemblance to civility vanished. Completely betraying her working class background.

'She killed my boy she did. She and her fucking sister!'

It was then that discrimination and common-sense reappeared, and Simon sprung out of his chair and advanced towards the unknown woman taking her roughly by her arm, whereupon he received a flurry of unexpected wild blows on his chest for his trouble. But his height proved at least to be an effective block between the two women, and before very much longer, the manager ran swiftly across followed by two gentlemen in long grey coats who dragged the screaming woman back. Then even further away for she would not stop her verbal abuse.

Thus began the short enquiry, and while a nurse attended to Avis' hot face, in her room on the first floor, bathing it with a lotion, the woman, who had calmed down considerably once she had been dragged shouting to the manager's office and ordered to sit, explained her actions. Clearly, in the eyes and ears of the manager, she appeared demented until he returned to the nurses room, and spoke to Avis.

Within another ten minutes a policeman appeared, and took charge of the situation. He was advised by the manager not to have the two women in the same room; therefore he took brief statements from them separately. When confirmed by others, and Avis' face checked and explained, he arrested Mrs Bywaters for common assault, and eventually, a van took her away.

The manager called for a clean blouse for Avis, and as her injuries were only of a superficial nature, amounting to nothing more than a sore chin and chest, with no damage at all to the other parts of her face, she was allowed to leave by the on-call nurse. As compensation, the manager sent for his own car, and one of his underlings drove them both back to 231 where they told their story to her speechless parents.

The case though never got to court, for Avis, with the support of her parents, decided not to press charges. Although the incident did not stop the Holloway Express from printing a small piece about two unfriendly women who had fought in the tea rooms at Jones Brothers' department store over the purchase of a dress. As usual, complained William, they can't get anything right.

Twenty-One

December was not a month to which the Graydon's were looking foreword. Christmas was one important reason, and Christmas Day especially, as that was Edith's birthday. Their Christmas of 1922 had not taken place as Edith was still in Holloway, and under sentence of death. Not a single card had been written except for the prisoner who received hand drawn ones only from her close family. No one had given any thoughts as to gifts. Which did not especially please Ethel's sister's children who, not understanding why, became miserable when told, 'they would not get anything from Aunt Ethel's family this year.'

However, when the festivities became displayed in the shops, the family agreed to make an effort, and a kind of begrudging enthusiasm began to move them. Simon, along with the boys was to spend the day at 231, and they told themselves that an effort ought to be made at least for the sake of their children who, although adults, still felt youthful enough to enjoy a good soirée.

What made 231 more crowded was William and Harold had also brought along their girlfriends. Newenham and Mary preferred to split the day between the two houses.

Unfortunately, it was quite impossible for the two, now related by marriage, families to spend it as one, as neither of their homes was large enough.

As it was, the dinner had to be split into two with the younger members enjoying it in the back room, while the older ones ate in the front. They kept the doors open though so they could shout merrily at each other, which Ethel didn't particularly like as she was still trying to impress Simon with the family's manners.

However, as the beer and shandy flowed, and positions of solitude and comfort sought after filling themselves, the last thing finally on the mind of Ethel was good manners, and she headed off to the kitchen for a good cry on the pretence of beginning the washing up. Avis had naturally sprang to her feet immediately, but her mother shooed her down, and told her to let her dinner die down before coming out to give her a hand. Which, when she did, to William's dissatisfaction, noticed that not one of the other three ladies offered to help except Mary.

After, and stoking the fire in both rooms, they all squashed together in the front, and played a few games before the young men got bored, and decided to play cards for pennies. William thought this was a good idea, so he joined them, and the male-female divide was complete until teatime when Ethel began to serve huge amounts of exactly the same food they had for their Christmas lunch, but cold.

Sometime during the evening though as the day wore on, and everyone began to tire, William called a halt to the proceedings, and raised his glass of beer in salutation.

'I don't need to tell you who I wish well on this, which would have been her thirtieth birthday. She is with us I'm sure in spirit, and I can say with assurance, that she is still missed, and still grieved by all who knew her. I have battled with my conscience, and with influences beyond my control over the past year, and it is difficult even now to realise that this very day, just one year ago, she was alive, but suffering so much.'

Here, William's voice began to crack, and he faltered whereupon Avis stood and raised her glass as well.

'So...happy birthday to my sister Edith. May she always be forever in our hearts.'

'I want to say something as well.' Ethel stood as well and took hold of William's hand.

'I had a cry earlier after dinner just as I expected me to do because we are not, after all, just celebrating Edith's birthday are we? What we are doing is commiserating with each other on the fact that she is not with us anymore. I don't care now how she died or really, what wicked men caused that to happen to her. They will get their just rewards when they meet the Almighty. But for now, she's in here with me, and always will be. But what I mean to say is, if my delightful daughter was here today, she would not like us to mope around unnecessarily. Edith was a delight, and often the life of the party, and she would have wanted us to be happy, of that I am quite sure. So please, drink to her memory and pray for her. Thank you.'

Ethel sat down, quite amazed at the length of her speech, and equally unexpected, William placed his long arm around her shoulders, and planted an embarrassing kiss on her cheek which broke the tepid atmosphere. Whereupon Newenham rose and offered to refill everyone's glass.

William's middle son, William or Bill as he was known, caught up with Avis in the kitchen a little later as she was washing plates. They were close enough for him to hug her in a manly and brotherly sort of way.

'I heard what happened between you and Freddy's mother. Did she really do that? Throw tea in your face?'

'She did. I think she wasn't in a proper state of mind Bill.'

'Simon says she was swearing something awful.'

'You could say that! The words she used...'

'Damn good job I wasn't there. Does she imagine that only her family has suffered? Stupid cow!'

'No Bill, you can't say that. It wasn't like a normal person shouting. She looked demented. She'd lost so much weight as well. So much I hardly recognised her. It was only her voice you see.'

'I think she was bloody lucky for you to let her off like you did. She ought to have got six months for that.'

Avis shook her head. 'Mum and dad agreed with me. What would have been the point though? Her life would have been ruined more than what it is already. We're all suffering Bill. I don't know how I've got through this last year. You and the boys haven't been here, but we've had our ups and downs I can tell you.'

'Well, I know we haven't been here sis, but we've missed her too.'

'I'm not saying you haven't Bill, but if it hadn't been for meeting Simon, I really don't know where I'd be.'

'He's a good chap. West Ham man!'

'Go on, get out of the kitchen. Here, take these cakes in will you? Mum made them yesterday, and they are so sweet! She must have put tons of sugar in them!'

Oddly enough, the postal system returned on the twenty-eighth, and one of the first letters to be handed to Avis was a hand written one with an unknown postmark because it was smudged. Taking her second cup of tea after breakfast, she slipped a finger under the seal, opened up the two sheets of folded paper and began to read. Then she put the letter down, and took a sip of tea before handing the letter to her mother who was gently rocking by the fire with Joey on her lap.

'Mum? Take a read of this.'

'Whose that from?' William was stuffing his pipe with tobacco. The first of the day.

'It's from Mrs Bywaters.'

'Read it out then.'

'Can I Avis?'

'Yes, of course mum. I was going to show it to dad after anyway of course.'

Ethel laid her cup on her lap, adjusted Joey so that his claws didn't pull on her skirt and angled the paper to the daylight so she could see better.

'It says, "Dear Avis, I'm writing these few lines to let you know how infinitely sorry I am for attacking you on that terrible day. I have no excuse, but to say that I was not of sound mind, and I deeply regret what I said and did. I can only hope you were not too badly injured. I have suffered nothing but embarrassment about the whole thing ever since and it has been on my mind to ask you for your forgiveness for some time now. Please believe me when I say I am so sorry. I have been away in hospital for the last four weeks, and I am under a doctor at the moment for nervous tension. I have been quite unwell. Your decision not to pro-secute me came as a complete surprise as truly I did de-serve to be punished. But not having to undergo that humi-liation certainly helped me to get back on my feet again. We are a tragedy. All of us. You lost a sister, and I a son and please, please believe me when I say that I do not consider anyone to blame for my boy's death, but the courts, the evil judge and those awful juries. Your family, like mine, is com-pletely innocent, but yet it is we who are now suffering as I am sure your family is. I would very much like, perhaps in the new year, after January, to write again if I may? Perhaps it would do us both some good to listen to each other's stor-ies. If you do not wish me to do this, please let me know. My most sincere wishes, Mrs Bywaters." Well! What do you make of that?'

'I think that's very courageous to write such a letter mum.'

'I think she must be off her rocker!'

'Dad! She's obviously ill. She's on her own you know. Least mum's got you. It must have been difficult to cope during the last year on her own.'

'I suppose so then. So, are you doing to write back?'

'I think I will dad. But not to ask her not to write again, but perhaps to even meet.'

'You're barmy after what she did to you. Just meet in a public place that's all.'

'Well, if I go, Simon will certainly go with me.'

'And changing the subject, I take it he hasn't yet?'

' No dad, no proposal yet. I've got a feeling he's going to do it after the ninth.'

'He should have done it at Christmas, in front of everyone.'

'He's too shy for that dad. How did you propose to mum?'

'Oh...let me tell her this', interrupted Ethel, 'Okay, we were playing tennis over Victoria Park when he said, "Ready?" and hit the ball right into my eye when I was definitely not ready. He was so apologetic that that's the reason I think he asked me because he thought he was going to lose me!'

'Now Avis, don't believe a single word what's just been told you. Yes, the tennis ball did knock her in the face, not the eye I don't think, but I already had the ring, I was just waiting for the right time.'

'I don't know who to believe! What a story!'

Twenty-Two

No snow for December and no snow for January 1924. The ninth came around extremely quickly the family imagined, and William and Avis both took the day off work. Simon joined them for breakfast, assuring them that he was truly part of the family now, but the boys were away, and had had commitments although Ethel told them that they ought to stop whatever they were doing at nine o'clock and say a prayer.

The usual eggs and bacon were cooked, and served by Ethel in a quiet mood and together, they ate in silence. At eight forty-five, they retired to the front room as they had done exactly one year previously, and sat listening to their same old clock. William spent a minute or two attempting to work out how many times it had ticked since it had announced his daughter's death exactly one year ago, but gave up. It was far too difficult without pencil and paper.

Avis' youthful imagination was at the hanging itself. A year ago, her mind could not have conceived of such a dreadful thing, but now, freed through time, and with time spent in the company of Ruth, she could imagine the horror of what Edith must have undergone, and it almost took her breath away.

Ethel began crying softly, and William placed his arm around her. Soon, as the hour hand reached twelve, she was joined by Avis, and when the clock chimed nine times, the three of them were hugging tightly. Only Simon sat alone, eyes down to the green and red frayed carpet. He had the feeling that, for that moment, he was not wanted. But he understood. And patiently waited.

After the ninth chime, they had slowly released each other, and some resemblance of normal family life, distancing and cold, returned, each with a single thought; that they were now into the beginning of a second year without Edith.

Avis had already arranged to stay home with her mother that day, and therefore Simon took himself off after another pot of tea had been brewed and drank. No one talked much about why they were there, and William took himself off to his shed where he continued his work oiling and maintaining his lawn mower. Simon called out to him before he left, but William didn't hear him. Never mind, he thought, I'll be back in a few hours.

A short while later, he could be found on a tram heading to stratford where he had to pick up a box of repaired bibles and hymn books for Father Clifford from Case and Son

Bookbinders in West Ham Lane opposite Queen Mary's, hospital. A little saddened by the beginning of the day, he sat back on the hard chair and stared at the endless poverty which was the area.

After washing up with her mother, the rest of the day was spent quietly, and diligently. They had finished a weekly wash, and cleaned the outside toilet before lunch. After which William decided to go for a pint to '*clear my head*' while the women took the afternoon easy, and spent the time darning in the kitchen talking about various non-confrontational issues.

William returned after a few hours, and as the light was beginning to fade, Avis put away her repair box as there was a knock on the front door. She smiled for she was expecting Simon back for tea before they were to go and see a film.

However, the person at the door was not Simon, but a tall, middle-aged gentleman wearing a raincoat and a serious expression. He coughed, as if to excuse himself and behind him stood a policeman.

'Good evening Miss. My name is Inspector Bryant. May I speak to...'

Here he held a piece of paper close to his eyes as if he had poor eyesight.

'...A Miss Graydon?'

'That's me.' She felt the first shimmer of fear run through her. 'I'm Miss Graydon.'

'I see. Is there anybody else in the house Miss?'

Ethel, who had been listening to these first few lines of conversation, stood in the kitchen doorway, wiping her hands with a teacloth.

'I'm her mother. What's this all about?'

'May I come in Madam? It's a private matter.' He looked over his shoulder into the street as he said it.

'Please go in there. I'll get my husband.'

Ethel hurried back to the kitchen where William was examining a dripping tap, trying to figure out if he was able to fix it or not.

'Why did you ask for me?'

The two tall men seemed to dominate the tiny room, and the inspector sat only at the request of Avis. The policemen did not. Soon, they were joined by William and Ethel who both wore the look of worried parents. The inspector stood again, and gripped his brown fedora to his chest.

'Thank you. May I ask if you are familiar with the personage of Simon Derry?'

'He's my boyfriend! What's happened?'

'I'm sorry to tell you that there has been an accident this afternoon at Stratford Broadway.'

A stunned second's silence.

'What? Is he all right then? Where is he? What sort of accident?'

William stepped forward, and placed his hand on Avis' shoulder as she had stepped forward towards the inspector. He then led her to the sofa where she sat.

'I'm afraid to tell you Miss that he is dead. It was a bad accident involving a tram and a horse. I'm so very sorry. This letter was found on him. It has your name and address on it. I'm afraid I cannot let you have it at the moment. It will be needed for the inquest. I'm so very sorry. Did he have any relatives Miss?'

Avis shook her head violently. 'He was an orphan. He lived on his own. I was going to be his wife.'

The inspector glanced at William. 'If you wouldn't mind sir. Might you write his address down here please? For official purposes.'

As Avis began sobbing quietly into Ethel's shoulder, the inspector decided it was time to leave.

'I'll see myself out sir, and again miss, I'm sorry to have to give you the news. I bid you all goodnight.'

Once the policeman had closed the Graydon's front door, and the men were walking back to their car, the inspector turned to him.

'You know who they were PC Brown?'

'Not a clue sir.'

'Well, you ought to. They're well known. That was the Graydon family. Remember Edith Thompson? My word! Didn't she die a year ago today?' He bit his lip as he attempted to remember.

'I couldn't say sir. So they're famous criminals?'

'No, you buffoon! It was their daughter that was hung. My word, what a day for them.'

Twenty-Three

Simon's funeral took place one week later, and was an extravagant affair paid for by life insurance. Every person who had anything to do with St Thomas the Apostle attended, and a collection of women took it upon themselves to provide tea and sandwiches after in the hall attached to the church. Simon was buried with his parents in the City of London Cemetery at two in the afternoon surrounded by over sixty people.

Avis' part in the affair was somewhat limited as while she was not family, she was recognised as the woman he would certainly have married. The sympathy for her was great by her churchgoing friends, but that overly strong display of understanding did not help her get through the day any easier. That morning, she had ruined two pairs of stockings whilst dressing, and she had spilt coffee on her blouse. Ethel had watched her sip her way through breakfast because she had been unable to keep down anything solid, and spent some quiet time with her before the car arrived.

Throughout that long week, since she had learnt of his death, Avis had literally taken to her bed on the advice of Doctor Wallis who came to administer to her. After the police had left, Avis fell into a kind of stinging panic from which she felt she would not recover, and it took a visit from the doctor and a mild sedative before she was able to feel better.

The realisation that she was doomed to spend her life without the one man she had found that made her happy, had barely sank in. Yet within a day, calmness of a sort took over, but it was not a normal serene woman that emerged from her bed but a breezeless automaton. A woman without a smile or a happy word.

She spent her days leading up to the funeral undisturbed by emotion but listless, only preferring to walk occasionally by herself over Wanstead Flats. Doctor Wallis, who became as concerned for her welfare as her parents, gave her a note excusing her from work for ten days. On those days when she did desire a little company, in the evenings, much to the relief of Ethel, Mary would join her on those walks, just to look after her. She reported back to Mrs Graydon that Avis remained as voiceless during those walks as she did when at home.

Avis had control over every aspect of herself except her happiness. Sadness poured out of her like an unstoppable stream, and by degrees, it broke Ethel and William's hearts, for they could do nothing but pray that her broken heart might mend. Avis' disconsolate personality, apart from being crushed, continued working though, and on the fifth day, she took up her knitting again, the very first sign that she was recovering.

She was the first to throw a handful of earth onto the coffin as it lay so deeply in the dry uneven sticky clay, but did not cry. Ethel believed that even then, the reality of what had happened, had not reached her fully. The day was cold, but at least it wasn't raining. That was what Ethel heard repeatedly as she mingled, and she thought, did it matter? These people ought to be grateful that they can actually pay their last respects to a place in the earth that they could visit.

Avis was taken by her arm by her father, and one of her aunts after the crowd had dissipated, and returned to the cars. No words were said, but she held on tightly to her father as she stepped back across the wilderness of crosses, dates of death and marble. It was a cold and horrible day. William wondered as he waited for the car, just what he had done to deserve this curse, this curse that had fallen on his family.

Avis was not able to attend Holloway for several weeks, and therefore wrote to Ruth instead, hoping that her letters might offer a pitiful substitute. Ruth, by way of a friend, wrote back offering her condolences, but it was some months before Avis again stepped over the threshold of

Holloway Prison. During which, to maintain their special friendship, no less than forty letters had been exchanged. Upon her arrival, some time in early spring, with those daffodils and white crocus' once again growing deeply in the Governor's front garden, it was brought to Avis' attention by way of a familiar face, a wardress, that just as she had saved, in a way, the prisoner's life, Ruth had now saved hers. It was a poignant moment.

Avis changed churches after Simon's death to St Francis RC church in Stratford because she could not bare to look at the organist's position without feeling so much sadness that she felt she had to burst. Everyone was so kind, but the memories were too much to bare. The new minister naturally had heard of the tragedy, and welcomed her without fuss or prejudice. It was in this church then that she continued to worship, study and make friends until her own death.

In the beginning of march, she received an unexpected letter from a local solicitor, W B Gowen, somewhat of a local curiosity, for she was a woman solicitor. She had an office above the White Swan in Stratford. In it, were details of the last Will and Testament of Simon Derry, who, to her amazement, had left the Windsor Road house, and all its contents to her, the delay being caused by a distant cousin whom Simon had never seen.

The solicitor requested a meeting which eventually took place, in the presence of William and Ethel also, and the keys were offered to her. Which she took. But only for an hour. For after she had taken her portrait, and found the engagement ring which was destined to be hers anyway, she walked to the nearest estate agents, and put it up for sale whereupon it was quickly sold, it being such a prime property and having an excellent location, to a sweet family of Germans who enjoyed living there until they were ousted out just before 1939, whereupon Herr Kaufmann, a teacher and a man of some perspicacity, sold it and moved his family back to the Fatherland. The money, in its entirety, Avis donated to St Thomas the Apostle.

Twenty-Four

Avis never fully recovered. Yes, eventually she laughed again, but was always haunted by the fear of loss, and therefore never quite trusted herself again in a relationship. Although an attractive woman, and still young, she was to forever remain a spinster, and a true friend of the Catholic church. When a man became interested in her, and it did happen occasionally over the following years, she had a sure-fire method of making sure he did not ask a second question, for she just flashed her engagement ring at them proudly...with a grand and triumphant smile on her face.

Mrs Bywaters made her peace with the Graydon family, and after an exchange of letters, a series of dinners were held at both the Graydon's and Mrs Bywater's house which continued for over a year. However, as they only had their deceased children to talk about, and that was their only point of attraction, they eventually drifted apart. Through a mutual friend, Avis used to hear how she and her family was, but the last time she heard about them was just before 1929. After that, her source dried up.

It was a testament to the love the family had, that on the commemoration of Edith's death, every year, special prayers were said, and flowers placed in a votive position by Ethel's little altar. Ethel Graydon herself died in 1938 at the age of sixty-five, and was buried in The City Of London Cemetery seventeen years after her daughter Edith was executed. Very soon after, Avis and William sold up, and moved to Gantshill in Essex. In 1941, between arial bombardments, Avis and her brothers buried their father next to Ethel, both parents, at their deaths, still at odds with the fact that their daughter's body had not been returned to them.

One person whom she continued to be friends with was her childhood friend and her brother's wife, Mary. Who eventually bore two children and who came to love auntie Avis almost as much as their own mother. It says much about Avis' personality that never once did she suffer from any form of jealously regarding her two nieces.

However, yet another death awaited Avis. A small one. Yet one with a strange twist. Her new friend Ruth, upon finishing her long sentence and, having adjusted by now to the accents of the Southerners, decided to settle in North London where she, with the help of the Prisoner's Reform Association, retained for herself a position in a rural gardening shop. Work she enjoyed a great deal as she had become fond of that activity.

However, some four years after she was released, a desperate letter from her family, sent her running back home to Newcastle. After calling in on Avis to say good-bye, she promised to return when her mother was better. However, Avis never saw or heard from her again. She stupidly and incredibly had taken no address, and knew of no other information except that her mother lived in Newcastle. It was yet another death of sorts, and the mystery of what happened to the young woman who helped her so much when it was needed was never solved.

Within a reasonable amount of time. For in the summer of 1958, thirty-five years later, when Avis was aged sixty-three, she was taking part in a ten day, round Ireland tour with twelve others from her church when, on the seventh day, their coach stopped at Dublin for a two night sleep-over courtesy of Adam & Eve's (Church of the Immaculate conception)

It was that evening that Avis, and her closest friend Mabel, took themselves off along The Liffey to buy some supper, and see the sights by the evening light. They decided on fish and chips, and found a suitable shop whereupon, they sat by the river, and ate in silence as they watched the sun go down in a magnificent show of colour.

The fish and chips were wrapped in newspaper of course, and having finished her supper, Avis was about to fold hers up, and look for a rubbish bin when a familiar face stared at her from the greasy paper. There could be no doubt, even given the amount of years that had passed, that it was the face of Ruth. Immediately she saw though the decades, and recognised the head and shoulders portrait instantly. Almost an old lady with silver hair, like her own, the image showed her smiling happily while she held a small dog to her chest.

Excitedly, Avis began reading until she saw it was the obituary page. Underneath was the information she did not want to read;

'Ruth Brown; In memory of a devoted friend and colleague who passed away after a short illness at the House of the Blessed Virgin Mary. She will be greatly missed by all Dubliners. Her welfare and experience offered to the Prison Welfare Benevolent Society will never be exceeded. RIP.'

Avis looked at the top of the paper, and saw it was just one week old. So therefore, impossibly, she had missed her by weeks. It did not take a great deal of time the next day, to discover where she was buried, and that very afternoon, Avis took a cab to Glasnevin Cemetery where, in soft sunshine underneath a canopy of high green trees, she paid her last respects. This was the woman who herself had showed such respect when she and her family were in the depths of so much despair. Chained and tethered no better than a dog, she had risked further punishment, and did what she did because it was something in which she believed. The gift of compassion. She did not uncover though why Ruth did not keep in touch after the family emergency.

Incurably, once again Avis' became sad as she thought of her sister, now thirty-five years dead, whilst kneeling at the little mound of earth, still too early on which to put a head-stone, and she dabbed at her eyes gently with a lace handkerchief. She laid flowers gently on top of the earth, and said the Lord's Prayer, and Simon came into her mind as well, suddenly remembering the only time when the three of them were together around that long brown and scratched table. Avis still wore his engagement ring, and it sparkled in the speckled sunlight which filtered through the thick oak trees. She wondered too what Edith would have thought of her once young lover. Avis eventually stood, and recognising that she would never visit again, said her good-byes before slowly walking away.

Avis Graydon lived out the rest of her life in Ilford, only a couple of roads away from the 1922 murder, and died 6 August 1977, aged eighty-one, fifty-four years after her sister, and was buried in the Roman Catholic cemetery in Leytonstone. To the very end, she prayed regularly for the soul of Edith who had become such a tragic figure of our modern age. Like her parents, she was never allowed to witness the final resting place of Edith. Even when the prison authorities moved her body on the night of 31 March 1971 to Brookwood cemetery in Woking, they did not have the courtesy to inform her. It was undoubtedly one of the final cruel acts of the entire tragedy.

The Letters

30 December 1922

To the Queens most Excellent Majesty Most Gracious Sovereign

May it please your Majesty to grant the favour of your Royal influence towards obtaining a reprieve for my unfortunate daughter Mrs Edith Thompson.

As a mother, you will well realise the torment through which I am passing knowing that my daughter is the victim of the most compromising circumstances but yet being absolutely innocent of the awful charge upon which she has been convicted, and I now appeal to you as Mother of the Nation to be pleased to show your gracious mercy towards one who, up to the time of this terrible catastrophe has always been a most dutiful and loving daughter and has always been the first to help others in the hour of their distress. I hope in your Royal mercy and graciousness you will not fail to hear this cry from the heart of a grief-stricken Mother in her hour of need, all of those three sons served their country in its hour of need.

I have the honour to remain your Majesty's most faithful subjects and dutiful servant.

Ethel J. Graydon

----

30 December 1922

To The Rt. Hon. Bonar Law Esq. M.P.

Sir,

Re: my sister Mrs Thompson

I beg you kindly to read this letter in the hope that some of the points will enable you to see my sister's character other than presented to the public, by the prosecution.

I can assure you Sir that my sister had no idea that her husband was going to be murdered, as if it had been arranged a fortnight before that. I should accompany them to the Theatre, & spend the night with her in Kensington Gdns, & she had no idea until she met her husband in the evening that I was not going to be of the party. Her husband telephoned me late in the afternoon & I told him that I had already made arrangements to go out for mother. How can they pass sentence of Death on her?

Doctor Spilsbury gave evidence that there was no trace of poison in the deceased's' body, how then can it be said, she poisoned him. Why was all the evidence of defence put on one side, & only the black side - the foolish letters of an over wrought, unhappy woman - placed before the Jury.

It is untrue that my sister was happy until Bywaters came into her life.

Mrs Lester can prove, & also others with whom she lived before, that she was unhappy; only her great respect & love for her parents, prevented her bringing her troubles home. If she had done anything wrong at any time, she would have told mother at any cost, also my brother in law, would have spoken to my dad.

I should like to say, that Percy Thompson being of a particular character had no friends of his own, & naturally very soon disagreed with my sisters friends. The man is dead, but why should he die blameless. His case was just the same as my sister's which you can see by the letters, not produced.

Mrs Thompson was hardworking woman, of a generous, loving nature & no doubt after Bywaters seeing her unhappiness, she turned to him for sympathy. Her great mistake being - afraid to confide in her family who loved her above everything. Why was it so emphatically said 'She incited Bywaters?' it is obvious her letters are answers to questions, where are Bywaters letters to prove his statement that Mrs Thompson is innocent?

Can it be my sister is insane! Is this question having the prison doctors attention?

If you had seen my sister at any time, there could not be any doubt in your mind that the verdict was wrong.

I beg you to show mercy on her, for her parent's sake, you are a father therefore understand their feelings.

We are helpless & know she is Not Guilty.

May the Great Judge of all guide you in coming to your final decision, to which the family are just clinging, as the last hope.

Committing the above to your kind attention.

I remain in anticipation

Avis E. Graydon (Miss)

----

21 December 1923

Dearest Mother and dad,

Today seems the end of everything. I can't think - I just seem up against a black, thick wall, through which neither my eyes nor my thoughts can penetrate.

It's not within my powers of realisation that this sentence must stand for something which I have not done, something I did not know of, either previously or at the time. I know you both know this. I know you both have known and believed it all along.

However, I supposed it is only another landmark in my life - there have been so many when I look back, but somehow they are not landmarks until I look back upon the journey, and then I know certain events were landmarks.

I've tried to unravel this tangle of my existence, this existence that we all call life. It is only at these times that we do think about it.

It has been an existence, that's all, just a 'passing through', meeting trials, and shocks and surprises with a smiling face and an aching heart, and eventually being submerged and facing Death, that thing that there is no escaping - no hope of defeating.

You must both be feeling as bad and perhaps worse than I do today, and I do so hope that this will not make things harder to bare, but I really felt that I should talk to you both for just a little while, after I was told the result.

Even now I cannot realise all it means: but, dearest Mother and dad, you both must bare up - just think that I am trying to do the same, and I am sure that thought will help you.

Edith

31.12.1923

To the Gentlemen of the Cabinet

Dear Sirs,

My husband & I were the aunt & uncle with whom Mr & Mrs Thompson spent the evening at the theatre, & I assure you Gentlemen, that from Mrs Thompson's manner, conversation, & also arrangements we all made to go to dances, dinners, & other theatres, during the season, it was absolutely impossible for Mrs Thompson to have entered into any arrangement with Bywaters to commit the crime. Moreover, knowing the late Mr Thompson very well, I say the lad's story is true & undoubtably he acted as he thought in self-&fence, Mr Thompson being just the kind of man who would bluff having a weapon.

But Gentlemen, my real plea is on behalf of the parents. By hanging the unhappy couple it is not them who suffer, but the family left behind. I know it is a difficult decision for you to arrive at, & possibly it will make a precedent for the abolition of 'Capital Punishment', but Gentlemen, being a new Government it is possible for you to do this. If burning at the stake was not a deterrent to crime, I am sure the more merciful way of hanging is not. These things or crimes are only committed in a moment of passion & not premeditated. The punishment of years of confinement is bourne by the offenders, but the punishment of hanging, is bourne by the parents and relations. May I therefore ask once more again for 'Mercy'.

Yours sincerely

L. LAXTON
(sister to Mrs Thompson's mother)

To the Weekly Dispatch
14 January 1923
Sir,

381

I had hoped at after the execution of my unhappy daughter, I should have been able to to retire into obscurity and try, if not to forget, at any rate to be forgotten.

Certain sections of the press, however, are still engaged in publishing intimate details of my daughter's life. May I, through your columns, protest against this?

Mrs Thompson sinned and she paid the penalty. How great the penalty was only those who knew and loved her can tell. Surely the decent thing is to let the past bury itself, if not out of pity for her, out of consideration for those she left behind.

Whenever I or any member of my family goes we are pointed at, steered at, photographed. My house is besieged all day and every day by anybody who is the victim of morbid curiosity.

During all these terrible weeks we have had no privacy, and now that we desire to go away for a brief period we are haunted always by the thought that we shall be known and followed.

To continue to rake up the past is only to prolong the agony. And when that past is almost entirely fictional I feel bound to protest.

Nine-tenths of what has been written about my daughter has been completely untrue.

Now that she is dead, cannot the lies cease? Cannot we be left to the privacy which I used to think was the right of all Englishmen to enjoy?

I am, Sir, yours faithfully

W E Graydon.

To the Governor of Holloway

20 January 1923

Dear Sir,

My Mother and Father have asked me to expressed their thanks to you for your kindness and consideration towards both our family and Mrs Thompson during the time my sister was in your charge.

There were very few visits passed that did not bring from Mrs Thompson some words of thanks due to you, and I only wish it was possible for me to adequately express the feeling of gratitude we have towards you, as well as the whole staff who came into contact with her.

Very sincerely yours,

Newenham E Graydon

To the Stratford Express

25 January 1923

Would you kindly allow me to use your columns in order to express my thanks to the hundreds of newly found friends in the district covered by the 'Stratford Express' who have so kindly sent me their sympathy and condolences during the agonising period through which my family and I have just passed. Verily one's true friends are not found until adversity's heavy hands descends upon one's shoulders. It has been the kindness of those unknown friends which has kept my spirits up so far, and my gratitude to them knows no bounds. I thank them all from the bottom of my heart.

Your Sincerely

Ethel J Graydon

20075696R00229

Printed in Great Britain
by Amazon